A. R. LATIF

Vultures in the House of Silence

The Servants Book 1

With prayers for the people of Palestine, Sudan, East Turkestan/Xinjiang, Somalia, Kashmir, and the Congo. Dedicated to everyone facing despair, who strives to bloom.
11/26/23

And what is [the matter] with you
that you fight not in the cause of
Allāh and [for] the oppressed among
men, women, and children who say,
"Our Lord, take us out of this city of
oppressive people and appoint for us
from Yourself a protector and appoint
for us from Yourself a helper"?

Qur'an 4:75

Contents

SOUTHEASTERN MESOPOTAMIA
The Tigris
Baghdad
The Euphrates
The Khaniqah
Mada'in
Karbala
Wasit
The Caravanserai
Najaf Kufa
Maqhar
Basra
The Persian Gulf
N
W E
S

V

Prologue

*The House of Silence had no roof — and only one circular wall—
coated in fungus. Its many residents lay on a musty stone floor.
Some were on their backs, others on their bellies; one rested on
his right side, face crumpled into the ground. In the early morning
light, the way they were dressed in florid fabric and sprawled about,
they might have been mistaken for partygoers napping after a long,
drunken night out. But they weren't sleeping—the only snoring
was the wind's occasional roar.*

*A hacking cough tore through the quiet scene. The sound came
from a skeletal boy lying on his back, who went on to wretch up
a bucket-worth of seawater. The liquid dribbled down his amber
skin and a few drops landed on his salted black hair.*

*Beneath a muddied robe of red, gold, and now brown, the boy's
fragile chest trembled as he recovered from the fit. He attempted
to raise a hand to rub his eyes, but neither arm would move. He
struggled to sit up, but his back didn't budge.*

*The boy craned his neck forward. He blinked several times at
the corpse by his feet—white grubs greeted him from holes in
the ruined skull like neighbors leaning through their windows to
wave. He turned his head as far as he could to the right, toward
the cadaver of a shrunken old man whose remaining fragments
of skin were a dull gray sprinkled with roving swarms of dots. He
looked down at his own stubborn arms which still refused to rise
and saw bloody knobs where his hands should have been.*

Choking back vomit was the only thing that prevented him from screaming. His mind tried to run from the open-air chamber of the dead, but it had as much trouble moving as his body. He slammed his eyes shut, but he couldn't flee from the foul fumes of rotten flesh or the stale aroma of barren bone.

Heavy panting pulled the remaining bile back from the brink. The boy's breathing slowly eased as he resigned himself to processing what he couldn't escape. He tested his tongue to see if it also didn't work.

"Am I dead?" he croaked. "Is this the punishment of the grave? Or Hell?"

Flies landed on him and buzzed in a noncommittal answer. He wiggled as much as he could, like a maggot poking through flesh, and they flew off toward less-resisting prospects.

The small triumph he felt at the insects' retreat was ruined by the descent of two shadows from a perch at the top of the wall. The vultures were an identical abyssal black, with soft, drooping feathers made cruel by sharp beaks and blank eyes. They ignored the old meals and perched on the new dish: the boy. Both leaned in for a nibble of his flesh despite his desperate squirming.

His pained "shoo!" was the loudest sound the House of Silence had ever experienced. The vultures craned their heads toward him as he spoke, then after a moment's pause, dove in for another attempt at pecking him clean.

"Stop!" he sputtered. Again, they ceased to bite him and stared.

"Get off! I'm not dead. . . I mean, I think I'm not dead. Don't eat me. Please don't eat me. . ." The whole time he spoke, they gave him a look that seemed almost inquisitive, with their heads tilted to the side. After a few seconds of quiet, they reared their beaks for another strike.

"What—if I talk, you won't bite?" The vultures stopped their

dive a centimeter from his sallow flesh and raised their haggard features to look him full in the face. Their heads dipped, as if in assent.

"Alright," he said. "Captive speaker rather than captive audience, huh? I could use some water before I begin. . ." One of the vultures swooped in toward his vulnerable neck during his prolonged pause.

"Oh come on, no breaks?" It reeled its head away from his jugular when he spoke again and reverted to a motionless state of attention.

"I'll tell you the story of how I ended up in this nightmare, though I'm not sure you can understand. There's a lot I still don't understand and there's a lot which makes even this seem sane. Let's see. . . It began like life itself. In a garden."

I

The Dream

Chapter 1

It was pitch black when Shaykh Nariman's aged voice floated past my door and knocked me out of bed. "Prayer is better than sleep!" he shouted with awful glee.

I was too drowsy to register what I was doing, but my limbs felt wet and chilled against the pre-dawn breeze, so I must have managed to get through the ritual washing. The Shaykh started the prayer on the cobblestones right outside the garden gate before I could fumble for the key.

I nodded off as he recited from scripture, seesawing between focus and utter collapse until the prayer finished.

The Shaykh turned around and faced me before starting his litany of post-prayer supplications. "Khurafa, my boy, come visit me today," he said after he finished. This was his twentieth time making that request in the past two months— I'd counted.

"I can tell you the story of Amir Hamza and how he van- quished a wicked dev—a giant, monstrous jinn," he said. "You've always loved that one. . . Or we can visit your parents." He whispered the last bit. His wrinkled, white-bearded face was blank, controlled.

"Aren't there a dozen stories of Amir Hamza fighting devs?" I asked, rubbing my eyes so I could watch for the quivering of his lips, or any tell-tale twitching of his wispy mustache. "I can't make it. I have some responsibilities today. . ." I felt guilty seeing that he didn't frown. After the first full month of refusals, he had stopped getting disappointed.

"There are many variations of the same story trope," Shaykh Nariman said, stroking his long white beard. "Amir Hamza, the hero, faces greater and greater threats, but by recognizing that *God* is far greater, he succeeds. . ." I choked back a yawn and he halted his lecture.

"Get some rest; I will come back to visit you later." He said, placing his right hand on his heart in farewell. Shaykh Nariman never shook hands. I always figured he had some kind of skin disease that stopped him from doing so. He was perpetually pale and pasty.

He turned back and let his gaze linger. "Have you smelled anything strange again recently?"

I shrugged in response. He walked off and I stared at my feet for a long moment.

"I should probably get to work," I mumbled as I noticed the molten colors of light crawling up from the horizon. I dragged my feet to the wooden garden gate, patted myself down to find the key with one hand, and counted out some of the things I had to do on the fingers of the other.

–Go to the baker. I had enough bread though, and I could pluck and eat an orange. With honey, if I braved the hive lodged against a corner of the wall today.

–Buy meat. In two months they must have cleaned up all the bodies. There was no way any seedy vendor would still be trying to pass off. . . Well, the meat would be only animal now.

–Gather seeds, fruits, and a few choice flower arrangements to bring to the market. The idea of taking anything out from the garden made my insides churn. I didn't have much, but I didn't need more money, no matter what my rumbling belly said. I only had to get food for myself, and the soil was kind, even when people weren't.

–Open the garden to the public again. Invite people in to visit. It wasn't ready though, and the last time someone I didn't know entered, things ended. . . poorly.

–Prune. I'd seen a vine trying to creep up the orange tree the previous evening and more than one spiky purple wildflower poking out from beneath a bush. I needed to apologize to them. No one deserves to be torn from their roots, not even wayward plants.

I found the key in a pocket sewn by my mom into the back of my chemise. I unlocked the gate and then stepped in with my right foot first, like it was a place of prayer.

I whispered what my dad had always taught me to say. "*Asalamualikum* flowers, *Asalamualikum* trees. Peace be upon you bees, and even you, weeds. . ." *All living things have a soul and will testify to your mercy,* he'd say.

I surveyed my little patch of paradise. A rainbow of tulips encircled the orange tree in the center, bowing in morning worship under the weight of dawn's dew. They bloomed brilliantly, as if the world hadn't ended two months ago.

The rose bushes against the walls glistened as the mist mixed with the rising sun. I looked away from the deep red of the petals toward the single bush of purple roses. My dad crossbred varieties for over a decade to get the color and it was worth the wait. The flowers were ethereal in the shade. He'd meant to start selling cuttings this year, but. . .

I turned to the nursery patch, like I did every morning. There were two pots there I'd worked on myself. The olive tree cutting that I'd half-buried in a mix of mud and sand was sprouting flat, light green leaves. Little nubs were growing out of its tiny trunk like pudgy baby fingers, but the rest of the cutting was lean and bent. It looked wise, like all olive trees.

The fig tree cutting was doing just as well; already four distinct branches bore its three-pronged leaves. Its trunk was beginning to thicken.

I poked a finger from my left hand into the soil of the olive tree pot, and a finger from my right hand into the fig tree pot. I felt around gently. Tangles of roots were everywhere. I tapped them ever so lightly and pulled a little.

They were strong.

I broke out into a grin. It instantly made my face ache— my muscles hadn't moved that far in weeks. They were both ready to be planted in the ground! And the olive tree cutting was ready *weeks early.*

I started with that aspirational olive tree. My heart sank a little as I moved it away from the fig pot but I brushed the feeling away. It was alright, they would still be in the same garden.

I brought the pot over to an empty corner of the garden against the wall, which was surrounded by herbs. Mint, thyme, and bishop's weed, among others. I'd already dug the hole a week ago, but I scraped it into a more even shape, exposing fresh soil in the process. I ran back to my house to grab some fertilizer and then returned to sprinkle it generously, scrunching my nose to avoid the smell. I lifted the olive tree cutting out of the pot, taking care to bring the soil with me and not tear the roots. I held it like it was a baby.

I moved it into the dirt and patted the ground down until it was flat. I leaned in, letting the leaves brush against my forehead. I breathed it in—I could smell a hint of oil and its characteristic odor similar to an apricot.

I got up to repeat the process with the fig tree cutting. It needed more room, so I'd moved many plants away from its designated corner, diagonal to the olive tree. I plopped it into the garden's dirt, taking extra care to make sure that the plant was upright and not leaning.

Stand straight young man! I thought with a small smile. My dad was never serious when he said that—his own back was always bent as he dug into the earth.

I brushed my hands together when I finished, letting the dirt flake off onto the ground. I gazed at my morning's work—but a thumping on the garden gate tore me out of my reverie.

Though the door was open, the pudgy son of the baker stood with his feet glued to the threshold. "My dad sent me," he mumbled. He had one hand outstretched, clasping a steaming piece of naan. The white and yellow flatbread was stained with little black crisps.

My mouth watered. I rummaged through my pockets and found a few copper *fils*. I handed him the coins with a quick thanks and went straight to eating. I didn't even bother to wash my hands—my dad would have joked that dirt is a great seasoning, and my mom would have shaken her head at him and then handed him a bowl of soil for his next meal.

The baker's boy didn't raise his head to meet my eyes—and I didn't look directly at him.

"Umm. . ." he said, "Khurafa, do you want to. . . " He didn't finish. We'd played together once or twice, months back. But now he was all too conscious of what he still had at home—and what I lacked.

It didn't matter. I couldn't even remember his name. And

we couldn't wrestle in the garden anymore anyway—too dangerous for the flowers.

He walked off and somehow I found myself right outside the garden, staring at his back. My mouth was open. I stuffed it with the last bit of naan and turned around, back into the garden.

The doves were tittering and the songbirds played timeless tunes. They sounded like lullabies. Bees roamed their marketplace in step with the music.

I yawned. It wasn't anywhere near midday yet and there was a lot to do, but I'd done some tending and my belly was the most full it had been in days. I'd earned a nap.

I lay down closer to the center of the garden. On a bed of flowers—well, not literally; I lay on soil and grass surrounded by flowers.

A white orchid leaned into my ear, whispering fragrance like a lover's secret. I'm not familiar with what that's like, mind you, but my mom always laughed when my dad used that description. There was also the breezy scent of honeysuckles in the air, though there was none around.

One hard-working bee landed on my nose, confusing the merchant with the merchandise.

I drifted off and the flowers faded, but the void of nothingness failed to greet me for the first time in months. Instead, I dreamed.

I was on the muddy banks of the blue-green Tigris river, standing by a throng of fishermen whose nets were tangled together. The breeze brushed the water, danced around the fishermen, and grazed me before fading into the palm trees. The sensation was pleasant, the playful push of a friend.

I looked down to see little pink drops flecked on my forearms.

I turned to the fishermen, taking in their statue-still sandaled feet, their rigid form, and their headless necks spewing fountains of blood into the wind. The fluttering flow was as hypnotic as it was terrifying.

The river tickled my toes, breaking the spell and leaving the dread behind. The water's touch was thicker and heavier than memory would have suggested. I waded in, in an attempt to wash away what I'd seen. The river coagulated around me, the blue-green turning dark scarlet like in one of Moses' plagues.

Nine dried, skeletal snakes slithered out of an indistinct carcass suspended in the center of the bloody water. They circled around me on their way to the shore, nine maws ready to bite, fangs bared, but pulling away at the last second. I flinched at their bite but couldn't take my eyes off them.

The snakes swam to the shore swiftly, and clambered out of the water. Some slithered, while others walked on makeshift legs and claws, formed out of the blood beneath them bubbling together into mangled flesh. Their wiry bodies filled out, their yellow eyes exuding hunger.

They tore the fishermen's nets and plowed onward.

I tried to follow them, to run and warn the city, to defend the fishermen's dead bodies, anything.

But the water pulled me in, eager to replenish the store of blood it had lost with their departure.

I started to dissolve into the scarlet river—

—And woke up, sweaty despite the cool spring air, a faint trace of blood lingering in the breeze.

The bee on my nose lurched into open space as I jolted to my feet. I brushed past the orchid and was shaking so badly I just missed stepping on a wayward tulip.

Images from the dream clouded my vision. The Tigris

turning blood red. Nine monsters gnawing their way toward me. The headless fishermen. *How many nightmares am I meant to live?* I stumbled out of the garden before I knew what I was doing. Tripping on the threshold wasn't enough to slow me, but when I reached the ramshackle houses that had survived the fall of the city I went still.

The trace of blood was gone and the bright glare of the morning sun made me blink at the fear I'd felt.

Before I could turn back, Shaykh Nariman hailed me. His face brightened upon seeing me, but the light tempered as he noticed my complexion. He hurried me toward his ruined shack by a pile of long-forgotten trash.

The heavy-set baker cut between me and Shaykh Nariman as I approached. His thick brow rose in surprise but he inclined his head to me—yet didn't acknowledge Shaykh Nariman at all. He walked off before I could thank him for sending the bread earlier.

I made it to the door of Shaykh Nariman's hovel and the stale odor of the garbage beside it contrasted so greatly with the flowers from before that I wavered, dismissing thoughts of retreat only because they'd be rude.

"Why don't you clean it up, Sidi?" I asked.

"Why should I clean when there are young folk like you to do it for me?" he said, his mustache curling as he smiled. "Though it has been a while since you visited. Meanwhile, how many times have I walked through the flowers to find you now? That's not good for my knees."

I lowered my head, trying to distract myself from the knot in my chest by thinking about how stepping on the soft soil was probably good for his knees, but he went "tut-tut" till I met his eyes. "I'll have none of that guilt now," he said. "I am inclined to celebrate you coming here but the set of your jaw tells me this is something serious."

He motioned for me to join him inside. As usual, his footsteps were silent. For an old man living alone in such dismal circumstances, he had an elegant way of carrying himself. His white beard was untrimmed yet it never looked disheveled. His clothes were clean, unmarked by a single mote, despite the dusty film covering his hovel. I wondered, not for the first time, if his peculiar living habits were why people always ignored him on the street. I don't think he'd done anything shameful in the past.

He saw me blanche at the sight of mold on the divan and gestured for me to squat with him.

"Well, my boy, you haven't left home or the garden grounds for anything other than necessities in the last two months. What brought you out when my words failed?" Shaykh Nariman asked, concern mixed with a salty sting.

"I—"I wasn't sure where to begin a response. I was *needed* at the garden. There were always weeds to pluck, plants to prune, and bugs to fight. I was never afraid of leaving the garden, I just felt like it was where I should be.

Shaykh Nariman took my pause as a request for advice. "Khurafa, my dear lad, your parents are in the garden of paradise." He began, a sympathetic smile on his face. "Making this one more beautiful won't make it Eden and it won't bring them back. You see it as your duty to continue their legacy, but boy, you are their legacy! You need to get out and be a kid— "

I blurted out the contents of the dream in one continuous stream of words—to forestall the lecture, I told myself. My cheeks were hot and flushed, first from embarrassment at cutting him off and then from reliving the dream. At the mention of the headless fishermen Shaykh Nariman frowned. When I talked about the snakes, his frown deepened into a scowl. By the end of my recollection, his face had turned so pale that for a second, he seemed transparent.

"Do you know what it means?" I asked. The widening of his eyes and the quiver of his upper lip told me he did.

He drew in a deep, heavy breath which somehow didn't set the dust particles in the room in motion. He launched into familiar territory, maybe to inform me or perhaps to comfort himself. The further he got into his monologue the more relaxed his voice became.

"You know there are some dreams that are real, visions from God embedded in symbols that we don't understand," he said. "Others are tricks from the devil. And the rest, the vast majority, are fantasies that our imagination concocts—"

I nodded as he spoke. This was one of his favorite subjects and why I'd reflexively sought him out. Comfort would be great, but I was looking for understanding too. He would go on at length about the importance of dreams, how close they can be to revelation. And he never shied away from expressing his mastery at interpreting them.

"So what does this one mean?" I asked. "Is it from Satan? Or my imagination? It felt so real though. . ."

"I rather wish it was a satanic trick," he said, his expression soft. "I'm afraid it holds some truths."

He drew inward like he was scrolling through texts beneath his eyelids. After a moment's pause, he gestured to a line of moldy volumes on his bookshelf. They were riddled with worm holes and covered with cobwebs.

"My eyes aren't quite as good as they once were," he said. "Would you mind picking out a book for me? The fifth volume of Tabari's history."

I brushed the spine clean and plucked the appropriate text from the shelf. A billowing little dust cloud trailed in the book's wake. "What am I looking for?" I asked, setting the book open like I was putting down a newborn. A couple pages slipped free and lazed their way, floating to the ground.

"It's a universal history, you know," he began. "Tabari wrote in the dark hours of the night, the whole story of the world as he knew it. He wanted us to learn from the past, to improve our present." The shaykh shook a finger in emphasis as he spoke. I could sense another lecture coming on, one he'd given me before about history being less about what happened and more about how we make meaning from it.

"Shaykh," I said gently, guiding him back to the topic at hand. "What about this text makes you think of my dream?" *What about it frightened you?*

"Ah yes," he said. "Look for a couple names. Year must have been. . . 119 hijri. Mughirah ibn Sa'id. And Bayan ibn Saman." He made a spitting motion after he said them, but his mouth was dry and no saliva came out. I let go of the book and rose to get him a glass of water but he waved for me to squat again. "Find it and read," he said.

It took several minutes of browsing before I came to a splotch of red ink which read "The Execution of al-Mughirah ibn Sa'id and Bayan ibn Saman." I speed-read the dark passages below it, my eyes skirting around the occasional discolored gap in the text. I read pieces out loud; the writing style was matter of fact, bland even, though the events were strange.

"As for al-Mughirah ibn Sa id, by all accounts he was a sorcerer. He was heard saying, "I will resurrect 'Ad and Thamud. This time they will destroy and not be destroyed.

. ." I paused for a moment, confused. "Resurrect Ad and Thamud?"

"The peoples who lived long before us," Shaykh Nariman said, "Giants, skilled builders who shaped the mountains, but were decimated by God for their pride. . ." He caught sight of my eyes drifting back towards the book. "Ah, you know that, of course. Can't help but teach, I'm afraid."

I almost mustered a chuckle at his self-evident remark and went back to reading aloud. "Al-Mughirah would go out to the cemetery to preach to his followers and locusts would swarm on the graves as he spoke. Al-Mughirah ibn Sa'id rebelled with his lieutenant Bayan ibn Saman, and seven other men who called themselves 'The Servants.' Their rebellion took place outside of al-Kufah. Khalid al-Qasri captured them all at the end of the skirmish. . . "

I glanced away from the book and saw that the Shaykh's eyes were closed, his lips moving silently.

I continued, "An eyewitness reported: 'I saw Khalid when he brought al-Mughirah and Bayan with seven men, all in chains. He commanded bundles of reeds and tar to be brought. Then he ordered al-Mughirah to take up a bundle, but the latter shrank from it and delayed, chanting under his breath and looking around wildly. Lashes were rained down on his head, whereupon he took up the bundle, embracing it. He was tied to it; then tar was poured over him and over the bundle. Then fire was kindled on that snake of a man, and he was consumed by the blaze. Khalid ordered the followers to their deaths, and they submitted to the sentence with smiles on their faces. He commanded Bayan, the last of them; Bayan hastened to come to the bundle and hugged it tightly. Khalid said, 'Woe to you! Do you act foolishly in everything? Did you not see this al-Mughirah and his end?' Bayan laughed in response and continued to do so until his lungs were burned to ash. Some claimed to hear words amidst the roaring of the flame: 'We'll see you when the world changes again and your saints are dead.'"

"And so it has come to pass," the Shaykh murmured.

"What does this have to do with my dream?" I asked.

"Your dream means that 'The Servants' have returned. And something must be done to stop them." Shaykh Nariman said, his eyes still shut, his nose drooping down in regret. "There were nine sorcerers—you saw nine snakes. They were burned alive on the shores of the Tigris, probably where you stood. They swore to return when the world shifts and the saints die. Fishermen are an old biblical metaphor for saintly folk, starting with the disciples of Prophet Isa—Christ himself. They were dead in your dream. And we've now witnessed the most devastating conquest in history; the Mongols wrecked the world two months ago and many of the pious have perished. The world *has* changed again."

"But it's been hundreds of years. How could they come back to life? Only God can resurrect the dead," I argued. What he was saying sounded more like the epic tales he'd tell me than any religious insights he would preach. But he'd been teaching me for five years, calling out only to me while other kids played. I had too much respect to be dismissive.

"They burned alive—their bodies were reduced to ash, but did they die?" Shaykh Nariman asked, opening his eyes just a crack, facing me. They were glassy and I could only see the whites. He was lost somewhere in the domain of memory. "Jinn possess people. You've heard stories."

I shuddered only slightly at the thought of the tales other

kids used to tell me of spirit creatures taking over people's bodies and overcoming their will. Those anecdotes always gave me chills that heroic battles against monstrous 'devs' failed to evoke.

"Why shouldn't men with black magic possess others?" He asked. There was a shade of awe in his voice, but his body shook as if he might vomit at the thought. "That, I believe, is how they survived. The nine of them worked together to possess something else—some*one* else. They escaped the coils of their mortal flesh just as it burned. Their host froze upon the possession, keeping their souls tethered to it but alive. But now the host is dead and they have been free to seek newer, more pliable vessels."

"How do you know that?" I asked. "And what kind of host would survive so long? That doesn't make any sense. . . "

Instead of answering, he made his way toward the door, beckoning for me to open it. His limbs shook with every motion. But his face was stalwart, jaw set as he asked his own question. "Do you think you can identify the part of the river where your dream took place?"

"I'm not sure," I said. "I was too distracted by the blood and snakes. . ." And the garden needed tending so there wasn't time to look around randomly. The vines on the orange tree and the intrusive wild flowers were waiting. . . I couldn't leave the plants all alone like that. I had concrete responsibilities to take care of first, a whole list I didn't complete because I was snoozing.

The practical demands of the day have a way of making dreams fade, though I suspected this one would stick around.

"I think I'll go back now Ya Shaykh," I said, turning away from the serious expression etched into the wrinkles of his face.

It all sounded like a child's fantasy. . . or a scholar's dementia. Still, I didn't disbelieve. I just needed to think things through, to digest. And I was sure I'd spotted mice in the neighborhood. If I wasn't careful they'd burrow beneath the garden wall.

Shaykh Nariman's wrinkles furrowed further and his lips pursed. "Are you sure boy? This isn't the sort of thing you forget about. What it means for all of us is harrowing. Can you walk away from it?"

"I'm not running away," I said. I knew the Shaykh tended to get a bit dramatic, but this. . . "If there is something that needs to be done, I'll do it. It's a lot to take in, I need to process." Weed the garden, weed my thoughts.

"I'll walk you back," Shaykh Nariman said. He must have known his presence alone was a form of persuasion because we trekked back in brisk silence.

I caught a whiff of the smoke before I spotted the trailing tendrils. My stomach growled loud but a second sniff stifled it. The fire wasn't from a barbecue like my appetite had thought; there was no taste of crisp meat wafting over me. I wasn't trying to claw my nose off, so the fumes didn't come from burning trash. In fact, the opposite—there was a hint of incense and an overtone of aromatic wood.

The tendrils led to a grayscale plume. I broke into a desperate run, leaving Shaykh Nariman behind and abandoning all the polite glances I gave to make sure his balance was steady.

I knew what the source was before I saw it. It hadn't been enough for the world to end two months earlier. Now *my* world had burned to the ground.

God's voice did not call out from the burning bushes but I could hear the orchids scream. Tulip petal embers waltzed in the haze. Palm trees became torches. The young olive and fig trees were blackened, bent husks.

My dream made me rise and run. But this time, the night-mare of reality brought me to my knees.

Chapter 2

My earliest memory is of my mom hefting me into the air and letting me sail ever so slightly into empty space before catching me. Up and down I went, chirping in delight like a chick discovering flight. The garden gate was shut, so her scarf was draped around her shoulders and her curly black hair bobbed every time she leapt for me. She flung me a little too far once, and my head bumped a rind hanging low from the orange tree. It was a squishy ball bouncing against my head—of course it didn't hurt. But I cried anyway, because I wanted her to pull me close, to dance between the daisies while cradling me, reciting her favorite poems into my ear like they were lullabies.

Now that same orange tree was a chandelier adorned with flaming, melting orbs. The heat turned my tears to mist while the smoke stung my eyes. I sank into the ruined soil.

"Maybe you can save it!" Shaykh Nariman yelled at my prone form. "Get water! Don't just sit there!"

On the third repetition, his words pierced the fog in my mind. I scrambled for a bucket, but in the end it didn't matter. The walls prevented the flame from spreading, but also created an oven. The blaze died when its fuel ran out and the garden my family had cared for, for four generations, died with it. I'd failed and I didn't know how or why.

****

I combed my fingers through the soot. Nothing survived. My calluses were raw and red with burns. Ash clung to me like a second skin. The scent of the non-existent honeysuckles taunted me.

I pulled myself to my feet, using the carcass of a grape vine for leverage. It crumbled under my grip. Something in me crumbled too.

I couldn't figure out how the fire started, why it burned so quickly, or how it decimated the roots. I sprinkled water throughout, but there was nothing to salvage.

I tried to find the fig and olive trees, to hold onto their charred wood at the very least. But they were gone now. Two small, blackened mounds were all that was left in their place.

I used my hands as shovels, pulling out clumps of Earth to check if any roots had survived. One hole, then another. I grabbed a scorched shovel to search deeper in the soil.

Shaykh Nariman watched me work without saying anything. He was slumped against a scorched wall. He looked worn, his limbs thinner than usual.

At some point a Mongol official popped his head in, but I didn't stop digging. He found nothing worth beating or stealing, so he left me to my misery.

The baker and his boy stopped by too, with mournful expressions on their faces and muttered words.

They left a few pieces of naan on a straw plate by the door. I had the presence of mind to pause my work and pass them a few *fils*, which they didn't refuse. Neither so much as nodded at Shaykh Nariman.

After I had dug my ninth hole to double check the roots,

Shaykh Nariman spoke up. "Khurafa, that's enough," he said firmly. He was standing—staggering, but standing.

I kept digging, tearing into the soil without even registering the blisters peppering my palms. He continued. "I'm sorry this has happened—but remember, your parents never expected you to take care of the garden alone. Maybe now you can turn your attention—"

"To *what?*" I screamed. "To that dream? To sorcerers and make-believe? Maybe there is dark magic, maybe that destroyed the—the—"

My eyes had regained enough moisture for tears to bubble. Every fiber of my being quaked in frustration and pain, but also in mortification. How could I have talked to the Shaykh that way?

He looked at me, the corners of his eyes crinkling in compassion, but he didn't embrace me or put a comforting hand on my shoulder. He hadn't done that even after what happened to my parents. Instead he spoke, taking my every word seriously. "Perhaps," he said, "it could be connected. The fire could be God removing your attachments. It could be a warning of what's to come if you do nothing. It could be an attack by the servants, though I don't know how they'd have found you. . . Or it could be a freak accident, pure chance. Its meaning is uncertain, but your dream's interpretation is not."

I balled my hands into fists but I couldn't punch a fire that was already extinguished. What good would it do if I did?

Shaykh Nariman spoke past all my rage and frustration. "Let's find the place in your dream. Please." The last few words he said under his breath. "At the very least it'll take your mind off of this."

I reflexively moved to pick the shovel up again but it clattered out of my grip. My fingers were trembling. I took deep breaths and thought of the bird's eye view of the earth like my mother taught me to do at times like this.

Shaykh Nariman stood there, arms crossed, expectant.

I'd need to start replanting but the soil was already ruined for this season. I could dig it up and dredge up new soil though, get things ready in advance. But the plants wouldn't be the same. The last flowers and shrubs my parents had planted, watered with their sweat and blood, were gone. The only thing they'd entrusted to me was ruined.

I met Shaykh Nariman's eyes. The orange glow of sunset reflected in them so it looked like they were burning.

Maybe God would reward me for listening to a scholar, however eccentric. Maybe the dream was true and all of this was punishment for not acting on it right away. Maybe doing something now could help me salvage the situation and bring the greenery back.

So many maybes.

I stared at the gaping holes in the barren ground, holes I'd carved. I wondered for a melodramatic moment if that's what my heart looked like.

"Let's go," I said, my voice a whimper. The Shaykh had repeatedly asked me to leave the garden for the past two months. He deserved better. I couldn't say that I was finally doing as he asked. There wasn't a garden to leave anymore.

I tried to spend the hike staring at the ground in anguish, but Shaykh Nariman's steps were so jittery I couldn't help keeping a hand outstretched and ready to catch him. He never took it. The firm line of his determined lips was as solid as his footing was poor.

I stumbled over some trash once as I watched him, lurching

towards a clump of rocks, mud, and slime. I managed to kick out my left foot just in time to restore my balance.

The riverbank near the city was never clean—trash, rotten vegetables, and runaway laundry all found their way to the shore. But the conquest had upped the ante on the pollution. I was beginning to think the most unrealistic part of my nightmare was how clean the river was.

The fetid smell of refuse was jostled by the breeze, sometimes overwhelming me and sometimes vanishing. And there it was again, piercing my senses, out of place—the scent of honeysuckles.

I'm not sure how I recognized the part of the river from the dream. It looked like any other spot; there was no distinctive bend or noticeable rocks, and there were no fishermen, headless or otherwise, lingering on the bank. But I knew. The water was blue and green, dyed orange from the sun's afterglow. When I closed my eyes I saw the pink and red. I opened them and the water was normal.

Beside me, the shaykh collapsed to the ground, planting his bony bottom on gravel.

Something caught my eye before I could turn to help him. And my balance gave out too. It was a day for wobbly knees.

It looked at first like a man in the river, but it couldn't be. The being was five times larger than the largest person I'd ever seen, with limbs more like tree trunks than branches and tusk-like teeth bearing out of a gaping mouth that resembled a wolf's snout. The creature's eyes gleamed yellow, and its skin was the translucent gray of a rainy day, covered with uneven patches of matted fur. With every passing second, it faded, becoming more see-through, like an after image.

It wasn't the size or the animalistic appearance of the

creature that had stolen the strength from my step. There was a rent in the creature's mountain-like chest, a massive hole with leathery skin torn outward, as if something had exploded out from the inside. Traces of dark blue blood leaking from the cavity shimmered, sizzled, and evaporated.

Before I could fully process what I was seeing, I'd crawled towards the water, preparing to dive and reach for the creature, whatever it was. If I could touch it, make sense of it, save it. . .

The tips of my fingers had just touched the water when the Shaykh's belabored shout broke my trance. "It's gone! It's gone!"

I eyed the spot where the bizarre cadaver had been, and he was right; the gradual vanishment had completed. I would have swum into open water and probably drowned. I'd forgotten in the cloudy cognizance of the moment that in real life, I could barely swim.

"W-what was that?" I asked, the words tumbling out though I'd already come up with an answer.

"A dead jinn," Shaykh Nariman said. "The 'Servants' possessed him and the act paralyzed both parties for centuries. And now it's over. They burst free and killed him. Jinn corpses don't last long in this world. But now you've seen one and you *know* the story is real."

For a moment the shaykh's whole body glimmered in the light, as if he were also see-through. But it was only a moment. He looked as tired as I felt.

The dream. The garden. And now an actual jinn corpse. Maybe I should have been surprised or rubbed my eyes out of my sockets in disbelief. But I just felt sluggish. There was a weight in my chest that I couldn't pinpoint.

The shaykh didn't say anything to me as we walked back. He

knew that I wouldn't be able to answer with more than a grunt.

I threw myself onto my bed in my tiny home right outside the garden's wall. The sheets were stained green and brown from all the times when I'd fallen straight to sleep after work.

I had the same dream again. But this time the serpentine creatures crawled all the way to the ruins of my garden and burrowed into the nine holes I'd dug. They gnawed on dead roots and then on me.

Chapter 3

The smell of soot filled my nose when I woke, though a hint of honeysuckle tempered the harshness. I yawned and swallowed a few white, ashy particles dripping through a leak in the ceiling. Even in the groggy moments of getting up, the garden's carcass followed me.

I opened my door only to see Shaykh Nariman resting with his back against the garden wall, eyes closed. I moved to close the door, but instead found myself biting my lower lip, trying to find appropriately polite words with which to scold him for not knocking and waking me. Of course, he'd never knocked in all the years I'd known him. A second glance at the soft, blank expression on his face made me brush away the words and walk out to him. He looked like some saint out of a storybook. The wind tickled bits of dust over the wall's edge, but none clung to him. I leaned close without brushing against him but before I could decide whether to whisper or yell, his eyes opened.

"Wanted to make sure you're alive," I said. "You barely breathe when you sleep."

I walked towards the garden gate which was pock-marked with burned-out holes and tar-black splinters. I paused before pushing it open; I knew what I'd see: The holes in the gate offered previews that the grass hadn't miraculously re-grown under the moonlight. My pause became a standstill. I bounced from one foot to the other and stretched both arms.

Shaykh Nariman lurked behind me like a shadow. "You need to tell others what you saw, to warn them about what's coming. You should visit the Mongol *Amir* and tell him."

I rotated each shoulder and then leaned toward my toes.

He continued, "The Prophet, peace be upon him, gathered the people and stood atop the hill and warned them. I am not saying you should do that, but surely the rulers need to know. Whatever travesties our new overlords committed, they'll not stand a threat to their rule. . ."

I took a slow, deliberate step towards the gate, flexing my fingers in anticipation of pushing ever so gently.

His voice became heated. "It takes time to process, to reflect, but in issues of truth and justice, one must act. . . "

On my second step, my foot sank into a lump of cinders and I slid forward, colliding head first into the gate and bursting it open. The charred wood bumped my head back and stopped my fall, but it crumbled into shards and rubble. The door frame dangled holding nothing but an image of ruin and the nine holes dug in the soil.

"Your duty to the garden is finished. Now you've been given a task by the divine Himself," Shaykh Nariman said. "Tend to the people with half the care you gave to flowers."

I faced him and rubbed my eyes before any tears could brim. I couldn't muster the words to apologize for trying to ignore him, but I didn't need to. He'd dealt with both my curiosity and my tantrums for years.

"I'm Amir Hamza off to fight some devs, right?" I mumbled. He smiled, wrinkles and dimples mingling in an expression of pure warmth.

I told him about the dream I just had with the reptilian Servants in my garden. His brow furrowed. "It could be Prophetic—further motivation toward action. Or, more likely, it is a normal nightmare brought on by the fear of the first dream. When you wake next, seek refuge in God and blow three times to the left. Do it for protection."

I stalked off to my musty room and smoothed the creases in my fanciest pair of clothes—a green embroidered kurta and refined shilwar that I'd worn at Eid the previous year. I'd wanted to spend the money on a singing bird which a peddler advertised aggressively, but my parents laughed and said enough birds came to the garden and performed for free. Why cage something beautiful when beauty is already bountiful around you? My parents bought the clothes and when I attended the festival, a blue bird landed for a brief moment on my shoulder. I touched the spot where it perched as I changed and could almost hear the echo of my mother's laugh.

Where would the birds go now?

After wearing the clothes, I marched out of my house so single-mindedly I had to loop back to close the door. Shaykh Nariman gave me another warm, grandfatherly smile and I lifted a hand in farewell.

As I cut through the city proper for the first time in two months, I relied on old habits, walking quickly and carefully. My dad had always said—*the best way to avoid getting robbed is to walk like you know where you're going and are almost there.* My mom would scold me about running and getting dust on my pants—the soil from gardening was ignored but street dirt always earned a tongue lashing.

I passed by several broken walls and more than one shop or stand left in pieces. I dodged mounted horsemen with disinterested glares who rode their heavily hooved mounts on ill-suited roads.

The city had changed. But the biggest difference from before wasn't the lurking presence of the new rulers or the occasional mark of destruction—it was the volume of the city's buzz. It was loud and bustling by average standards no doubt, but Baghdad was never an average city. People had died, people had fled, and the change in numbers was audible. A million chuckles, boasts, and brash remarks, had dwindled into thousands of murmurs.

The rivers of people on the streets and seas of humanity in the squares had turned into a few streams and ponds. I crossed without slipping and drowning in memory.

The palace jutted out from beside the Tigris River. The marble patio which had risen over the river had collapsed right down the middle. Many of the columns of the main structure were askew and more than one wall had been picked clean of tiles. Two of the arched doorways to the courtyard were rubble, but a third stood firm, the floral patterns woven into its sandstone barely cracked.

A complex of hide tents covered the husk of what had been the most beautiful gardens in the land. My parents took me many times to the hill closest to the walls so I could spy the heavenly floral arrangements of the royal gardeners in the courtyard. My mom would sigh and mutter verses to herself and my dad's eyes would light up with the ambition to someday surpass those hedges. Now all the bushes were gone, their remains munched on by massive stallions out to pasture. The Mongols wouldn't just change the population of the land, they'd change its vegetation too. They would devour the cities and their horses and herds would eat away the countryside.

"They're gog and magog, you know," a passing old man with wild hair, wilder eyes, and a missing arm said as he read the distaste on my face. "A tribe from the end of the world, come at the end of time. . . They'll consume everything, just you wait."

A grown woman, his long-suffering daughter probably, hushed him loud enough that it drew more attention.

"What? Can't speak the truth anymore?" he whined as she pulled him away.

I approached the remnants of the garden walls, trying to figure out the most effective way to gain an audience. There was a line to meet with a minister and lodge complaints, but most of those in it were hardy men. The way they shifted about, it didn't seem they expected to have much luck getting what they wanted. I looked out to the river and for a moment it seemed to shimmer red.

My stomach churned as I walked toward the line, and bumped into a frowning serving boy. A plate of pomegranate-dyed beef strips tumbled out of his hand and cracked on the ground.

"Great," he huffed. "I'll get chewed out for the food being rejected and *now* for the plate breaking. Why oh why are their tastes so bland? "

"Ah—I'm sorry. I can pay for the plate. That was my fault," I said, fishing into my pouch.

The serving boy looked up and down at my outfit and frowned. "I doubt it. This is the most refined porcelain, imported from the far east. It's worth more than my monthly salary, I'll tell you. It doesn't matter though. I'm quitting. The cooks send me to serve the savages, the savages spit on the food, and I'm the one who gets chewed out. 'Their tastes will change, you're just not presenting it well enough' the cooks always say. So why don't they present it to those monsters themselves then?" He tore off his embroidered apron and lacquered skull cap and stormed off.

"Are—are you sure?" I called after him. "Won't they look for you?" He ignored me and marched away. I picked up the apron and cap, unsure whether to chase after him or not. I saw the line, unmoving and now growing. "I seek forgiveness from Allah," I whispered, slipping the apron on.

The odds of someone quitting so theatrically and providing a ripe opportunity like this had to be slim to none. I could imagine Shaykh Nariman flailing a finger in the air and saying, "God is aiding you, paving your path! There is no coincidence!"

A long whiskered cook came by, dripping ladle still in his hand. He took one look at me wearing the apron and holding the hat, and glanced over the cracked dish on the ground. "So you're the replacement then," he said. "Put the hat on. They won't say no to a bowl of fruit at least. Though I'm sure they'd much prefer dried horse's milk. I can't even begin to. . ." He walked off.

"What about the plate?" I called out.

"We'll talk about that when you come to get your salary," he said, taking long strides towards the palace kitchen. It had been ransacked like the rest of the complex but was the first place to be repaired, I quickly found out. The cooks had convinced the conquering khan of the merit of their cuisine— diplomacy by the mouthful—but the *amir* he had appointed to the city was less cultured and his men were getting upset stomachs.

In a few minutes I was bearing a platter of sliced apples topped with honey. I walked past menacing guards wearing leather jerkins and bearing twisted knives. Their eyes didn't even register me. I slipped through the flap of the largest tent, which was made from the hides of a dozen beasts. I smelled cloying odors of jasmine perfume and musk mixed with an abundance of horse. The aroma of conquerors settling in our lands. The combination was jarring, but I could smell the potential . It wasn't a cheap, gaudy smell—it was just real.

Inside the tent, a huge man squatted on a mass of lion's fur while yapping commands to a small, jet black dog. The dog sat and stretched its limbs lazily, tongue lolling as it failed to follow or even register its master's commands. The man—the *amir*—yapped at it again with a bemused smile on his face. I couldn't understand the commands spoken in his language, but it seemed he was personally training the puppy, rearing it into one of his proud hunting dogs.

I set the platter down before him and he scooped up a handful of apples slices while gesturing for the dog to scrape up the remainder. Could a man who cared for an animal be all that bad?

I cleared my throat and looked at the puppy so I wouldn't lose confidence. "O great Amir, my name is Khurafa and I am a humble gardener. I wanted to pass on a warning about a seditious group of sorcerers called The Servants—"

I went on for a few minutes while his dark eyes pierced me. I was beginning to sweat, cracking like the plate that got me through the door.

When I finished, the tent was silent except for the expectant slobbering of the dog. The khan scratched its back and spoke slow words I could make no sense of. Then he barked out a boisterous laugh.

It occurred to me that he might not have understood me at all, that a new ruler from distant lands wouldn't know the language of his subjects. "Ya Allah. . ." I whispered, pleading. The amir smiled— fear at least was a universal language.

A measured voice came from behind me. "What he said was: Do the assassins among your people kill by talking targets to death?"

I turned and took in a tall man with an exquisitely trimmed brown beard and a lavish robe of deep red and brown. "You should probably run, boy. I doubt the puppy will be able to chase after you like its older peers."

"But I—" I gulped realizing who I was talking to. "Honored Vizier, I have a message to convey, you see—"

"Yes, yes, I heard everything." He said with a rueful smile on his face. "These days are filled with endless doomsday prophecies, new rumors of myths and monsters." He paused. "The time of the Hour is known only to God. The masses worry when they should work. But normalcy takes a while. I have to say though, I haven't heard of Mughirah and The Servants since reading Tabari as a child. This is certainly a new conspiracy theory. I rather like it. Asking the Mongols to stop the end of the world, rather than saying they are the end of the world. . . quite audacious."

"It—it's not made up, sir. My shaykh said—" I tried to explain with recourse to Shaykh Nariman because I had no proof of what I saw in the river.

"Boy, tell me." The minister said, lowering himself eye-level to me, while the amir watched with a toothy grin. "Why did your shaykh not come himself? Why send a boy—whose story would inevitably sound like a tall-tale, a fantasy—when he could have brought his own gravitas?"

"He's. . . he's old and doesn't travel much," I struggled to come up with a better answer. It *was* weird though that Shaykh Nariman hadn't followed me. He was old but he'd gone to the river. He could have come here himself along with me. He'd seen the jinn too.

"I'll let you go as it seems you may have been tricked." The minister said softly, "Though of course we'll have to see if the *amir* agrees." He launched off into the Mongols' language, speaking with the exact accent I'd heard the khan use. In mere months he'd mastered their tongue. . . or he had been brought with them from their earlier conquests.

The puppy was dancing around the tent floor while I stifled a yawn waiting for the amir's answer.

The little creature nipped at my toes. The amir eyed it while responding to the minister.

"Hmm," the minister said. "It seems that because Dolchen, his puppy, likes you, you are free to go with your head intact. You should thank your benefactor."

I scratched the puppy's head with both hands.

"Umm, I took this job because a serving boy quit. But there's a plate I broke that I'm not sure I can pay off. . ."

"A bit too honest, aren't we? Perhaps your parents taught you too well." The minister eyed my calloused hands, a tiny bit of soil stuck in my nails despite my scrubbing. "A gardener? It's too bad these gardens are not what they were. Run off now. Don't worry about the plate. I have many that can replace it."

"Thank you."

"Infidels may have taken over, but principles of justice and mercy need not be lost. Give it time and we'll see normalcy, you'll see." There was a glint in the minister's eye as he shooed me away.

Chapter 4

By the time I made it back to Shaykh Nariman's hovel, my fancy clothes were stained with samples of mud and dust from around the city. My mom would have scolded me if she could have seen me.

Shaykh Nariman's door, as always, was half-open. I called out and no one answered.

In the days before I'd holed up in the garden, I would always leave and come back later when this happened. But now, after the minister's questioning, I had a sinking suspicion that the shaykh was using me somehow. He'd taught me and talked to me so freely for so long that the feeling seemed unworthy, but the world had ended and the garden was gone. Could I be surprised anymore?

I decided I wanted the doubt dealt with right away; I felt guilty being suspicious of him at all. I called out his name once or twice more, and after hearing only silence, I entered the house without permission.

"Shaykh Nariman! I let myself in!" I yelled as I went from decayed room to decayed room. Dust and mold dominated every surface. There were blackened remnants of fires from passing squatters and broken glass from wild youths who broke in to carouse while the shaykh was away.

I kicked myself again for never taking the initiative to clean things up for him and being too caught up in myself to pay attention to his living conditions. A room with a stained bed teemed with bugs. Falling bits of the ceiling had disturbed their environment, but no person had. The bed hadn't been slept in for a long time. And Shaykh Nariman was nowhere to be found.

I saw only a single recent set of footsteps imprinted into the dust as I exited. They were small, hurried, and unaccompanied. I recognized them as my own.

I walked outside on shaky legs. I knew people could be dirty, and I knew an ascetic like Shaykh Nariman might ignore discomfort in his surroundings. I'd seen that time and again in his sitting room, but this was something else, and it flew in contrast with the dignified way he carried himself. Did he sleep in the room? I considered the distant look that was sometimes in his eyes and would have wondered if he slept at all if it hadn't been for this morning.

The minister's questions needled me and I was hyper-aware of the dirt on the floor, so I opted to search for Shaykh Nariman outside rather than wait for him to return.

I went to the baker whose shop was closest to the hovel. The wafting aroma of warm bread erased the fungal sting left on my senses.

"Excuse me." I swallowed before I could salivate at the sight of fresh bread. "Do you know where Shaykh Nariman is?"

"Shaykh Nariman?" the baker said, scratching his beard and sprinkling it with bread crumbs. "It's been a long time, Subhan Allah." Had it been a long time though? He'd seen Shaykh Nariman and I together only the day before.

The baker pointed past the last row of houses, toward the

grove of palm trees marking the graveyard. "I'm sure you'll find him there. Please do give him my greetings." He didn't offer me any naan this time.

My feet, which had been fleet until this point, grew heavy as lead. It had been two months since I'd entered the graveyard. My parents would take me there often when they were alive, to plant flowers around the tombs 'so the plants can pray for the deceased.' A hint of guilt pricked me for not planting anything at their plots, but I shook it off. It was in the flowers we'd planted together that I felt their presence. Graves were places of absence; gardens were promises of things to come.

But the flowers were gone.

Weeds peeked out of several graves. Since my parents became residents of the graveyard, it had ironically lost its most devoted casual caretakers. I couldn't see Shaykh Nariman standing anywhere and figured that he might be crouched or sitting by a tombstone, so I scanned multiple rows. Some graves had unmarked rocks, others had slabs engraved with cursive writing, and one or two elaborate marble steles stood out in the otherwise humble environs. A lingering smell of incense and musk oozed from some of the stones.

"Peace be upon you, people of the grave. . ." The flowers had at least jostled in the breeze when I greeted them. The dead were silent and still.

I skimmed the names even as my eyes darted around looking for Shaykh Nariman.

I began to recite the Fatiha; I didn't want to be in the graveyard but I couldn't not pray for those I visited. "In the name of God, the most Gracious the most merciful, praise—"

And then I found him. Or his name, at least. On a grave. With a death date 12 years prior.

"What the—" I muttered. His name wasn't so uncommon and there were so many dead. But the peculiar coincidence was compounded by a whisper in my ear.

"How did it go?" Shaykh Nariman asked, from right behind me. I hadn't sensed him or heard his footsteps at all. His sudden interruption of the graveyard's stillness made me flinch a little too hard, and trip backward.

I fell right into Shaykh Nariman—and *through* him, like passing through a warm wind. I caught myself and tumbled to the side, landing atop an especially gravely grave and scratching my knees.

"I—I passed through—"

Things came together, tidbits of information I'd always known but never linked together. Why no one ever greeted the shaykh, why his place looked like no one lived there. Why he couldn't speak to the khan or the vizier. Why he never touched me. Why he somehow always looked so clean, as if the dust passed right through him. . .

I looked at the stone with his name on it again and reached out to grab his wrist. He tried to pull his hand away but I slapped it from above and below. My hands clapped together, the sound echoing across the steles and slabs.

"You're a hallucination," I said, a chill spread through my entire body, starting from where I was supposed to have touched him. "You're not real."

I must have imagined everything—not just the shaykh who conveniently gave me answers and looked out for me when the rest of the world forgot, but the creature in the river too. The story I'd told the khan was pure fantasy. It was the coping mechanism of a kid who'd lost his parents and then seen the only place he cared about burned to the ground.

"Come now," Shaykh Nariman said, stifling both a chuckle and a yawn out of respect for the serious environment. "I meant to tell you a long time ago, but I never really got around to it—"

I vomited onto the grave of whoever the real Shaykh Nariman had been, watering the weeds with the little sustenance I'd consumed over the last day.

"None of that please, son," the fictitious Shaykh Nariman said, stepping forward. "You're not seeing things that aren't there, you just see more than most people—smell more—"

I circled around the gravestone. It was a flimsy barrier to protect me from my own mind.

"Think boy—did you know all the things I've told you over the years? Did you know where to look in Tabari? You were chosen for something great, granted a great responsibility. And I'm not surprised precisely *because* you've always been able to see me," he said.

I stuffed my hand against my ears, but couldn't drown out the illusion. "Boy," he said. "I am a jinn."

I gritted my teeth and glared at this rebellious product of my own imagination. "But you're totally immaterial. And I thought jinn have powers—"

"I'm old," he said, his stern expression replaced by a wrinkled smile. "That's why I don't have much power. A normal jinn would be able to fully materialize and take on a human form, or possess a human even, without too much trouble. But at this age, the most I can do is maintain an illusion which you can only see because of your firsat. The Amir wouldn't have been able to see me. . . "

"A *firsat*?" I asked; his teaching tone caught me off guard. I was so used to it from him that I responded on instinct. If he was a hallucination did that mean I'd spent years lecturing myself?

"Let me not get ahead of myself." He said. "I am the real Shaykh Nariman. I was able to maintain a material, human form until about twelve years back. After that, I feigned death. But out of sheer habit, I kept up this illusory form. I was alone with my studies for a few years, but then you were able to see me and I was excited—excited to impart knowledge, to still participate with and interact with humans.

I'm sorry. I'm sorry I didn't tell you. As you can see, this sort of thing is not easy to tell and I feared you might act out if you knew, or avoid me."

He put a hand to his non-existent heart, and bowed his fictitious head.

"So you either don't exist or you deceived me," I said, unsure whether my mind or my mentor betraying me was worse.

"What is a *firsat*?" I asked.

"Some people are given the divine gift of *baraka*, of blessings. It may be earned or it may be granted without any action—God gives as he wills. You know this of course. A firsat is a manifestation of baraka, an ability to see things deeper and more truly. This entails seeing or sensing jinn and other beings that might be invisible to a normal person. But it also includes a form of extra-sensory perception that varies for each individual. You've heard of people reading faces and figuring out personalities or predicting a person's behavioral patterns from their palms? Usually those are scams, but there are some saints whose firsat used to take those forms."

"You're saying I'm a con artist," I said. I sat on the gravestone and wondered if my imagination was trying to come up with a career change now that the garden was gone.

"I don't think your firsat goes in that direction." He said. "You've told me before about smelling things that aren't there—distinct, floral scents in the distance. That is certainly a confusing thing for a gardener." He was talking about the aroma of honeysuckles, which had been tugging at me for days. It wasn't the first flower I'd smelled out of nowhere.

I'd thought hallucinating smells was a weird occupational hazard, but now it seemed hallucinating images was a logical progression."What am I smelling? People's personalities?"

"I don't know," Shaykh Nariman said, scratching his imaginary white beard. "Well, I don't know for sure. But I have a theory. That your firsat entails noticing baraka through smell. Something blessed by God emits those scents that you can perceive and others can't."

"I. . ." my voice tapered off as I considered what the jinn—or my hallucination—was saying. I'd followed an imaginary scent once when I was a kid. It led me to the carpet of a far off mosque. My parents found me curled up asleep after a full day of scrambling the city to find me. After the scolding I got that night, I never followed one of those scents again. Though I complained about them to Shaykh Nariman from time to time.

"I think you were chosen for this, Khurafa," Shaykh Nariman said. His voice was solemn and his jaw set.

"What do you mean?" I asked, but I knew what was coming without using any magical abilities of perception.

"The dream, this possible ability of yours, and the fact that I'm here—that we encountered each other and know each other. It's destined. I was alive when the Servants attempted their revolt. I was far from things, but I can tell you their power was real, their threat was apparent. At that time, there were many spiritual adepts and heroes. But now so many have died.

If you can find those with baraka like I suspect, you can bring together people who can stop them." He said, clasping his hands together.

"So either an ancient jinn is telling me I'm special and chosen, which probably means I am, or I've lost my mind and I'm living in a delusion," I said. I was starting to miss the red river nightmare and its terrifying simplicity.

"Which would you rather believe?" Shaykh Nariman asked.

"I'd rather have proof that I'm not crazy. I'd like to know if I'm needed to help the world—or if *I'm* the one needing help."

"That can be arranged in two ways," Shaykh Nariman said. "If I take a smaller form, I can become fully material. You can feel that I'm solid and *know* that I'm real."

"If I'm hallucinating scents and sights, a false sense of touch wouldn't be much of a stretch," I sighed.

"How does anyone know anything?" Shaykh Nariman began. "If we can't rely on senses, do we rely on reason? But how do we know our premises are true? Suhrawardi spoke of experience. . ."

I couldn't pay attention to his latest mini-lecture. At the first natural pause, I asked, "What's the other way to make sure I'm not hallucinating?"

"We follow your firsat to find a source of baraka to combat The Servants. The power of what we find will prove this is not imagined," he said.

"Where is this 'baraka' scent supposed to lead? Some magic flower that will defeat the bad guys?"

"No—think of who might be a source of baraka. A normal person perhaps, or a saint. Someone so beloved of God that baraka overflows around them, that miracles happen in their presence. When the Servants last thrived it was the saints of the time who stopped them, even before the government caught them. Imam Jafar Al-Sadiq, for example."

"The Saints are all dead," I argued. "That's why the Servants returned—because they've been killed in the conquests?"

"It is true that quite a number are gone now. But the world remains, so there must be many alive who God loves deeply. And saints spending day and night in devotion are not the only ones who might help. When I could still interact with humans, I heard of a group of holy warriors, of ghazis—men and women blessed with baraka, who dedicate themselves to fighting supernatural evils."

"Heroes. . . like Amir Hamza and Rustam." I said. If I was hallucinating, I might as well hallucinate something fun.

"That's correct. And your firsat will find them." Light shone in his illusory eyes. "But first I should probably transform into something material. It will need to be small and mobile. . ."

"How about a mouse?" I asked.

Interlude

The boy—Khurafa—shook his head a little as he reflected, launching a miniscule cloud of dust beneath him into the air. The vultures leaned in, tightening the grip of their talons.

"I don't know why I chose a mouse. Maybe I was thinking of that line of Rumi's poetry my mom taught me.

'Why with our brains don't we see/

That the mouse's guile destroyed the grain?'"

The vultures loosened their grip and shifted their positions ever so slightly.

Khurafa smiled as he continued, his expression matching his age for the first time. "He actually did it! I looked away as he transformed. He didn't crawl out of a pile of his own clothes— apparently what he was wearing was part of the 'immaterial illusion.' His new form was not what I expected.

Brown and gray fur, a tiny muzzle, a little button nose, and itty bitty paws. Shaykh Nariman was a cute, elderly rodent.

I didn't have too many positive experiences with animals before then. I mean, of course there were endless birds in the garden, so much prettier than you all. And there were bees. But other creatures I had to be wary of. Squirrels could dig holes, mice would eat things, some bugs would nibble away leaves. It was a constant battle—man and plant versus world.

But I didn't have anything to protect anymore. Except, maybe, the world.

Anyway—"

II

The Journey

Chapter 5

I chased the scent of honeysuckles through streets cluttered with rotting trash and squares filled with the debris of civilization's collapse. Broken homes, shattered cobblestones, tattered pages in the wind. The worse the scenery got, the stronger the smell became. When I started the search, it floated from several blocks, but now I could tell it was emanating from one person. One very agile person.

"What holy man wanders through the seediest parts of the city? Or is my imagination trying to get me mugged. . ."

A fountain on a nearby wall spewed a brown stew. I debated how safe it was to drink while my panting slowed.

The jinn-mouse Shaykh Nariman chirped up from within my pocket as I took a tentative sip. He lifted his white and gray-furred snout into the air while his ears sagged downwards. "Isn't that exactly where you'd find a holy man? Helping indiscriminately! With God—"

I coughed up a mouthful of rust and the soupy flavor of whatever animal died in the pipes. He continued while I spat away the taste. "With God as his protector, the dangers of this world are nothing. And why shouldn't one of the most impoverished be one of the most blessed by God? But of course, it need not be a Saint—it could be someone like you, simply granted a firsat—"

I jumped up. The honeysuckle scent was close. I whirled around to see two lumbering men, curses on their lips and fire in their eyes, running in the direction of the scent.

I followed the thugs into the alley, staying several steps behind them, and hid behind a pile of some indistinct, fuming mess.

Holding my breath, I peered past the pile toward whichever holy man radiated honeysuckles.

A girl around my age strolled to the end of the alleyway. She stopped moving, back turned towards the thugs, and took a moment to stretch her limbs and touch her toes.

I squinted. Her clothes were ragged and she wore no shoes. The thugs were nearly on top of her.

She yawned and it was like a hundred honeysuckle petals fluttered in the breeze. There was no mistaking it: She was the source of baraka. And she couldn't be less concerned about her impending doom.

Maybe she was one of those holy fools—people whose minds were so lost in the divine presence, they were no longer all there mentally. It would explain the random wandering around the city. I clenched my fists; maybe my hallucinations brought me here, but I wasn't about to let a helpless girl get hurt.

The larger thug announced their presence before I could call out a warning. "How about we don't just take what you have, but we take you instead? You'd be worth something at the slave market; with the Mongols around, no one checks for origins no more," he said, peppering his words with multiple grunts.

The girl snorted. "All you'll be taking is a nice, long nap."

What? I almost said it out loud.

The two of them closed in on her, sneering. "Scream and we'll give you ten times the beating."

"You'll be the ones screaming," she said, and lifted up a hand to cover a second yawn. She was definitely a fool but maybe not a holy one.

Fool or not, it was wrong to threaten a girl.

"When Amir Hamza saw a dev, he charged no matter how big it was. . ." I whispered to myself.

I plucked a shard of a broken wood from the trash, swiveled around the pile, and rushed at the thugs, wielding the shard with two hands like it was a sword. It crumbled in two against the head of the first thug, who staggered from the blow, but didn't fall.

Both thugs reeled on me. I tried to weave out of the range of their fists, but they weren't the unmoving vegetation I was used to. A body blow drilled me to the ground, but I managed to shout a pathetic "Run!" at the girl while grabbing the leg of the smaller thug. He kicked me with his free foot, but I kept my grip tight while seeing stars.

I was no Amir Hamza.

"That definitely didn't go as you imagined, *hero*," the girl said to me, finally turning around. She skidded under the grasp of the larger thug and leapt on the back of the one who kicked me. She tightened her arm around his neck. The larger thug moved to pry her off his friend, but she shifted her weight and her victim slumped away, out of his reach. I let go of the leg. The girl hopped off her target before the larger thug swiped at her again.

I crawled to my feet, ready to tackle one of the ruffians, but paused in awe of what was happening. The girl weaved through their punches with her eyes closed. Both men rushed her. She dropped to the ground at the last possible moment. Their heads slammed into each other. She launched into a series of punches before they could collect themselves.

The larger thug bellowed. "What? That's not even a bee sting! You little punk." He launched a sweeping blow and again she ducked. She slipped her leg behind his knee and toppled him right into his recovering friend. She picked up the more stable half of my failed wooden weapon and beat it into the temples of her assailants over and over. It crumpled between her fingers but the damage was done. The two thugs were dazed and moaning.

"Don't stand there with your mouth open like an idiot," the girl said. "Help me grab their goods."

"What?!" She wanted to steal? She was neither God-touched nor a saint.

"Me, a saint?" The girl snorted. "Guess not. But is it stealing if it's from people who were trying to rob me?"

"I didn't say anything about a saint," I said as the girl searched the two men. She pocketed the coins she found.

"Thanks for the help!" She said, "Don't wait for them to get up." She ran off.

"Wait!" I yelled. One of the thugs roused himself enough to grab my arm. I yanked my arm as hard as I could but his grip was like iron. Shaykh Nariman hopped out of my pocket and bit the man's finger with his tiny yellow incisors, breaking the grip. I scooped Shaykh Nariman up and hurtled out of the alley after the girl.

Adrenaline from the fight kept the ache from settling in, but I slowed down as thoughts percolated through the blood pumping exhilaration. Shaykh Nariman had bit the man, which meant the mouse-jinn was real, right? Hallucinations can't bite people. Or had I been the one to bite the guy? I had the urge to spit again.

I followed the scent of honeysuckles, weaving through streets, skating by a vegetable stand, hopping over the rubble of a fallen dome, and sliding past a cloth-laden mule. I finally caught up to the girl sitting on a street corner counting her take. I got a good look at her so I could find her by more than just smell if the need arose. She had curly black hair, olive skin, and a hooked nose. Her eyes were the color of limes, and when she looked up at me, her expression was just as sour.

"You led those idiots right to me," she scowled.

I turned around, and sure enough, the two thugs were huffing and puffing in their pursuit. Their faces were bruised an angry red.

I balled my fists and bellowed a war cry—this time I'd hit them and they would go down. Before I could launch any pathetic, heroic attack, the girl screamed in a pitch several times higher than her actual voice. "Help! Those men, they're trying to snatch me and my little brother. Please!"

A bulky watermelon seller approached the two thugs. An elderly aunty swung her bag of groceries like a weapon. A one-legged survivor of the war wielded his cane like a sword.

"W-wait!" The larger thug sputtered. Before he could call us thieves, the girl grabbed my wrist. "Let's go," she said, dragging me away.

We came to a stop in a previously run-down neighborhood, now further devastated by the conquest. "Alright," the girl said. "Why were you looking for me? I know you've been chasing me."

I reviewed everything in my mind. The worry about hallucinating clouded my thoughts, but I plowed past it. "It's a bit complic—" I began, but she put a hand up to stop me from speaking.

"Nevermind." She shook her head. "I don't want to know."

"But the fate of the world might be—" She gave me such a withering look that the words died. This was harder than talking to the Mongol Amir.

"Don't want to hear it, Khurafa. The more I think about it, the more messed up it is to think that you've been following me. You were a help—sort of, but that doesn't change the fact that you're a stalker," she said, backing away.

I tried to object but couldn't muster anything more than mumbles. If I'd been hallucinating everything, she was right. "B-b- but wait, how do you know my name?"

She turned away without answering.

"Stop!" Shaykh Nariman interjected, poking his head out of my pocket. He stared intently with his beady black eyes. "God has granted you a gift, whatever it might be. Do you really want to run around indulging in a life of petty thievery when your fate is so much more?"

She squinted for a second, but there was no look of shock on her face.

"Did you not hear him? Or see him?" I asked. "A talking mouse! For God's sake—"

"You're crazy," she muttered, and left.

"So you really aren't real." I stared at Shaykh Nariman. He gave me a quizzical look that would have been impossible on an actual mouse.

"You're not real," I whispered.

In my mind I could see the garden, the ashes that awaited me now. I could taste their parched bitterness and there was no destiny to wash them away.

I accosted the first people to pass by—a middle-aged couple heading towards the market. "Do you see this mouse?" I plucked Shaykh Nariman from the pouch and dangled him before them like he was a toy.

The thick-bearded man flinched and stepped back while his wife leaned forward and stared. "Yes, what about it?"

One of the knots in my chest loosened. "Talk to them," I whispered to Shaykh Nariman. He stared at me with uncomprehending, beady rodent eyes. "TALK TO THEM!" I yelled in desperation.

He bit me and the couple walked off in wide-eyed alarm while I nursed my finger and fought back tears.

"Even those without a firsat could hear me if I spoke in this form. It would be dangerous to talk in front of strangers—who knows how they might react?" Shaykh Nariman whispered. The sympathy in his voice deflated my frustration. "I spoke earlier to convince the girl; I'm not sure why she lied, but I imagine an experience like she had today unsettled her. And perhaps it disturbed you as well. Do not give up—there will be more smells to investigate." Was I imagining a feral mouse comforting me?

I walked home in a slump, my feet dragging against broken cobblestones. My whole body ached but my head especially pounded like a drum. I collapsed into my bed despite the muck on my clothes. Shaykh Nariman, my imaginary jinn, scampered off like any normal mouse would.

I didn't pursue him.

I dozed off, convinced I was a victim of delirium and not destiny. The serpentine forms of the servants didn't plague my dreams. Instead, the void embraced me, though its empty arms brought no comfort.

***

The thugs from the previous night must have found me and were trying to get into my house. That seemed to be the only explanation for the thunderous banging at my door. I curled up on my bed and considered my options: slip out a window in the back to escape, open the door as they rammed into it and hope they lose their balance, or bundle under the covers and wish everything away.

That last option was the most tempting, but it hadn't regrown the garden or shown me whether I was 'made for great things' or plain old mad. My body ached and the red swelters on my skin throbbed as I debated what to do. The wounds reminded me of the costs of foolish bravery, but part of me saw them as badges of honor.

I picked up a bowl to use as a cudgel and moved to the door. I was a lion stalking prey in the tall grass.

"Don't be so melodramatic!" a voice called from beyond the door. It was sing-song, mocking.

I opened the door and the girl from the day before was standing there, arms crossed and foot tapping against the ground.

"I'm thinking of going to live with my grandmother in Isfahan and I suppose I could make a few detours along the way. So let's follow 'these scents' or whatever," she said. "We're looking for story book-type characters, right? Saints and gazis?"

". . . What?" Maybe she was God-touched and crazy after all.

"Where's the jinn mouse?" She asked, eyes darting around my room. I would have felt ashamed under normal circumstances having a stranger look at my meager, ash-stained possessions, but I was too bewildered to care.

"Right here," Shaykh Nariman said, crawling over from a sooty corner in my room. "How is it that you know what we are trying to do? And why the change of heart?"

The girl sighed. "I never dream—*never.* Sleep is the only time all the thoughts are quiet. But last night, I had the same nightmare Khurafa had, with the bloody river, the monstrous servants, and all." She shivered.

"How do you know about my dream? How did you know where I live? What in God's name is going on?"

"You told me. And for what it's worth, you're not hallucinating. Though it was funny to see you think you are." She snickered.

"You cut me off when I tried to speak—I never said anything out loud yesterday!" I raised my hands to my head, I was on the verge of tearing my hair out.

"It's her firsat," Shaykh Nariman said, pink paw raised to his petite chin. "What is it exactly? Can you hear thoughts?"

"I'm not keen to advertise that," she said, "but I don't exactly hide that I have an unusual level of insight."

"You can read minds." All her odd behavior suddenly made sense.

"You let me think I was hallucinating on purpose! You knew how important this task is because I was thinking about it! Why you—" Indignation stifled awe.

She snickered. "I'm sorry about that. Sort of. The whole 'mission' thing seemed pretty outlandish, though I could tell you believed it was true. The mouse actually turning out to be a jinn was a surprise. It was the dream that really convinced me though. Mind you, I'm only in this till Isfahan. If you want to meet truly pious people you should see my grandma there."

My first attempt at recruitment succeeded. I hadn't lost my mind.

My whole body relaxed and I would have fallen to the floor in relief if I wasn't worried about the girl laughing at me.

So it was real. I had a prophetic dream. Wicked people with massive power were out there conspiring and I was chosen to do something.

The old stories were real—and I was in one of them.

It hit me fully then, the duty before me, the momentous nature of the task God had granted us.

But I had something else to take care of first. I didn't know how this mind-reading stuff worked, but I imagined the nastiest, most fly-ridden trash.

The girl yawned at my attempted vengeance. "I have to save this helpless girl," she said in an artificially high voice, mocking a thought I'd had the previous evening. She pantomimed thwacking a thug with a stick.

I scowled. She definitely wasn't a saint. I wasn't even sure she would help us against The Servants. But God gives baraka to whom he will and it would be wrong to reject opportunities he provides. That's what Shaykh Nariman would have said if he caught me griping about it. She must have read my mind, because she rolled her eyes.

She walked off and I remembered my manners. I turned to Shaykh Nariman and looked at the ground—out of shame, not just to see him. "I'm sorry for thinking you weren't real and for treating you like I did. Thank you for your patience with me."

"My dear boy," he chuckled. "I thought you would think I was a manipulative mastermind when you found out I wasn't human. Not that you'd think I wasn't real. I much prefer the latter."

"You don't have to be a mouse if you don't want to."

"Ah, but I'm growing to like it," he squeaked. "And it helps to have a material form. When I don't, I feel like I'm about to fade away. . ."

***

The girl's name was Zakiyya. She started her tenure with our group by asking for a couple days to settle affairs. It turned out that it was less about sentimental goodbyes with friends and more about selling things she couldn't take with her. She had me lug them around as she negotiated with merchants. She looked discreetly over her shoulder the whole while.

The knick knacks I carried carefully in the crates included some fine porcelain and a silver knife. "It's been in my family for seven generations!" Zakiyya said about the latter as she tried to squeeze a few more dirhams out of a merchant; she flailed the knife around to emphasize her words. She ended up saying a lot of things had been in her family for increasingly long periods of time.

I was beginning to think she'd stolen everything and was making things up.

"Don't say anything," she muttered.

"What do you—" And then I remembered. She could read minds. It would take some time to get used to that.

My cheeks reddened a little. She'd heard me accuse her of stealing. A *whack* drove me out of my embarrassment even as it reddened one cheek even more.

"Your thinking is distracting. Rid yourself of thoughts, focus on God, whatever it is you pious types do," she said.

"Did you really just slap me?" I'd almost dropped the boxes

I was holding. "Because I couldn't control my thoughts? How many folks control what they're thinking—" She raised a hand before I could finish as a merchant returned for another round of haggling. I shook my head in muted disbelief.

The load I was carrying lightened and then disappeared completely. Zakiyya was good at getting deals. It hadn't occurred to me what an advantage reading a trader's mind would be in any transaction. If it had, Zakiyya would have threatened me with a slap and said skill mattered too.

She went off to take care of some tasks on her own and I kept thinking about the probable thefts she'd committed. Shaykh Nariman was at my place, napping. Becoming a mouse seemed to have increased his need for rest. Or maybe he always needed so many hours of sleep—I'd never been around him quite this much before. If he'd been there, he would quote that old adage at me: "If a friend of yours does wrong, make seventy excuses for him. If your heart cannot do this, then know that the true shortcoming is yours." Zakiyya wasn't exactly my friend. Was she off for one last caper? Could her joining us be a con?

I trailed a good way behind her, far enough, I hoped, that she couldn't hear what I was thinking. She looked over a gaggle of tiny children and presented them a handful of coins. I could see the glint in her hands. She gave them instructions of some sort—advice on how to spend the money? Strategies for pick-pocketing? A verse that Shaykh Nariman often quoted came to mind. "Oh, you who believe, avoid suspicion. Indeed, suspicion is sin. And do not spy on or backbite about each other . . . "

I felt a twinge of shame for trying to read her lips. She was probably aiding orphans.

She turned and stalked over to the pillar I was hiding behind.

"You're not stealthy at all," she said. I began to come out from behind my failed vantage point, suitably chastised, apologies on my tongue—and right in time I tripped over a loose rock. Zakiyya's wicked grin turned into a laugh. I dusted myself off with as much dignity as I could muster.

"Let's head back over to Shaykh Nariman and catch some sleep," I said, changing the topic. Being holier than thou and suspecting others was as bad as stealing, worse probably. I was tripping and falling in far too many ways.

"I can't read his thoughts, you know," Zakiyya said as we walked. "Shaykh Nariman, I mean."

"Huh?" After what I'd just berated myself about, I was willfully obtuse. "Well he's a jinn, that makes sense."

"What's he really after?" she mumbled.

I raised an eyebrow. "What do you mean? He wants to stop The Servants."

"How am I supposed to know that if I can't hear it in him," she said.

"Most of us can't hear people's thoughts and have to trust them anyway," I said, feeling mollified.

She called it a night and I rubbed my eyes. I didn't have anything left to take care of and little to pack.

Still, I made a pit stop at the baker's home, which was a small, rectangular sandstone living space attached to a large, vaulted clay oven. A few bricks covering the oven were chipped.

I knocked twice before the baker's son opened the door.

"Huh—Hi," he mumbled, looking at my feet.

His father towered behind him. "Shop is closed for the evening son," he said stiffly. "Everything okay?"

"Yeah . . ." I said. "I'd just wanted to . . . I wanted to buy some bread. But it's okay if you're closed."

The baker's eyes softened. "We have some unsold pieces. Maybe a little stale," he said. He shooed off his son to some back room. We stood in awkward silence as we waited, the baker inclining his head toward me.

His son came back with a few pieces. I reached into my pocket and picked out a few fils and handed them over.

"Thank you," the baker and his boy mumbled in unison.

"No, thank you," I said, meeting their eyes. "Peace be upon you . . . and goodbye."

***

I slept fitfully that night. The nine serpentine creatures crept over the land, north, south, east, west. I saw one climb jagged gray peaks. Birds fell from the clouds like acid rain and the mountains crumbled.

Another entered the sea and stained the water a dark crimson. Fish floated to the toxic surface, bellies up.

The forests fell, the fields died, the winds went silent, and the lights in every city went out. The last of the nine monsters approached me, mouth open wide. The girl had already been devoured—the remnants of her flesh strewn in gooey splotches.

I was the final bite.

Chapter 6

"I seek refuge in God from Satan, the rejected one." I whispered the phrase thrice.

I packed and rushed out. Shaykh Nariman and Zakiyya were waiting.

"So all we have to do is follow any distant scents I pick up on?" I asked Shaykh Nariman. I pretended nonchalance but—*we were going to meet real heroes and saints!*

Zakiyya raised an eyebrow at my thoughts while Shaykh Nariman nodded.

"Bismillah!" I grinned. "From the south there are smells. Not flowers. They're more complicated, fancy perfumes and maybe incense. There's musk mixed with sandalwood, a strong whiff of apple. They feel aged."

"And the scent of Zakiyya, it was 'fresh?'" Shaykh Nariman asked.

"That's right," I said.

"Have you smelled something like this before—an aged scent without a source?" Shaykh Nariman asked, whiskers drooping.

"Um . . ."My forehead wrinkled. "Well, now that you mention it. I pick it up around the city sometimes. From a few of the graveyards . . . The tomb of Abdul Qadir Gilani had an incense smell but I thought that was because the caretakers were burning a lot of the substance . . ."

"How far away from Gilani's tomb were you smelling that? A block? Way farther?" Zakiyya scoffed as she ran through my thoughts. "But I guess you wouldn't realize that isn't normal if you've never known otherwise . . ."

The lapis lazuli dome above Abdul Qadir's had probably been crushed by the Mongol raid. It wasn't so far away but I never bothered to check. My mother had me deliver flowers there and to the grave of Umar Suhrawardy to the North. On a couple occasions she took me as far as Shaykh Maruf across the river and even all the way to Adhamiya and Kadhimiya to give specially arranged bouquets. I relished those old, elegant scents. Those places were the farthest from home I'd been.

"You are picking up on the baraka of the dead," Shaykh Nariman interrupted my reverie in his pedantic way. "Saints who are no longer with us, great imams of the past. They were blessed in life and a remnant of that blessing persists still. But it is tied to the places they reside and won't be of use to us."

Shaykh Nariman saw my crestfallen expression and adopted a gentle invective. "To the south is Karbala, Kufa, and Najaf. They house the graves of great luminaries: Imam Ali, the heroes who accompanied Imam Husayn, even some Prophets. They are worth visiting but right now we need mobile, living sources of baraka. I believe in you, my son. Filter out the aged smells. Can you find a fresh odor, a source that has not passed on?"

I closed my eyes in concentration and sniffed up a gnat. After a wicked sneeze, I got something. The pure, clean smell of myrtle floated above the muckish odor of sewage and rotten meat polluting the city.

Zakiyya raised an eyebrow. "What's myrtle?" She asked. "Oh, a tiny tree with white flowers." She read my mental image before I could answer.

"It's coming from directly east this time. Not as far as the aged smells."

"A living source then, God-willing." Shaykh Nariman squeaked, his beady eyes now wide. "You wished and God granted, immediately. How merciful is he?"

I glanced at the few belongings I scrounged up for our unclear quest: a couple dried flowers planted and preserved by my parents after I was born, a few bits of stale bread, a clutch of coins, and two changes of clothes. Zakiyya's bag was puffier; she had far more clothes, which just barely muffled the jingling of the many coins from her sales over the previous days. Apparently her rags on the day I met her were a costume used to garner sympathy from strangers.

I stopped by the shredded garden gate and took one long look at the ashen remnants of my old life. I whispered the classic prayer for the deceased, "From God we come and to him we shall return."

I'd see the flowers again in paradise along with all the generations of family that planted them. *Inshaallah.*

In the meantime, new duties beckoned. The seeds of adventure were planted and I needed to water them. The whole world could depend on the fruit of our labors.

The burden was heavy but my steps were light.

We took several shortcuts across the city that Zakkiya suggested, including an uncomfortable number of twisted alleyways selected to spite me. We marched through broken mosques and ravaged homes to avoid street traffic. Eventually we slipped out a battered wooden gate through a gap where two planks should have been. The wrecked city wall it belonged to looked like an assortment of enormous toy blocks swatted by a giant, angry child.

The Mongols were starting to clamp down on people fleeing the city. The ruined capital was too important a location to depopulate further. Our possessions were meager enough to make it look like we were going on a short trip rather than moving, and with Zakiyya's mind reading, we strode by a checkpoint on the road out when the guard was most distracted.

"He's daydreaming about frolicking with the sheep. They really did give swords to a bunch of herders," she said in disbelief. "What's that about moving versus traveling? You think you won't come back?"

"Did you have to read my thoughts too?" I asked in exasperation.

"You think so loudly it's hard not to. We can communicate quietly this way. And trust me, I'm not interested in your deepest darkest secrets." She pretended to yawn. "I'm sure they're boring."

"You mean I can communicate and you can listen in smug superiority." I grumbled. "That's not right. It's an invasion of privacy!"

Zakiyya shrugged.

"Which way now?" Shaykh Nariman asked sleepily as he snuggled in my pocket. His new small form came with creaturely capriciousness and a need for intermittent rest.

Zakiyya answered for me, "Farther east. You know, I think I know where it's coming from."

"Where?" I asked. I'd sniffed like a hound and here she was stealing my thunder.

She smirked—she could hear my annoyance. "There's a khaniqah not too far away. A sufi lodge that survived the invasion. I overheard people mention it. Seems like an ideal place to find someone favored by God."

After an hour of trekking, Zakiyya kicked a stone in the road. "So . . .What do The Servants want?"

"What? I mean . . . they're bad guys," I said. "Pious folk in the past opposed them. They wanted to resurrect Ad and Thamud!"

"Yeah," she said, swatting the stone aside. "But why? What did they *want*? What was their ultimate goal?"

Shaykh Nariman interjected. "Power, influence, terror, and control. That's all we know. It's all the histories say and it's all I remember from my experience at that time. They were secretive about what they were trying to bring about."

"Rather vague, generic villains then," Zakiyya murmured.

"You only saw the jinn corpse in my thoughts," I protested. "You didn't witness it. They're not cliche. They're really, truly wicked."

"Mmmhmmm," Zakiyya murmured, unconvinced.

My nose led us to the exact place Zakiyya predicted.

The Khaniqah was a square, brown stone structure. The classic open-air courtyard had been turned into a closed building. The arched doorways into the courtyard were covered with mismatching gray rocks.

An extremely tall, wool-cloaked woman exited the structure and caught sight of us.

"She's going to bring us in there whether we want to or not," Zakiyya sighed.

"Children!" the woman called out. "Please come inside!"

Shaykh Nariman ducked deep into my pocket, pushing himself against the lining. The woman smiled as she approached, but there were hard lines in her face and permanent furrows in her brow. She didn't seem the sort to take kindly to a friendly pet mouse.

The lady herded us in through the single open doorway. The calligraphy above the arch was freshly carved. "La illa hu," 'None but he', a statement derived from the slogan of faith, "There is no deity but God."

We followed the woman's directions sheepishly—aunty-style authority is a frightening thing. She introduced herself as Naama.

She led us through a maze of narrow, gray stone passage-ways. Aside from the scent of myrtle that only I could detect, there was a staleness in the air, offset by the gentle smoke of the torches on the walls and a light glow of frankincense burning in some distant chamber.

We reached a clean-shaven servant whose round face was pale as the moon. He plucked away our bags before we could protest. Zakiyya frowned as her coins were pulled away. I pressed my hands against my thin coat protectively, not wanting them to take Shaykh Nariman.

"His mind was so blank, I didn't know he'd take our things," Zakiyya whispered. "But they will change our clothes; the lady, Aunty Naama, saw you touch the coat. She thinks it's dirty."

"Can we get our bags back?" Zakiyya asked Aunty Naama with a voice more high pitched than usual. "All I have left of my parents is in there." She scrunched her face up in a pout verging on tears. *Con-artist.* She kicked my shin and I suppressed a grimace.

"Oh child, possessions are tethers to this world, but do not worry. We're taking them to your rooms. You could use some rest tonight." Aunty Naama patted Zakiyya's head and then ruffled my hair. She frowned as she started measuring the length of my locks. My mom had cut my hair three months back and I hadn't trimmed it since.

Aunty Naama was too close for me to whisper, so I thought rapidly. *The impression I'm getting is that they're a little zealous but nice and well-intentioned.* Zakiyya tilted her head slightly in the barest nod.

Ok this mind-reading stuff is convenient. Her lips curled upwards. *Still an invasion of privacy though.* Her lips flattened into a stiff line.

We reached the end of a narrow stone hallway, replete with dramatic echoes. Attendants guided Zakiyya and me into separate chambers. My eyes widened in alarm as we shared one last look, but Zakiyya tapped her skull and mouthed the words, "It's good you think too loudly."

A silver-haired grandpa fussed over me and helped me out of my coat. I'd heard of rich people with servants who changed their clothes for them, but I'd never experienced anything like that. From the corner of my eye I saw Shaykh Nariman slip into the shadows.

I was dunked into a bath for a brief moment, the sudsy aroma mixed with the scent of myrtle hanging thickly in the air. The former seemed fake compared to the latter.

I was outfitted in soft gray robes, a shade lighter than the stone. I moved my hand to scratch at a sore spot from the fight in the alley way, but the elderly attendant swatted my wrist away.

"This world is a place of discomfort. Best to start getting used to it now." He winked.

I was ushered into a chamber where a thickly bearded man

sat, his hands lifted to the sky, palms open as he made prayer supplications. "Ah, it is good to see you, young one," he said, lowering his hands. "You came seeking refuge from the world, from pain, from suffering. You came for solace and for God and you have found them both."

"I'm looking for baraka," I said. "For a living saint if there is one around."

"You've found it. Our leader, the illustrious Sidi Saf son of Sayyad, is a light in the dark earth, hope in a sea of despair," he said. "The miracles he has worked will amaze you, the insights he has shared will change you."

"Can I meet him?" I asked with bright-eyed eagerness and a quickening pulse. There was a saint here! And he had followers—maybe a secret order of people ready to fight monsters was based within these walls!

The man gave a hearty laugh that made his beard bob. "You can meet him this very day! Though your eyes may not be able to handle the light he gives off." He added the last bit in a teasing tone.

The man spoke to me at length about the many signs of the end of the world appearing in the world today. Rivers drying up, plagues breaking out, and wide-scale slaughter were high on his checklist. He talked about the importance of holding on to the rope of God; I found myself nodding along. He finished with moisture in his eyes. "It's in the darkest moments that God sends his aid and that we who seek it must stick together."

He offered me a drink of milk sweetened with honey—which I chugged. He brought me to a richly carpeted room where followers leaned forward on their knees, murmuring mantras. I copied their motions as best I could while stifling a belch.

I spotted a group of women forming in the corner. The

smallest figure, clothed in a full body black burka that only revealed her eyes, raised her index finger when my gaze passed by her. She wrote something swiftly in the air but I couldn't make it out. *Zakiyya*, I realized. I attempted to project my thoughts at her. *It seems their leader Sidi Saf could be the real deal. It feels like the scent is coming from the very foundation of this place. Maybe all the followers are infused with baraka! I feel like we've hit the jackpot.*

Her head fidgeted and she gestured something, but I got distracted. At that moment, the light murmur of recitation stopped as a figure swept into the room and everyone stood up.

"Sit, my beloveds," the figure, Sidi Saf, said in a sonorous voice that filled the room. It was warm and commanding, deep with rich, sweet tones.

When everyone was seated, I was able to get a good look at him. His beard was immaculate—long and trim without a single loose strand. Above his hawk-like nose, his eyes were pools of brown molasses. His lips crinkled as he smiled. All the welcomingness of a grandfather was combined with the regal bearing of a king, yet somehow he looked to be no older than his 30s.

So this is a saint.

He beckoned an elderly man forward, whose sagging skin was as loose as his gray robe. With trembling, liver-spotted hands, the man struggled to carry a heavy cloth bag jingling with coins. When he dropped it at the saint's feet, golden dinars jumped out.

"Brother Usman donated his life's savings to our community in hopes of greater wealth in the life to come." Sidi Saf's smile was radiant as he looked upon his wizened follower. Brother

Usman's face was choked with emotion; tears leaked from his eyes. He hardly had to lean to kiss the back of the saint's hand. "The poor will be fed and the ill will be cared for by means of his sacrifice."

An attendant scoop up the fallen coins and carry the bag away as the old man rejoined the congregation. The show of generosity was astounding but the leadership and community that caused it was even more incredible.

A couple walked towards the front—a balding, squat man wearing the same gray as I, and a tiny, demure woman cloaked in black. They held hands as they knelt before Sidi Saf, heads bowed. "May your union be blessed, Aslam and Tahira," the saint said to the newlyweds, putting a hand below each of their chins and lifting their faces up. "May you have happiness and progeny, laughter, love, and light."

The couple's hand-holding tightened. They backed away as a large woman in the same formless black approached the saint. A cry escaped the newcomer and she swayed.

Sidi Saf himself propped her up. "Mistress Haniya's husband walked with elegance into the garden of souls," he announced. "We look forward to meeting him in brighter pastures. May he be embraced in mercy and sheltered in kindness. We shall see that you are provided for madam." He gestured toward an attendant and some of the coins that Brother Usman gave earlier were placed into the mourning woman's hands. A few women stepped up to Mistress Haniya and helped her back to the congregation.

"In this period of loss, gain too is at hand," Sidi Saf said, his gaze sweeping the room and inundating it in warmth. "The world ends but it also begins anew. All you who are here are seekers who found what you sought. Two new seekers have joined us today; they are young but that makes their resolve all the more impressive. Come forward, my children. Khurafa and Zakiyya."

My breath caught me in my throat. He knew about us—knew our names and was calling us to him. I stepped forward and his followers split open a path for me like I was Moses cutting through the sea. Zakiyya joined me. She gestured frantically but my vision was glued to the saint.

Sidi Saf put a hand on our heads; I could feel the callouses in his palms, the blemish and bruises of years of labor. Somehow his touch was still gentle. I sniffed—there was a hint of an oil cologne on him and the aroma of myrtle floating from below his feet.

"What ails you, my children?" he asked.

My tongue was heavy and I blanked on how to start. He pinched my cheek and I instantly felt at ease, not even annoyed at being treated like a kid. I took a deep breath, but Zakiyya elbowed me before I could begin.

She looked the saint squarely in the eyes and then turned towards the followers, intense focus on her face. The room was hushed but she could hear the thoughts behind every bated breath. She was stealing my thunder, but considering the size of the crowd, I didn't mind.

"How did you pull it off?" she wondered aloud. "The charisma, I get. The situation, the chaos, that makes sense. But what was it that really convinced everyone that you're holy? A fake miracle. But how did you pull it off?" The faces of the followers twisted in horror, or anger, but the leader's face was serene. I had a sinking feeling in my stomach. What was she trying to pull?

"He is a monster," Zakiyya said. "There is a darkness in

him that would haunt you if you knew. How many of you have been forced to give up their life savings and abandon their children, like Brother Usman? How many of you have been threatened into marriage with his elites, like Tahira? How many dissenting voices have been killed, like Mistress Haniya's husband? How many of you has he abused while saying you're chosen— "

"Oh child, what has possessed you?" Sidi Saf said softly, cutting through her rant like a knife through butter. He tapped her shoulders and Zakiyya went rigid as a board. Her face froze, her expression caught between confidence and fear. Her arms were stuck to her sides.

"Whatever Satan seized hold of her is resisting removal. I will heal her personally." He said. He looked at me kindly and ruffled my hair. "She will be fine, don't worry."

"Move Zakiyya! What are you doing?" I whispered. She was as unresponsive as a statue

My heart beat a mile a minute.*Was* she possessed by something? I saw only beauty and kindness in this place, but she'd turned every interaction sour with a few words. She could read minds, but how could I tell if she was telling the truth? Could Sidi Saf save her?

I looked into Zakiyya's unblinking, frozen eyes. The icy horror there was real. And so was the unspoken plea.

Seventy *excuses*, I reminded myself. *You recruited her, now trust her.*

"She's right, isn't she?" I reeled on the supposed saint and summoned all the righteous indignation I could. The top of my head barely came up to his chest but I tried to push him.

He poked my forehead like a doting parent quieting a tantrum and I went rigid as a statue. There was no gradual spread of ice in my veins. My bones were instantly immovable rock, my flesh petrified.

I tried to scream, but nothing came out. Every fiber of my being shook, but my body was still.

He hadn't tried to exorcize Zakiyya— he froze her. And now he'd done the same to me. She was right. Saf was no saint, but he had powers. And he used them to make us prisoners within ourselves. There weren't people fighting monsters within these walls but there *was* a monster.

"I will purge them of what pollutes them after our gathering is finished. Everyone keep these lost souls in your prayers." He turned toward us as we were hauled away over the shoulders of some attendants. He bared his perfect white teeth.

My sight was blurry by the time we were set down. I heard the echo of footsteps receding and through the blur I detected a drastic change in illumination. A draft pricked my skin. We were placed together in a cellar, surrounded by moldy boxes and aged knicknacks.

It took me a moment to realize my muscles were not completely unmoving—I could breathe, however weakly, and I could think. I organized my thoughts in case Zakiyya was paying attention, *was it poison?* I still tasted the sweetness of the milk and honey on my tongue. He wouldn't have poisoned us *before* we resisted him. And he didn't pinprick us with anything, I would have felt that.

Zakiyya? Can you hear me? Are you okay? Do you know what's happening? I was lying on my back and couldn't turn to face her. If she fidgeted in response I'd never know. I began to wonder, how long could I go with my eyes open before I'd become permanently blind? How long would it be before bugs came and tried to eat me?

I would have gasped if I'd been able to. *The attendants took our clothes!* A little *sihr*, a little black magic, and maybe this was possible. I heard stories of the use of hair tied into knots of ropes to make someone sick, concoctions to force someone into false love. Those were always stories, but unless this twisted man who preyed on children was blessed by God, *sihr* had to be real. I tried reciting some verses of protection, but my tongue could not move. I thought them instead, over and over—*I seek refuge in the lord of the dawn. I seek refuge in the lord of humankind.*

It sounded like tiny rain droplets hit the ground. Pit-pat. The footsteps of something small. "I attempted to hide," a squeaky voice said, "and this body was drawn to the dankest place with the greatest number of stale snacks lying about. Lo and behold, I find you all here." Shaykh Nariman brushed against me and I felt a surge of hope.

"Well, get up then. Say something . . ." Shaykh Nariman circled Zakiyya and I. "What happened to you, why can't you . . ." He tried prying my arms out of their outstretched position but nothing happened.

Shaykh Nariman paced around the room, skittering over the ruins of rotten crates. My eyes were drying out and it was dark, but I could make out a stick leaning against the wall in my peripheral vision. It was coated with dust and mold fused it to the wall it rested against, but somehow its form held after God knows how many years of abandonment.

Shaykh Nariman flitted up the stick, nibbling away the mold and spitting it out with little raspberry sounds even as particles of every kind of dirt clung to his fur. Shaykh Nariman gave a push and the stick plopped down to the ground, the top bounced against my chest. A cloud of brown and gray particles filled the air.

"Let's see if I can use the stick for leverage," Shaykh Nariman said. "Fit it between your limbs. Don't have the strength to push hard but maybe . . . "

Some of the dust wafted down by my nostrils, landed on my pupils, and seeped into my mouth.

I coughed, I sneezed. My eyes fluttered.

It took me a few seconds to realize I could move.

"How . . ." I wondered out loud, blinking away the remaining dust. I swiveled towards Zakiyya, "Can you move?" I asked. No response.

"Was it the dust?" Zakiyya was just as coated as I had been, and still she remained inert. A scent cut through the mildew smell of the room. Myrtle! It was the stick—no, *staff!* Now that it was cleaner I could make out the way the top was thicker than the bottom. How did it end up down here? It was the source of baraka that had drawn us to this place.

The scent seemed to come from the ground because the staff was in the cellar. I plucked it up and poked Zakiyya.

She sputtered and spat.

"We're in a grungy basement. But on the bright side, I found the source of baraka!" I said, as she recovered. "I'm wondering how an *object* becomes blessed. Because it was used by the pious, maybe?" I was blabbering, giddy that I could move and she was okay.

"You were right about the leader Saf not being a saint," I admitted while she was still unable to rub it in. "But when did you figure that out? And why did you make a scene like that?"

"I tried signaling to you, you just didn't pay attention," she said as we made our way to the door. "Saying anything out loud would have drawn suspicion. This is a cult, dressed up as a normal Sufi order. They start bringing you in with niceties and by the time you realize how screwy it all is, you're in too deep. Luckily, I can read minds, so I figured that out before getting sucked in. The terror in those people's minds . . ."

"Why blow up at him when it could endanger us?" I asked, ignoring her jibe as the giddiness faded.

"You were about to tell him about the Servants," she said. "Somehow that seemed like the wrong move. He could use that to wring out more from his followers with a story like that. Or maybe he'd help the Servants, I don't know. I had to stop you. And the whole situation just pissed me off. You couldn't hear his thoughts. There was some sick stuff . . . Anyway, your attempt at helping was stupider than what I did. Seriously, you wanted to prove you trusted me so you pushed him?"

My face got hot but she shushed me before I could protest. "Someone is within earshot now," she whispered. "Okay," she said after a moment. "Now they're gone." It must have been terrible to play hide-and-seek with her when she was younger.

We tried the door. It was locked. We pushed, but it was too solid. Shaykh Nariman positioned himself between the small gap separating the floor from the door.

"I'll search for the key," he said. "Stay put and decrease your volume. We don't want them to know you recovered."

"Okay," I said. I thudded the staff gently against the door, a thump of encouragement.

The door creaked where the staff had touched it and a vertical crack ripped through it.

The door split completely in two.

I dropped the staff in shock but caught it before it hit the floor. Now I was worried about tearing the ground apart.

There was a banging sound in the distance. Someone heard the wood splinter and was on their way.

"It divides things," Zakiyya muttered. "It split the invisible bonds holding us and now it split the door. A staff that splits things . . . Don't tell me. . ."

The noises moved closer. There was shouting. "We need to get out of here," Zakiyya said. She grabbed my hand and yanked me toward the wall opposite the door.

"Split the wall," Zakiyya commanded. I dashed forward, raising the staff high behind me and swinging toward the wall in one smooth motion.

But of course, my foot slipped on a slimy broken crate in the middle of my heroics. I caught myself with both hands. My relief at not crashing face first into the ground was undermined by a cracking sound.

My right hand had flailed as I slipped and the staff sailed free. Its tip poked the spot where the ceiling and wall met.

The stones rumbled, like an ancient beast waking up. A storm of soil leaked through the crack in the wall, then burst through like a wave. It filled the room and smothered us. The crack in the ceiling buckled. Rocks plummeted down, followed by furniture and screams.

***

A sharp pain in my forearm brought me back to consciousness. The first thing that came to mind were the screams I'd heard earlier. They weren't mine, and they couldn't have been Zakiyya's. Our mouths had been filled with soil.

I opened my eyes and saw in the pink and orange glow of dawn that I was only half-buried. Shaykh Nariman rested on my arm. He'd bit me.

"You're alive. Thank God." His whiskers sagged in relief.

I opened my mouth to ask what happened and dirt poured out. I spat for a moment before I could ask, "Where's Zakiyya?"

"Right here, you clumsy idiot," she said, poking the soil with the staff. It burst apart in front of me, parted into two halves. I struggled up through the opening. She offered the staff to help me to my feet. My hand trembled.

"It's not dangerous if you handle it right. It doesn't split things unless you want it to. You were eager to get past the door when you tapped it. Using it as a walking stick should be safe," she said.

I stilled the trembling and grabbed a hold of the wooden lifeline, pulling myself out of the remaining dirt.

"At least, I think?" she said as I scanned our surroundings. "I tested it out and that's what seems to be the case. And if it's what I think it is, I'm definitely right. Amazing really—an old relic, stuffed away and forgotten in a basement."

"No basement anymore," I said, horrified by what I could see: The wall that had blocked our way had toppled, but so had half the structure connected to it. The basement was filled with soil and stone debris, including the entire kitchen of the Khaniqah. The floor above us completely collapsed.

Shouts broke through my awe. "How did we survive?" I asked as Zakiyyah dragged me away.

"It'll take them a while to sort through the rubble," she said. "The area around the fallen floor—the basement ceiling—is unstable now, so they'll be cautious too. With any luck they'll think we're dead and no one will chase after us. And before you ask—no one left behind is injured." She grimaced .

I nodded with a dumb semblance of comprehension and asked again, "How are we alive?"

"I'm alive because I dove for the staff and used it to split a massive chunk of rock before it smashed me to smithereens," she said, unfazed by what she was saying. "The ceiling would have split cleanly in two halves, but when it split, the weight distribution was uneven, and it caused the rest to crumble . . ."

"I'm not going to understand architectural talk," I huffed.

"That burst of soil—it inhibited your movement. And because of that you stayed cemented to the one spot where rocks didn't topple. The exact starting spot of the split," she said. "There really shouldn't have been that much dirt pouring through. The building is old and its foundation is unstable."

"It's the will of God," Shaykh Nariman pronounced as he moved from my shoulder to my pocket, burrowing into the dirt lazily rather than pushing it out. "The two of you are meant to do great things, and it wouldn't do well for you to be smothered or smashed here."

I cast a glance at Zakiyyah, expecting her to roll her eyes at Shaykh Nariman's melodramatic words. But she only shrugged. "You came back for us," she said to him. "Thank you."

She wasn't suspicious of him anymore! She frowned at my happy thoughts. I didn't care. In the end, we trusted each other and came out alive.

She glared at me.

We trotted along the road, no destination in mind except for *away*. I was hungry and thirsty, my body a mass of aching sores. I was beginning to understand why I'd never left the area around Baghdad before.

Shaykh Nariman fell asleep to the rhythmic movement. I was a pretty good pack animal, all bruises aside.

"He saved you and now you can't doubt him," I whispered.

She stared at my pocket to make sure his squeaky snores were legitimate.

"Someone doing nice things for you isn't a reason to trust them. If anything, it makes them more suspicious," she said softly.

"Why are you telling me this?" I asked. "Do you trust me?" Why would she?

"Your mind is like an open book. The handwriting is scribbled but it's really large." She shrugged.

"So you're saying I'm simple?" I whispered heatedly.

"That's right. Too simple to deceive." She gave me a wicked grin, but it was half-hearted.

"You can literally read minds. Who could've broken your trust to make you so suspicious?" I asked. *Husn al-dhann*, thinking well of others, should go both ways.

"Reading minds doesn't mean people won't betray you," she said, so silently that I had to lean in to hear. "It just means you know they're betraying you."

Chapter 7

"We'll have to stop somewhere to get supplies," Zakiyya piped up after several aching miles.

"But our money is gone," I lamented. She raised an eyebrow. "*Your* money, not *our* money," I amended.

"Shaykh Nariman retrieved some of my possessions before he found us." *So that's the real reason she thanked him.*

"You had time to reach for coins before everything fell down on us?" I asked, raising an eyebrow.

"I have two hands." She gave a weak smirk.

"When you said there was no one seriously injured who we left behind . . ." I began to ask.

"I can hear thoughts, and pain expresses itself in thought. It doesn't feel very good." She looked away at the sandy hills and stubborn shrubbery that dotted the side of the road.

"But there was someone outside the door when everything fell apart," I said slowly. "What happened to him?"

"He got lucky; he was right outside the area where everything collapsed."

"Thank God," I sighed in relief. Shaykh Nariman poked his head out of my pocket. I expected some spiel about praying even for one's enemies, but instead he shared a long look with Zakiyya.

"What about those people he was manipulating? The old man, the woman forced into the marriage— all of them?" I asked.

"It was all we could do to save ourselves," Zakiyya said. Her lower lip twitched. "I imagine his authority was damaged by all this."

We settled into a sleepy quiet for the next hour, ambling along. Zakiyya froze mid- step and raised an open hand. I tried to stop, but slipped on loose pebbles. Only sticking out the staff at the last second kept me upright. I teetered, drowsiness replaced by alarm.

"What—" I began, but she gestured with both eyebrows toward a collection of palm trees and boulders off road. I followed her lead, crouching out of view

"Someone from the Khaniqah is looking for us," she whispered. "I think it's Aunty Naama. I could hear her far off, but I don't think she saw us." The neigh of horses followed her words.

I sneaked a peak past the rocks and vegetation and saw the tall, severe-looking aunty. Her eyes scanned the horizon, a hunter seeking prey. Around her were two men, armed with swords and a whip, her hound dogs. They moved away slowly.

I cringed, ducking back. My heart was thumping so loudly I was afraid they would hear it.

We stayed still for another half hour before Zakiyya let go of a long-held breath and moved on.

"The road will fork up ahead, she's going north; we should keep toward the southeastern path for now. It seems most of the folks they sent searching have gone toward Baghdad rather than away from it," Zakiyya explained.

"Well, that's one way to decide our route," I said, sniffing for baraka without success.

"We're moving away from your grandma now, aren't we?" I asked, pretending nonchalance.

"It can't be helped," she sighed. There was another question I wanted to ask, but I stifled it. She could hear it in my thoughts.

A little while later, right before dark, Zakiyya exchanged some of her coins for food, clothes, and a satchel from a wagon heading in the opposite direction from us. The clothes were mismatched and oversized, but one can't be particular about fit on the road. I think Zakiya haggled up—the wagoneers saw two ravaged-looking children and wanted to help. They would have given us a ride if we hadn't been headed the opposite way.

"The roads aren't always safe, little ones," the merchant leading the wagon said. His skin sagged on his once thick frame. War had ruined business.

The waggoners opted to camp for the night and we joined them, though Zakiyya insisted we sleep a little ways away. She didn't trust them either.

Shaykh Nariman curled up in the tan, knotted hemp cloth satchel Zakiyya had bought. It was thin and worn, but he found that comfortable. "It's just like me," he chirped before nodding off.

I closed my eyes and saw a serpentine creature claw its way out of the rubble of the Khaniqah. It scanned the gray expanse with yellow, slit-like eyes. I pressed myself to the ground, praying that I would not be seen. It stopped swiveling its head and licked its lips with a long, forked tongue, coated with blood.

It was facing me.

***

I sought refuge in God as I woke.

We began walking at dawn and left with rudimentary good-byes to the wagoneers. We didn't even exchange names.

To distract ourselves from our sore legs, Zakiyya and I rehashed what had happened in the Khaniqah.

"It sounds like the Servants aren't the only evil about," Shaykh Nariman said, pulling at his whiskers, "but I can't help but think they're all connected. Good comes in many forms but wickedness is always one."

I shrugged and my mouth dropped open. There it was—strong, distant, but alive. An aroma like a lush green field. "Tulips," I said, breaking out into a grin.

"Which way?" Zakiyya asked.

"Still southeast," I bubbled with excitement. I forgot the pain in my legs and skipped much of the way toward Mada'in, a city complete with mosques, madrasas, ancient ruins, and a hospice. It didn't have Baghdad's recent rotting smell. The river stink was also minimal, though we were next to the massive Tigris. I risked a glance at the water and it was cleaner than I'd ever seen.

The aroma of tulips floated from around the city. We walked by a massive arch left by a forgotten empire. It was so high up, like a twin of the heavens. Zakiyya rolled her eyes at my cringy poetics, but she was amazed too. The ruined palatial building attached to the arch only made it look larger.

"Something this big must have been built by jinn," I said.

Shaykh Nariman's scoff looked more like a whiskery pout. "As much as I'd like to claim credit for my kind, this was the product of human ingenuity . . . and madness." He pushed against the cloth of the satchel, away from the ruins.

Zakiyya and I lingered in awe but the scent drew us away. It came from all around, but there was one spot where the fragrance was most dense.

My anticipation built. Baraka was oozing from many things—maybe a group of people! *Heroic fighters for truth and justice? Maybe those legendary gazis Shaykh Nariman spoke of?*

I guided our little group to a quiet bookstore by the grand mosque. There was no group of people that I could see through the windows. The baraka was coming from objects.

Shaykh Nariman squirmed with joy like the true nerd he was. I had to pat him down and whisper, "Come on, Shaykh, if they see you, we'll be kicked out."

"Can you imagine?" he squealed. "A baraka-filled book! These eyes can still read." He loved books; it must have been frustrating to not have the materiality to take care of the ones he'd kept in his hovel. Or did he think dust deserves to read too?

We entered, and the shopkeeper glared at my oversized sleeves and thin travel bag. My shalwar wasn't dragging on the floor only because I'd knotted it a half dozen times.

"Blessed mornin' to you. Looking for something in particular?" the man asked gruffly.

"Just browsing," I said, glancing at every stack of books. My dad would have laughed if he'd seen my clothes, not judged.

Zakiyya struck up a conversation with the shopkeeper that let me sniff around. The tulip scent mingled with old paper and long-dried ink.

I patted Shaykh Nariman- he was wiggling too much at the sight of certain titles. I muttered, "I doubt we even have enough to buy the book we're looking for, let alone anything extra . . ." Shaykh reigned in his ageless curiosity and stopped squirming.

My eyes blurred from all the reading. Titles like *Kitab Al-Ittar*, *Kitab Ibtal Al-Qiyas*, and *Kitbal Tashrih Al-Hayawan Al-Mayat* made my head ache. The shopkeeper didn't organize the works by categories like scripture, poetry, or law, or by author. Did I have to open all the books to find a stronger whiff of baraka? What would the shopkeeper say if I perused every text and didn't buy a single one?

"Hey," Zakiyya poked me. "'Uncle Hasan' says he's got an interesting new acquisition." She waved a hand toward the shopkeeper.

"Oh?" I crinkled my nose to avoid sneezing out dust mites. That must have looked like condescension because Uncle Hasan glared again.

"Lots of interesting acquisitions really—a horde of books rescued from Baghdad's destruction made their way here. But this one's something special," he said. "I sold it and now unfortunately it's found its way back to me. It's a book of poetry about death. Very old, I think it's the author's own copy." The shopkeeper's affected disinterest veered into excitement.

"Is that what makes it special?" I asked.

"Jubayr, an old copyist in town, was scrapping the manuscript to make palimpsests." I gave him a blank look, and he continued. "A palimpsest is where you rub away the text, scrape the paper clean, and reuse it."

"Alright, and . . ." I said, half-turning back to peruse another stack. The snotty-buyer stereotype seemed to be helping our investigation. Maybe ill-fitting clothes was a rich people fashion out in the provinces?

"Well, we found Jubayr, the copyist, with half his face scraped off. Mirror image of what he'd done to the book, except it was flesh and skin gone rather than words from paper." Shaykh Nariman went still in my pocket.

"He . . . died?" I asked as a chill crept up my spine.

"Had his funeral yesterday. No saying how it happened really, but the book was open and a few palimpsests were already made. No disrespecting the dead, but he didn't recognize its value. The poetry is pretty good, though its topic was too timely." The shopkeeper, Uncle Hasan, finished his story with a quick prayer for the deceased that was marred by the glow of morbid fascination on his face.

"So, that book was passed on to you and it's for sale? Can I see it?" I asked, reaching for another stack of books though I wouldn't be able to pay attention to what they said.

He pointed to a cellar door. "My daughter Ruya was checking it out. You can bother her."

We lifted the latch and climbed down creaky stairs into a book-filled hovel lit by dim candles. A gangly-haired, lanky-limbed girl sat on the floor, engrossed in a shoddy manuscript. She looked up the instant before Zakiyya spoke.

"Your dad told us to ask about a recent poetry Diwan you acquired. Do you have it here?" Zakiyya glanced at the uneven piles of books.

Shaykh Nariman muttered something about books getting moldy when left like this. I coughed to hide his squeaky voice. He was one to talk.

The girl, Ruya, skimmed a paragraph before responding. "I—uh, don't, don't have it," she mumbled. "A—a relative of the deceased wanted it, so I gave it away for free. But—but he's out of town now."

"What's the name of that relative? Where did he go?" Zakiyya asked, narrowing her eyes.

Ruya's dilated eyes widened further. "Umm . . . I don't . . . remember."

"Come on," Zakiyya said. "Did you really give it away? Why did your dad tell us to come down here?"

"Please don't tell him I gave it away!" Ruya yelped. "He thought it would sell well."

"We were really interested in buying it." Zakiyya shrugged, but continued to squint. "Any other interesting titles? How about that one you're reading now? Can I see it?"

"Uh—uh n—no this is mine, for my studies," Ruya said, hugging the book. "But—uh—my, my dad has a book signed by Imam al-Jawzi. Ask—ask him about it."

"And don't tell him about you giving away that diwan?" Zakiyya asked, in a parting jab.

"P—please. I'll—I'll tell him soon." Ruya gave Zakiyya a nervous smile of gratitude. "Now p—please, I need to get back to my studies."

We walked up the stairs. "What did you get off her?" I whispered to Zakiyya.

She whispered back, "Not everyone is an open book like you. I know she didn't give the poetry book away. And when I asked about that manuscript she's holding, she closed up like a clam."

I scratched my chin in thought. "Is there something suspicious about it?"

"Maybe," Zakiyya considered. "Could be that's her diary and it's filled with embarrassing stuff. Either way, we should keep an eye on her. But, let's see what we can find out about that creepy poetry book first."

Questioning the townsfolk about Jubayr, the unfortunate elderly copyist who'd died, resulted in angry scowls. Apparently

Hasan, the bookseller, was the only one around who openly reveled in the macabre. Luckily, angry silence accompanied crystal clear pictorial thoughts. Zakiyya's sly expression morphed into a grimace after one of the passersby turned out to be the local doctor. "Didn't want to see that . . ." she mumbled. "His face . . . Ya Rabb ."

With the collage of images and snippets of words she accumulated, Zakiyya located the copyist's home. His matronly daughter answered at the third knock.

"What do you want?" she asked. Her once-round face looked deflated.

"We want to offer our condolences," Zakiyya said, glancing at my satchel. I pawed Shaykh Nariman into my hand and slipped him down by the threshold while Zakiyya occupied the woman's attention.

Zakiyya softened her voice. "Is there anything we can do to help?"

"My father's face is still missing," the woman snapped. "Think you can find that? Otherwise just leave us alone." She grasped the edge of the door, ready to slam it in our faces, then stopped. She sighed. "I'm sorry. I'm not myself. You were being kind. So many people have already helped, but now I want some peace and quiet."

"We understand," Zakiyya stepped back. "May your father be in the highest level of paradise." We walked off and waited in pained silence

A few minutes later Shaykh Nariman nudged against my leg, a shard of parchment in his mouth. He spoke through gritted teeth. "She was bawling after you all left, though there were no tears left. She might have seen me if her face hadn't been in her hands."

I plucked the parchment from his mouth. He spoke more comfortably. "No fragment of his face was left behind, but some of the shavings he made from trying to clear pages of the book were still on the ground. I did not see any words on them."

I lifted the yellowed parchment to my nose and sniffed so hard that I had to sneeze it out. "Fading fragrance of tulips," I said.

"That doesn't make sense," Zakiyya muttered. "A book imbued with baraka being associated with a brutal death doesn't sound right."

"The death could be a coincidence—or messing with a book like this has consequences?" I looked to Shaykh Nariman for an answer.

"We don't know enough yet," he chirped. "But I can't imagine baraka being harmful. Most things have a dual potential—for good and evil—but something blessed is usually purely good." He swiveled his tiny eyes on us and smiled mischievously. "Blessed things, not people, I mean. But let's watch the bookseller's daughter—she must know where the book is. And that other text she was holding . . . "

"Kind of hard to stalk a bookworm who's in a closed-off room," Zakiyya said. "Huh, *bookworm*, that's an idea." She gave Shaykh Nariman a meaningful look.

Shaykh Nariman's tiny eyes widened. "Oh no no no . . . I can't change forms very easily anymore—I'm too old. And a worm? I'll be stuck like that for a day at least. If I'm squashed . . ."

I patted Shaykh Nariman's cute snout. "Sidi, you're strong enough not to get squashed. And imagine—you'll get to literally spend time *in* books!"

Cornered by my enthusiasm and Zakiyya's badgering, he agreed with a sigh. "Might keep your spirits up at least," he grumbled.

Shaykh Nariman transformed in the privacy of the satchel. "We are all worms groveling in the dirt before the majesty of God," he announced in a warped, tunneled voice when he finished.

"And yet still, God always notices us . . . You've lost weight, Shaykh Nariman," I said, tapping the satchel which was now considerably emptier. "Thanks for doing this."

I turned to Zakiyya. "The bookseller is going to think we are up to something if we sneak our way inside."

"I'll ask him about the Jawzi text his daughter mentioned. That should get him excited enough for you to slip the cellar door open."

***

The bookseller showed Zakiyya his prized text. She amped up the ooohs and ahhhhs to provide a distraction for me to reach the cellar.

She's read many minds, but how many books has she actually read? I thought. Her eye twitched, but she kept talking.

I began to lift open the cellar door so Shaykh Nariman could slither in, but it slammed open. I fell back, causing a stack of books to sway. Ruya peeked her head out.

"G—going for food," she said to her dad, who was still engrossed in sharing the details of his treasure. Ruya stared at me with glassy eyes. The same shoddy manuscript was wrapped in her arms.

"Sorry," I stammered. "The door swinging open like that startled me. . ."

She walked off without responding, stroking her book's

ravaged black cover. I felt the satchel—Shaykh Nariman was already gone. I caught sight of something crawling up Ruya's arm.

I moved in close to Zakiyya, who seized the chance and leapt out of the bookseller's show and tell. "I don't think I have the money for this right now, but I am very interested. Let's keep in touch?" she said. The bookseller's excitement soured.

We shadowed Ruya to the evening market where she grabbed a warm, spiced meal that made my stomach rumble. She clutched her book even while eating.

We followed her back to the shop, and retraced every step in case Shaykh Nariman had hopped off on the return journey.

We found nothing except a dropped dirham I scolded Zakiyya for pocketing.

"Maybe he doesn't want us to know what he's found," Zakiyya thought aloud.

"You think he'd betray you while he's a worm?" I asked in exasperation. "He literally took the most vulnerable form possible." I scanned the ground again. "Wait—worms are pretty slow, aren't they? If he didn't hop out it would take him a while to get away."

We mulled around for a couple hours. Zakiyya scouted near the bookshop to see if she could hear Ruya discovering Shaykh Nariman or retrieve useful smatterings of information. Her expression curdled. She didn't learn anything.

"He's not back . . ." I stated the obvious. I gulped. "You think he was smushed?"

"Can a jinn really, truly be smushed?" She wondered. "A being of smokeless fire? How does that even work?"

"Well, how does he take a physical form at all?"

"Whatever. We need to do something." She said, brow

furrowed. "Assuming he didn't just leave us . . . "

I responded with a sigh and muttered, "I know you're worried about him too . . ."

Ruya exited the bookshop. She was stifling snobs and snot. She made no move to wipe her face. Tears dripped onto the mass of papers she carried in addition to her book.

She looked down at her book through bleary eyes and stopped dead in her tracks. She whirled on us hiding in the shadows.

"Why are you following me?" she demanded.

I cast a glance at Zakiyya hoping for her verbal gymnastics but she was frowning. No thoughts to read?

I opened my mouth to make up an excuse, but Zakiyya recovered and plowed forward.

"That's the poetry book, isn't it?" she asked, gesturing to the mass of papers in Ruya's left hand. Not much of a book anymore. "Why did you lie to us?" Zakiyya's accusatory tone was worthy of the town judge.

"It . . .what are you . . ." Ruya stuttered into silence beneath Zakiyya's weighty glare, the sort aunties practice for years. "I . . ." Ruya glanced at her book. "This text killed Jubayr," she said, shaking the stack of papers in her other hand.

Zakiyya grimaced—that gruesome image, at least, leaked from Ruya's thoughts.

"It killed him," Ruya said, her voice growing more steady. "It killed him and I'm going to destroy it so it can't do that to anyone else." There was a flash in her eyes—certainty . . . zealotry?

"How do you know it was the text that hurt him?" Zakiyya asked with aunty-like command. "Why couldn't it have been a freak accident?"

Ruya opened her mouth to answer, then abruptly stopped. She paled and clutched the book she'd been cradling so tightly, the veins in her hand popped out.

"This is how," Ruya said, raising the book she held so dear. She stretched it out towards Zakiyya and looked like she would vomit. Zakiyya had to peel the girl's fingers off the book.

Zakiyya brought the book to me. Together we glanced around for a light source sufficient enough for us to read by.

"There's no need," Ruya muttered miserably. "You can always read the book."

I opened the book and squinted at the title. *Kitab Shahadat al-Hazred. Kitab al-Azif. The Book of the Testimony of al-Hazred. The Book of al-Azif.* There were words on the page, too blurry to read in the dark, but I could see them in my mind. As if they were emblazoned over my thoughts.

The word is a powerful thing. The word is the first thing, God's original creation. His utterance began reality. And for us too, words bring worlds into existence. The swirl of thought and emotion becomes concrete in speech. Writing binds words, makes them resistant against time. It transmutes wind into stone.

Some monsters live in that swirling space on the threshold of speech.

"That's . . . but how . . ." Zakiyya shuddered.

"Is this what it's like? When you read thoughts, do they appear in your mind like this?" I asked, my hands shaking.

"No, it's always separate, like hearing or seeing something outside of yourself. I can always tell where my thoughts end and another's begins. But this breaks the barrier . . ." Zakiyya said. I only half-listened as more words pierced my mind. If this wasn't baraka-based, something miraculous, then I didn't know what could be.

Some monsters are bound in books. They must be found. They must be destroyed.

"What does that mean?" I asked.

The words on the page twisted and melted and new words popped into my head.

There are demonic books, written words that birth great evil. They are tormenting this city.

"But who are you?" I asked. "*What* are you?"

I was a manuscript once, of a great scholar, long gone. His name was al-Hazred. He poured love into writing to me, imbued me with righteousness and hope. God blessed the endeavor and gave me consciousness.

I cast a wide-eyed glance at Zakiyya. She didn't meet my eyes. She was glued to the book, transfixed. The pressure on my mind was minimal now, like scribbles on the corner of a page. But for her, it was an invasion.

"Then the death . . . . It was caused by one of these wicked books? And there are more out there?" I asked. Shaykh Nariman was right: Great evils were waking up everywhere.

Ruya answered in time with the text. "Yes, and I need to track them and burn them." She said, flinching as she looked at the stack of papers that had torn apart a man's face.

The other texts are in this city. Many works, scattered. But with one, major source.

"The bookshop?" I asked. Ruya hugged herself as I said it. "The Mongols destroyed so many libraries in Baghdad. But some of the books surviving the devastation made it here, didn't they? And people have been buying them, redistributing them . . . But which ones are corrupted? And how will you deal with them?"

"I'm going to burn the shop." Ruya said. Her family's

livelihood, her father's life's work. She'd destroy all of that?

"You'll burn them all?" I asked. "That's . . . so much knowledge will be lost."

"You think I haven't th-thought of that?" Ruya said. "You think it hasn't torn me apart? But I hesitated in listening to the *Book of al-Azif*," she gestured to the text held by me and Zakiyya, "and then that old man died." The tears and snot made sense now. Destroying even one book was anathema to her, but burning that many?

"What about other books, the ones your dad sold? What if they've been taken out of town?" I asked, the implications seeping into my mind. Jubayr damaged the wicked text and got hurt. Maybe if other owners didn't do that, they'd be okay. Most people keep the books they buy as is? Right?

"Does your dad have a list of sales?" I asked.

Destruction is painful, but darkness must be purged—

Zakiyya cut the *Book of al-Azif* off. "Where is our friend?" she asked. "The bookworm. You should have seen him. He was investigating."

She'd said 'Friend!'

"A worm is your friend?" Ruya asked; this confused her more than everything else going on. "I didn't see a worm."

Nothing passed between my pages, the *Book of al-Azif* assured us.

"Then if you burn all the books, he'll burn too. We have to find him!" I declared.

Worry not. The *Book of al-Azif* wrote in my skull and on the page. *Jinn are made of fire. The measly fires of this world cannot hurt them.*

"That makes sense," I said. "But just in case we have to find him and we need to take care of any other books that are outside the shop . . . "

"And we need to burn this one," Ruya said, gesturing to the poetry text. That's what she'd left home to do. She accepted our help easily. Holding this burden all alone must have made her feel insane.

I gave the *Book of al-Azif* back to Ruya and followed her.

Zakiyya whispered into my ear, "We never said that the worm was a jinn."

Chapter 8

"Now you know what it's really like to have your mind read!" I said.

"I only read what's on the person's mind at the moment. I wasn't thinking about what Shaykh Nariman *is*." Zakiyya whispered fiercely.

Ruya and the *Book of al-Azif* were several paces away by the bookshop. I'd persuaded Ruya that we had to gather the other deviant texts first before burning them all at once.

"Maybe it figured out that Shaykh Nariman's a jinn without mind-reading," I suggested, lowering my volume. "How else would a bookworm be sentient?"

"Maybe," Zakiyya muttered. "Shaykh Nariman wouldn't like this plan. He'd hate for books to burn."

"He's not here right now," I said. "The first step is for us to correct that. We can deal with the complaints later." Since when did she care what Shaykh Nariman likes?

Zakiyya gestured towards Ruya and spoke up. "You and I can search for Shaykh Nariman." She pointed to me, "You and the *Book of al-Azif* can look for wayward texts."

"But . . ." Ruya tried to protest at the separation from her precious manuscript, but Zakiyya's affected aunty aura allowed no argument.

"I think you'd be better at stealing books from unsuspecting owners than me," I said, plucking the book from Ruya. Zakiyya swatted at me half-heartedly. There was too much of a compliment in the insult for her to strike hard.

Ruya unlocked the front door of the bookshop and came back a few moments later with a list of her fathers' latest sales. She started to explain where each was located, but I waved her off. I could smell the tulip scent around town clearly. The monstrous books were mimicking a smell I'd been so sure was pure and blessed. The thought made my stomach churn.

Zakiyya followed Ruya into the book stacks. I left my staff with them so I'd be able to carry more texts, and instead took the satchel. As soon as the oil lamps in the neighbors' windows winked out, I set off.

This is sacred work you are doing, Khurafa, the Book of al-Azif told me. I didn't need to open it anymore to 'read' the words. I was glad for the motivation, but it made me miss Shaykh Nariman more. I whispered all the details of our journey so far. The *Book of al-Azif* was silent for a moment before I felt pages changing beneath my palm. *A great evil has awoken. There is little doubt. I am eager and honored to help confront it. Do you know yet where the Servants are?*

"I don't," I said as we approached the central mosque. I could make out the scent of tulips emanating innocently from within. Ruya's father had donated a couple works to the mosque and sold several more.

I walked past the minarets' moonshadows through the mosque's arched courtyard gates. They were open at night; the place of worship doubled as a refuge for all.

At the end of the courtyard there were two buildings attached to one another. The smaller structure radiated different shades of aged incense—it was a tomb complex, with *baraka* coming from the deceased. I squinted in the moonlight to make out the names inscribed on the door. I only caught the first, "Salman Al-Farsi." A companion of the Prophet, peace be upon him, was buried there! I gravitated toward it but the *Book of al-Azif* interjected forcefully, *Not there.*

The larger structure was the mosque itself. I fumbled around the entrance and found a half-molten candle left behind by some pious person praying late at night. I stepped gingerly onto the mosque's carpet, following my nose, with a small flame in one hand and the *Book of al-Azif* clutched close to my chest. I caught a whiff of perfume in the carpet and the tang of sweat and mold from all the bare feet that had walked there since it was last washed.

It didn't take long to find the fragrant, monstrous texts; I took a moment to sift through the pages as I grabbed each of them. A collection of sayings of the Prophet, peace be upon him, a book of stories about pious predecessors, a dense law text, among others. My satchel was swollen, and I had two texts swung under my arm with the *Book of al-Azif*. I figured it would protect me from any scary supernatural shenanigans. "These books don't seem evil . . ." I said.

The smallest bit of wickedness can be hidden within the cloak of goodness, the *Book of al-Azif* responded. *A single changed word can change everything. Imagine passing off a lie as the words of the Prophet, peace be upon him, or a holy man?*

"That makes sense," I said, rising to go. *There are more books here, take them,* the *Book of al-Azif* said.

"I found all the ones that are different," I said. I hadn't explained my ability in my summary of events, and it seemed it couldn't read minds because it didn't know until that moment.

I began to move when another smell broke through the deceitful aromas of tulips and the honest scent of incense; a sudden wretched and smoggy stench. The carpet was on fire! The candle had tipped sometime after I set it down to look at the books. I wasn't sure how I'd missed the flame earlier.

Thoughts of the ashen garden flashed through my mind. I dropped my satchel and all the books, and jumped on the flame. I smothered it with my clothes, reducing it to embers and then to nothing but a scarred patch on the carpet's geometric floral patterns. I'd succeeded in stopping a blaze from being born. This time.

I retrieved the books and rushed out. Had one of the wicked manuscripts done that? Started a fire? But that would have risked its own existence . . . Maybe the books could tell I was taking them outside, that they would be safe from the flames?

Why did you set the monstrous texts down away from the fire? Do you not wish to destroy them? The *Book of al-Azif* asked me.

"Yes, but I don't want to risk you! And I think they caused that fire." I said. I was hoping that Zakiyya and Ruya were having a better time finding Shaykh Nariman than I was nearly burning everything down.

Hauling the books back to the bookshop was slow-going. Knowledge is weighty . . . even corrupted knowledge.

After several minutes of labored walking, I dumped the texts unceremoniously on the ground outside the bookshop. I felt guilty as I did so, imagining Shaykh Nariman's disapproval.

Zakiyya poked her head out. "No luck yet," she said, "but we're still searching."

You should burn these books immediately, the *Book of al-Azif* pulsated the idea to me.

"Not now," I muttered. "Let's gather everything first." I

didn't want Ruya to go through the pain of burning books more than once.

I looked at Zakiyya, "Should I leave the *Book of al-Azif* with you? Maybe it can help find Shaykh Nariman?"

"No, that's okay," Zakiyya said quickly. "In fact, maybe you should leave it aside somewhere safe? Away from anything that will be burned or anywhere it might get lost?"

"No, it's helpful," I said. But really, I just needed the company. It wasn't a substitute though. "Find Shaykh Nariman," I pleaded.

I followed the scent of three more books, each in different buildings within the same neighborhood. The first was inside a pottery shop. I broke the lock and stumbled in. I was proud that I didn't break any ceramics in the process. The tulip-scented text I found was tiny. There were drawings amidst its prose. A star-shaped bowl, a pitcher that looked like a donut. "A book of designs?" I guessed softly.

If so, imagine what the vessels made from them could do, the *Book of al-Azif* warned. Its words were red and bold in my mind.

Before I could answer, there was a creak. I didn't know whether it was a teetering pot or person. I shut the door as quickly and quietly as I could, and darted off outside.

I was panting by the time I made it to the second manuscript. This one was inside a home. I tested for an open window, and it occurred to me that if I didn't get caught tonight, there would be an uproar tomorrow. Stolen books across town! A fire at the bookshop! But then again, how many people read every day? How long would it take people to notice the stolen texts? I was channeling Shaykh Nariman's book obsession at this point.

I must have muttered some portion of my sullen thoughts

because the *Book of al-Azif* answered. *Better that knowledge is lived than read,* it said. *How often are we slaves to the written word?*

I found an open window and slipped into the house without incident. The thunderous snoring of the homeowner masked my footsteps. People sleep better outside the big city. The insidious manuscript in question was on a floor pillow in the sitting room. By the hefty weight I could tell it was probably a law treatise.

I hopped back outside through the window and stuck my landing. There was another open window on the first floor of the house containing the last book, and I climbed through in seconds, feeling proud.

My self-congratulations were premature. The third and final manuscript was more tricky to retrieve than the rest, and its location was a snarky rebuttal to my lament about people not reading. The scent of the third book came from right beside—or maybe on top of—someone mumbling meaningless words from peaceful dreams. The book's buyer had fallen asleep in bed, with the text.

"What do I do now . . ." I whispered. I could make out the dark shape on the bed through the moonlight creeping in from the window. It was a child wrapped around a rectangular object.

The *Book of al-Azif* offered no suggestions. After a few tense moments of indecision, I heard the meaningless mumbling slow as the child fell more deeply asleep.

I took a long, silent breath and reached into the bed. The child's sudden snore made me jump. I stuck a hand out onto the bed to catch myself and the blanket muffled the sound of the impact. The child squirmed.

I slowly, carefully, tried to pry the book out of the kid's grip. The child murmured, "no," and I thought my heart would stop, but then another snore kickstarted my pulse. I had the evil text, and the kid wasn't awake! I couldn't wait to tell Zakiyya! Who's a better thief now! Actually, wait, that wasn't something to be proud of.

I extracted myself slowly from the bed, inch by inch, the kid's text in my hands. And then I stopped. I could hear the wind, I could sense the soft dance of leaves outside. I could feel my every breath. Adrenaline had spiked my senses to their peak.

But I couldn't hear anything from the child anymore, I couldn't detect the slightest movement, the smallest indentation of the chest or gasp of air."Hello?" I whispered, "Are you breathing?" There was no response.

What are you doing? The *Book of al-Azif* asked. *There is a time for concern and a time for haste.*

I shook the child gently and then with greater force. "Wake up," I said, my whisper rising in volume. "Are you alive? Wake up!" I put one hand to the child's chest and couldn't feel a heartbeat. I pressed the other hand to the kid's chest and pumped. At this point I'd dropped the text I was stealing. I pressed down again and again, my mind swirling with prayers, my voice raised, "Wake up! Wake up! In the name of God, please wake up!"

There were murmurs in the distance, the sound of the parents stirring. I didn't care if I was caught, though a mean, selfish part of me wondered if I would be blamed for the child's death.

I shook the child, nearly screaming, "Please!" and the limp body banged against the evil text I'd dropped. And then, as if all the tension in the world had unknotted, the child sputtered and took a desperate, fulsome gulp of air. My limbs went slack in relief, but I still grabbed the wicked text and slipped outside the window. I crouched under the window sill though the *Book of al-Azif* screamed for me to leave.

"Are you okay, little one?" the child's mother said, yawning.

"Mama," the child said. The words meant the kid was alright. I ran off as the kid blabbered. "Nightmare, mama! Papers all over me—couldn't breathe, but then—"

"What was that?" I said, when I finished my jog. "Was the text suffocating the kid?"

The *Book of al-Azif* answered, *Without a doubt. We must burn it and be done with it.*

I emptied my satchel as soon as I made it back to the bookshop and set everything in the pile of stolen, malevolent texts, except for the *Book of al-Azif*, which I clutched tightly. "We should burn these right away," I said to Ruya and Zakiyya.

"We haven't found Shaykh Nariman yet," Zakiyya said, her voice higher than normal.

"Not the books in the bookshop then," I said. "But the texts I've stolen at least. I—I saw one try to kill a child, and I think another tried to start a fire. If we delay, who knows what they'll do." The *Book of al-Azif* blazoned words of agreement in my mind.

"Let's find a place somewhere farther out so the fire doesn't draw attention," Zakiyya said, twirling a loose curl of hair.

"Yeah, I can do it. You can keep searching—"

"—If they're so dangerous, we should do this together," Zakiyya interrupted me. "Bring the poetry book too," she commanded Ruya. The girl lifted the mangled text and a chunk of the book pile without a word. In fact, I might have heard a whimper.

We walked a few minutes away to the ruins of an old house that Ruya knew of. The shadows and scattered rocks should have been spooky in the dark, but I was reminded of Shaykh Nariman's house.

"Start the fire first before throwing the books in," Zakiyya said. Ruya and I obliged. I clutched the *Book of al-Azif* while I worked the flint. I wasn't sure why I was still holding it, it just felt like the right thing to do.

The fire grew. I set the *Book of al-Azif* down reluctantly and selected three texts to throw in.

Right before I threw them in the rising blaze, Zakiyya pushed me! I skidded over a rock, toppling to the ground away from the fire. The texts scattered over the rubble. I lifted myself up, ignoring the stinging in my knee.

"What are you doing!" Ruya screamed. My surprise at her challenging Zakiyya turned to horror as I saw what she meant. Zakiyya tossed the *Book of al-Azif* into the fire.

That's what I got for trusting someone who trusted no one.

"No!" I cried, rushing forward to scoop it out, heedless of being burned. She blocked my path and pushed me back again.

"Just wait," Zakiyya said, holding her hands up to keep me away. I saw Ruya's terror transform to rage. She charged Zakiyya, but Zakiyya stuck out a well-placed foot and tripped her, planting Ruya head-first into the ground.

Fiery, searing words tore into my head from the burning *Book of al Azif. Save me! Save me! What have you done?*

I scampered past Zakiyya in desperation. "It has baraka! It can help, it—"

"It doesn't have the smell, does it?" Zakiyya said, her eyes burrowing into mine. "And all the books we're supposed to burn. They do."

I stopped moving and looked at her, registering the tired relief in her face.

Ruya rose and struggled internally, her hand reaching out toward the fire, then drawing back. Love for the book that had asked for her help, hate for it controlling her.

"I had trouble reading Ruya's mind earlier because she was always holding the book. It made Ruya bring it near Jubayr before he got hurt! It wants to destroy books—to destroy knowledge salvaged from the savaging of Baghdad. It's manipulating Ruya . . . and you. It hurts people, to goad us into destroying other books, or to sow chaos . . . I couldn't tell you my suspicion because you were always carrying it."

"If it has that power," I asked, "then why didn't it destroy the other books by itself?"

"The baraka in those texts must stop it," She said. Beside her, Ruya collapsed to the ground; her internal battle over what to do resulted in self-defeat.

"It was torment for her," Zakiyya gave her a pitying look. "She followed the book, but the pressure of its writing on her mind . . . She must have known something was wrong, but she's weak to authority, and the book exudes it."

I felt a stab of guilt for not figuring this out—just enough guilt to smother my anger at Zakkiya acting without trusting me. I also felt some shame. Was I weak to authority too?

"It had nothing to do with trusting you, you dolt," she scoffed, checking on Ruya. "I wasn't sure if it could read minds, so I couldn't tell you! And I needed it away so I could think—"

"You didn't trust the book, and you were right. That doesn't mean all your suspicions are right though!" I said heatedly to Zakiyya, staring at her. Flashes of orange, red, and yellow lit her up.

"You're . . . on fire," I said dumbly. And then I rushed to her, trying to bat away the flames. "You're on fire!"

If I burn, you're going to hell with me, the book—the obviously, utterly demonic book—screeched in our minds.

"No!" I screamed, and Zakiyya's relief and triumph gave way to wide eyes and her own scream. She tried to fan away the flames. She rolled on the ground, but it did nothing but make them grow. As the *Book of al-Azif* burned, so did she. The fire licked her flesh hungrily.

The garden burned and I'd been helpless, and now Zakiyya was burning. She couldn't die, I wouldn't let her die! But it didn't matter how much I tried battering the blaze engulfing her, the flames wouldn't stop.

I *was* helpless again.

"That's enough of that," a warped voice said from where the *Book of al-Azif* continued to shriek. Something wiggled out of the burning book and tore its spine apart. We felt a final screech rip through our minds as the tiny interloper destroyed the *Book of al-Azif*, and the flames on Zakiyya immediately died away. She groaned, and might have cried had the fire not dried up her eyes.

"How badly are you burned?" I asked. "Are you okay?"

Before she could answer, the small creature that had ripped apart the book, reached us. A bookworm. "Are you alright Zakiyya?" Shaykh Nariman asked.

"I'm . . ." she began discordantly. She looked down. The burns were minor, hardly even bruises.

"But how is that possible?" she said. Her eyes made it to the ground. Her foot was touching a lump of papers that I dropped when she'd pushed me earlier.

"The text . . . the poetry manuscript . . . It must have protected you," I said. The tulip smell wasn't deception. It was real, honest baraka.

"Then why didn't it protect the scribe?" Zakiyya asked. "Oh. He was tearing it apart, so the protection waned . . . "

"And the other baraka books are like this too, though maybe to varying degrees," I said, thinking back to the kid who hadn't been breathing. When the tulip-scented text I'd stolen touched the child, the suffocating stopped. And the child had only stopped breathing in the first place when that text was removed. The sentient *Book of zl-Azir* must have tried to kill the child and burn the mosque—maybe to get me to destroy books faster because of their alleged wicked acts.

Zakiyya was the first to break out of the spree of speculation. "I knew you'd be in there," she said to Shaykh Nariman, a smile lighting up her face more than the fire could.

"You're lucky these flames aren't hot enough to burn even an old jinn like me," Shaykh Nariman said. His voice sounded like it was coming through a tunnel again, a result of altering the worm form to allow speech.

"Please turn back into a mouse," I said, making the request to distract from my giddy, stupid smile. Shaykh Nariman was okay! And Zakiyya trusted him! For real this time! AND SHE WAS GLAD TO SEE HIM!

"Shut up Khurafa," Zakiyya muttered. Was there red in her cheeks?

"I will turn back, I will." Shaykh Nariman said. "The book trapped me when I crawled into its pages. Brought me deep into its words, somewhere not fully on the material plane. Burning weakened it and got me out."

"Glad I was right," Zakiyya sighed.

"How'd you know I smelled baraka on the other texts? I thought the *Book of al-Azif* blocked most of your mind reading?" I asked, while helping Ruya to her feet. She seemed too out of it to remark on the talking worm.

"You think *really* loud, remember?" Zakiyya said with an unsteady smile. I decided that she meant I think clearly. Whether or not that's what she intended.

"I need to return these books," Ruya spoke at last while looking at the pile of texts on the ground. "I was going to burn everything. Does this mean . . . does this mean I helped cause Jubayr's death?"

"You were being manipulated," Zakiyya said, giving Ruya's shoulder a firm squeeze. "You were able to resist in the end. If you hadn't, or if you'd saved the *Book of al-Azif* from the fire, we might all have died."

The call to the morning prayer echoed in the distance. I crushed the dimming fire under some stones. We picked the baraka-laden manuscripts up by the ember light and scampered off before anyone could investigate.

"We should return them," Zakiyya said.

"I don't mind doing it!" I said. Returning books was morally easier than stealing them.

"I don't know," Zakiyya said, reading my thoughts. "You got lucky grabbing the texts in the first place."

"She's right—rely on the mercy of God but don't needlessly test it," Shaykh Nariman said.

"You at least could believe in me, Sidi," I muttered. But my sourness was fake. We'd protected knowledge and come together. I believed in us.

In the end, I returned the heavy load of books to the mosque right before the prayer started, while Zakiyya returned everything else based on my scattered thoughts. From the smile on her face when she made it back, it was clear she had less trouble in her slinking around than I did.

***

We returned to the bookshop to check in on Ruya and she greeted us outside with a book in hand. "A thank you for saving the texts," she said, "and for saving me."

Zakiyya took the book from her and riffled through it briefly. I saw a few headings and recognized it: *Stories of the Prophets.*

Zakiyya caught me looking and handed it over. I hugged it for a moment and breathed it in. It smelled more heavily of tulips than anything else in town.

"You carry it," she said. "Now let's find a place to sleep." In her palms she clutched a small pouch of coins that Ruya had discreetly slipped into the manuscript. Typical.

I could feel Shaykh Nariman squirm. Being trapped in a demonic book hadn't diminished his enthusiasm for the written word. I wasn't quite as excited. Shaykh Nariman had told me the stories of all the major figures from Adam to the Prophet Muhammad, peace be upon him. I wanted to learn something new. But it had baraka, so there was that.

"Don't be so full of it," Zakiyya said. "I'm sure Shaykh Nariman would say that you can always learn something new from the same old stories."

"I would," he whispered. "And some collections of the stories of the prophets actually tell slightly different versions of the same— "

"Ruya!" I called out to avoid an argument. "Where did the sentient book come from? Was it in the texts your dad obtained from Baghdad?"

"No . . ." she said, standing on the threshold of her

113

bookshop. "There was a man who came by several days ago. He wore a cowl so I couldn't see his face fully. He was tall, and I think there was a scar on his cheek. He looked around for a while and then left the book behind in the store. I tried to find him afterward, but he was gone, nowhere in town. And then the book started talking to me . . ."

"The man with the cowl. He could be one of the Servants, sowing chaos," Shaykh Nariman interjected. "Or someone affiliated with them."

"Was al-Hazred one of The Servants?" Zakiyya asked. "The supposed author of the book?"

"It's a bizarre name, al-Hazred," Shaykh Nariman said. "I recall it though I can't say he left much of an impression in any histories I've read. He lived in the late 7th and early 8th centuries so he was a contemporary of the Servants but wasn't one of them. He was a 'wannabe.' Never a sorcerer at their caliber."

Something made by a wannabe had almost destroyed us. So what could The Servants do?

"You all look as tired as I feel," Ruya interjected, shaking away her residual fear. "Do you want to nap here? My father is out."

Zakiyya bolted to the book-buried basement. I moved more slowly, careful not to trip on any piles of texts. I curled up against a wall, nestled against a few ancient titles, and drifted off immediately.

***

I was in a library, maybe even a house of wisdom from the old days. Books were piled on floors and tables, big-bearded scholars sat on soft rugs peering at texts beneath their noses, illuminated by warm candles. Students struggled to carry multiple manuscripts, and one child flung a book at her peer and ran before getting scolded.

A wall burst open, and the scene froze. A serpentine beast tore through, biting flesh and pages with equal relish. It grinned at me, blood and ink dripping from its fangs.

It shrieked as a small manuscript in front of me began to glow.

Chapter 9

The wind rammed my satchel into my side; it hurt a little, with the weight of the *Stories of the Prophets* book behind it. Maybe it was pushing us forward. Zakiyya looked at me with weary expectation in her eyes.

"Are you catching a whiff of anything?" she asked as we ambled outside Ruya's place.

"From the north east, kinda smells like catnip." I wrinkled my nose in satisfaction at the mint-like fragrance.

"How far north east?" she asked, as she watched me stretch my legs.

"Can't be sure," I said. "Might as well get walking . . . But hey, that's in the direction of your grandma, isn't it?"

"That's right," Zakiyya said. There was the ghost of a smile on her lips—a muted hope.

"Why do you want to go to your grandma?" I asked. "What happened . . . to your parents?" It wasn't the sort of question one voiced after the Mongol conquest, but we were close enough now. I thought.

Zakiyya's expression darkened. "Same as yours," she said quickly.

I felt a sinking feeling in my stomach at the reminder.

"I'm sorry," I said. Shaykh Nariman poked his head out and

stared at her. His whiskers bristled in the wind.

"How did you survive? Were you dodging horsemen on the street?" I asked; it was an easy sight to imagine. But what do thoughts in another language sound like? And are horse thoughts neighs?

"No, I was unconscious for most of it," Zakiyya said. She looked at one of the many loose rocks on the street and kicked it off to the side. No quip about my musings.

"What? Did you get hit on the head?" I asked.

"No. It would be hard for anyone to hit me."

"Then . . .why . . ." my voice faded as realization dawned on me.

"You could hear everything . . . the terror, the fear." I whispered in horror.

Zakiyya was silent for a long moment before she spoke. "Everything that happened around me, within a few blocks. I could hear it. So loud I couldn't block it out. A thousand people screaming inside, worrying about their children, their homes, their lives. Everything was bloody and bruised. But the people hiding were even worse. Their anxiety about being found. I felt it, a thousand times over. Everyone's anxiety. And so yeah, I passed out."

"I'm glad you're alive."

"Uhuh," she said, not looking at me. "Me too. How did you make it through?"

"Oh umm . . . I was in the garden," I said, the blood draining from my face. "The—the flowers distracted them, you know?"

Zakiyya could read my mind, so she knew not to say anything.

"Be careful with the positioning of the book in the satchel," Shaykh Nariman piped up, breaking the pained silence. "You might hit me. Although if it were time for me to meet my creator, death by text would not be so bad a way to go." His whiskers twitched.

I switched the shoulder that the satchel strap rested on.

"Also—" Shaykh Nariman began in a sterner tone of voice, "you have a little more money now. Don't walk. Join a caravan in that direction and disemark when the scent starts to go off course. It is safer and faster than traveling by foot."

Zakiyya and I shared an "Oh . . . duh" look.

I couldn't help feeling a twinge of nostalgia. I'd never joined one, but my mom used to send me to meet caravans entering Baghdad from the eastern gate. I'd carry bundles of carefully plucked flowers, and merchants who had forgotten gifts for their wives or children would practically pelt me with coins. I was giving the flowers away and not selling them, but the merchants didn't always give me time to explain that. My mom called it our family's contribution to the 'social commerce' of the city, whatever that meant. She had me donate the coins I'd receive.

Caravans had dwindled since the conquest and I'd stopped going to greet them.

Zakiyya flicked me on the forehead and I broke out of my reverie. I kept my eyes on the ground.

"Alright!" I said, forcing enthusiasm until it became real. "To the mosque or market?" I asked. They were two of the largest clearinghouses for joining caravans. Merchants worked in the market, and they often made it a point to make prayers before embarking on a journey that could end at the swipe of brigand's sword or in the depths of a ravine.

"You're being pretty morbid today," Zakiyya said, shaking her head as she read my assessment of travel. Her black curls broke free of the gray scrap of cloth she'd used to tie them up. She scowled and re-tied it.

She was the one who had almost been burned alive but I was the one still affected by it.

"Hope is the core of faith," Shaykh Nariman said automatically, Zakiyya's proclamation sparking concern.

"Yes, of course," I agreed with the rodent shaykh. I felt a little guilty thinking of the burnt section of the mosque's carpet and hoped Zakiyya would pick the market as our recruiting ground.

"To the market,"Shaykh Nariman squeaked at the same time that Zakiyya said, "To the mosque!"

She was clearly hearing my thoughts and knew it was two against one. She eyed my frown and sighed. "I've been picking things up here and there. Someone in the market is asking about two unaccompanied children. And that someone is an unusually tall woman, accompanied by two men."

I gulped. Aunty Naama was still after us. "Don't worry," Zakiyya said. "Let's just figure this out fast."

We entered the mosque in time for the noon prayer. Shaykh Nariman slipped out without explanation before I passed the gates.

Zakiyya scanned the rows of worshippers from outside the mosque door and pointed out which trader I should pester. She joined the group of women in prayer.

I managed to corner the merchant in question after the prayer finished. He was an energetic young man with a scrawny brown beard. I started asking him questions and found that I was being interrogated in return: "Northeast? Where are you heading? What city?"

I squinted to make sure I didn't recognize him from the

creepy Khaniqah we'd wrecked. "I don't really know yet. I'll know it when I see it?" I answered truthfully.

"Are you running away, son? Is someone threatening you? Are you shirking work or running from your parents?" he asked. A journey without a clear destination was a bit strange, but still, his barrage was unnerving.

"N–no," I said, as I failed to come up with a more substantial answer. The weight of the Stories of the Prophets book saved me; it jingled a few of the coins that Zakiyya had grudgingly let me carry.

The reminder of money toned down the trader's questioning. "I'm heading to Rayy, and there should be space. For you and your young sister. But honestly I won't know how much to charge you unless I know how far you're going."

An uncle who was intensely reading the holy scripture shushed us and gestured with his head toward the courtyard. We slipped outside, and Zakiyya joined us as we ambled over to the well for a drink.

I breathed a sigh of relief, which she must have heard because she barely stifled a snort. "I hope my *little brother* hasn't been giving you too much trouble," she said.

"Well, the ambiguous destination is a little concerning," he said. He gave us a closer look. "And you both look rather young to be traveling alone without an older relative. And. . . you don't really look related."

Zakiyya gave him a deep frown which she transformed into a look of profound sadness. "We share only a father. He traveled northeast but disappeared somewhere en route a month back. We believe he left a sign that we would recognize, something carved on a tree or a signpost in town. Going in the general direction seems the best way to find it."

The trader nodded sagely, but there was a gleeful light in his eyes. "I see," he said, stroking his feeble beard. "Well, in that case, how can I take pay? Helping kids find their father! My name is Jamshid. I'll be happy to have you both join my small troupe. There is space on the pack animals. I plan to pick up more goods than I sell."

He beckoned us to join him in an expedited visit to the tomb complex. We ducked through the sandalwood door frame into a domed chamber housing three large, box-shaped cages covered with lattice work laced with celestial geometric patterns. Within the cages were the tombs, each covered with a lush green cloth. The incense flooding the room was intoxicating; some of it was real, some of it was from my baraka-sense. The graves practically oozed aged aromas of blessings.

Jamshid, the merchant, placed a hand on the cages and muttered greetings to the deceased holy men and then prayed to God for success in his upcoming venture. I put a hand to my heart and inclined my head in respect for the dead. I was feeling dizzy when we made it back into the open air.

Jamshid gave us instructions on where to meet, and Zakiyya and I headed off. I felt a ticklish presence and noticed Shaykh Nariman crawling back into the satchel and nestling against the Stories of the Prophets book after we'd passed the mosque complex's gates.

Zakiyya eyed the satchel as soon as we were alone. "You avoided the old arch," she said to Shaykh Nariman. "And you didn't join us at the tombs. Don't jinn like to live in graveyards and ruins? You could have found some of your relatives there!"

"My relatives are all gone," Shaykh Nariman said, bobbing his snout out to face her. His whiskers dipped in a sad smile.

I elbowed Zakiyya. "How'd you get the merchant to agree?"

"He was fixated on mystery. His mind was filled with over-imaginative speculation on what we were doing. Clearly he wanted a sense of adventure on his first trading mission," she said matter-of-factly. "I gave him that taste of adventure and the chance to feel like a hero. Of course he ate it up. Also, I caught something about his father passing away being the reason he's taking up business, so I played up on the theme of kids in need of their father."

"Devious," I muttered. She slapped me absent-mindedly. There was more pride than repentance in her face.

"So you picked him because you knew it would be cheap?" I asked.

"Well . . ." Zakiyya smirked. "We also needed someone who I could tell was already heading northeast. Asking around too much and drawing attention to ourselves would make it easy for the Khaniqah lady to find us." The merchant's mind clearly wandered way too much in prayer.

***

Within an hour, we were trundling along on a horse. As the faint scent of catnip continued to grow stronger, I tuned out of the trader's monologue on all the great merchant ventures he had planned.

"BANDITS AHEAD!" Zakiyya shouted just as I was beginning to nod off. I was nearly jolted off the horse by her volume, too shocked to feel vindicated for my earlier pessimism.

Our trader friend had more animals than merchandise, but far fewer guards than the number of goods warranted. I should have realized this would be a problem when we set out, but I'd gotten too caught up in the success of snagging a ride.

The single, white-haired man-at-arms, Jiddi Muqbil, shuddered at the size of the band of highwaymen. He lifted an open palm in warning, trying to halt them with it, as if it could push them away. It seemed he would have better luck relying on the bandits' respect for their elders than on his own strength.

Being cheap comes at a cost, I thought toward Zakiyya. She gave no response, in body language or otherwise.

"Stay back!" Jiddi Muqbil cried out. "Let us be about our business."

"I'm afraid this is *our* business," one of the bandits said jovially, while stroking his well-oiled hair and waving his scimitar. He was a walking stereotype, the exact caricature of a bandit I thought of every time Shaykh Nariman mentioned one in a story. I could imagine the smell of his unwashed, sweaty clothes and gangrene breath. Scents of violent desperation.

"Is that laughter to prepare yourself for the guilt?" Zakiyya said to the bandit.

Hey! The one girl in this group really shouldn't bring attention to herself. These are bandits, the things they could . . .

Zakiyya ignored me. I gripped my staff tightly, thinking quickly, *if you want us to run, lift your right ring finger, if you want to fight, your pinky finger.*

None of her fingers twitched. I remembered the thugs in the city and quieted my thoughts.

Shaykh Nariman tensed. He'd remained silent the whole trip with Jamshid so close by, but I had no doubt he would bite any bandit who got near us now.

"Hello little one," the walking stereotype said. He looked Zakiyya up and down carefully as he approached, his dull blade still reflecting speckled patches of light. "You'll fetch a fair price, assuming you don't make us hurt you."

"Your mother would be ashamed of you," Zakiyya said,

meeting his eyes; her lips twitched up as she spoke. "*Is* ashamed of you, actually. Her callous fingers were weaving that rug, working so hard to get your family out of poverty. And you threw all her hard work for a clean life away. The rug was various shades of red, wasn't it? As if she knew how much blood would be spilled by your hand."

The bandit paused, the blade jolting in his hand at the sudden stop. He looked at Zakiyya in confusion. I could see a fire of rage in his eyes, clouded by a shadow of fear.

"What was the last thing she said to you?" Zakiyya asked, a malicious smile taking over her face, her eyes wide in exaggerated glee. She inflected her voice with a rural twang. "I thought of stranglin' you once when you was crying as a babe. Mad, crazy thoughts, like a mother gets after months of no sleep. Course, even thinkin' bout that scared me. But now I wonder how many lives I woulda' saved."

The bandit saw more red than shadow. Anger won out. He charged and Zakiyya twitched her pinky. I brushed the ground before us with the staff right before the bandit reached us, tapping the ground as gently as I could. I pulled the staff back with all the rapid vigor the tap lacked. I wanted to stop the guy, not tear him into pieces. I stepped on something uncomfortably squishy as I moved away.

Step back carefully, there's horsedung behind you, I thought as I began to put space between myself and the bandit, rubbing my shoe against the road to clean it as I did so.

Zakiyya lifted her foot backwards over the fly-ridden pile of brown muck. The bandit's right foot sank into the new pothole the staff made; his forward momentum didn't stop despite his leg being caught. His upper body sailed forward in an arc. He plummeted into the ground, face landing with a squish, then a scrunch as he slammed into the cushiony dung and then the gravel.

The fall didn't loosen the bandit's grip on his blade, but his attempt at breathing through poop-clogged nostrils did.

Zakiyya knelt beside the bandit, moving with elegant fluidity. She gently patted the back of his head, then rammed it to the ground before he could recover.

"Let's see," she said, her tongue tracing her lips. "How many have you killed? Oh, seven people. And you vomited the first time. You still get a little bile in the back of your mouth when you think of them. And what do you think of your men?" She lifted her other hand and pointed to each of the other bandits in turn. "Savage, stupid, really stupid, oh . . . you're scared of that one, this one is a coward, and . . . you abuse that one because he tries to be kind and it pisses you off that he's not as ruined as you."

I angled the staff toward the man's head as he got to his knees. The red in his vision was gone and hot tears feebly washed his feces-stained eyelashes. His mind was stripped bare before Zakiyya's onslaught. Every question she asked brought thoughts unbidden to him and she exposed him with unrelenting malice. At that moment even I shuddered.

Zakiyya waved her hand at the bandit she declared was abused, a scrawny man holding a sword in limp hands. "There are better ways to feed your little sister," she said. She looked toward the coward, a hulking bandit in worn leather breeches, who was looking down at his own feet and trembling. "You want to run. Go, leave. Leave before your bladder starts leaking." He took a step back and then turned around and broke into a run. The savage, a gaunt man with a wispy stache and hollow eyes seized the coward by the shoulder.

Zakiyya chuckled, looking directly at the one who the leader was afraid of. "You've always wanted to lead this group. Even now you want to take control. A knife in your hands and what can't you handle? But this is something you don't understand . . . You want to kill what you can't comprehend, but deep down you know you're more likely to be destroyed by it."

"Witch," the leader—the stereotype—said, coughing out crap as he spoke. But even he limped backward, away, his leg sprained from the pothole. The others broke into a tenuous run, all except the scary one and the savage. The former offered his shoulder for the leader, swinging an arm behind him to steady him. The leader flinched at the contact, but allowed himself to be helped.

"He's still deciding whether to kill you," Zakiyya called out; it wasn't clear whose mind she was reading or which of the two she was talking to. The scary one converted the arm behind the leader's back into a snaking chokehold in response to her words; the leader slipped out his injured leg and twirled it around the gaunt man's left leg. They toppled into a heap, grappling in a tangle of limbs. Moments later, scarlet streaks scarred the sky . One—or both—decided that using weapons was better than wrestling.

The savage lifted his ax and bounded towards us. "This is YOUR DOING!" he bellowed.

Zakiyya opened her mouth to get in some final jibe that might dissuade him, but before she could say anything, or attempt to preternaturally dodge, she scrunched her nose, and yelped, "Achoo!"

The sneezes continued. She shook violently as she failed to hold back the next one and stop death from barreling towards her. "Achoo!"

Now? Really?

I moved to step in front of Zakiyya and swing the staff, but I stumbled over a rock. The staff sailed out of my hands, nowhere near the savage; it landed horizontally, so the tip didn't conveniently rent the ground in two.

The savage was upon us. He didn't slow his momentum as he swung diagonally. He could take us both out with one, clean sweep, lopping off my head and cutting through Zakiyya's torso.

My rush of adrenaline slowed time, but only my perception of it. I couldn't push Zakiyya out of the way or dodge. Instead I got to see the rusted ax head edge towards us. Death, inevitable. It was bizarrely beautiful.

I thought my last words, because my lips wouldn't move fast enough. *There is no God but—*

A thin line of brown blurred past us before my thought could finish. Jiddi Muqbil's arrow took the savage in the chest, with a heavy thump, and the bandit staggered backwards. His swing didn't stop, but it went wide, a hair's breadth over us.

Jiddi Muqbil raised a shaking fist. Age had dimmed his speed but not his aim. He knocked another arrow and buried it in the savage's face.

"God have mercy," Zakiyya said, now that her sneezing fit had finally subsided.

***

Jamshid the Merchant had fallen from his horse in an effort to evade the bandits at the very start of the conflict. The guard splashed water on his face and when he finally blinked awake, the guard offered a raspy explanation for the grisly scene before us. "Killed one, two turned on each other over some grudge, the rest ran." He said nothing about Zakiyya, his lips closed so tight his wrinkles were doubled. He wouldn't even look at her.

Jamshid accepted the good fortune without surprise. "You've earned a bonus then," he said, choosing to sound magnanimous rather than grateful.

Zakiyya snorted and whispered to me. "The old man will suggest getting more guards next time, but this only increased that fool merchant's confidence."

I chuckled, more from relief at being alive than Zakiyya's remark.

Chapter 10

As it turned out, the close brush with death put Jamshid the Merchant in a reflective mood. His rambling died away, though Zakiyya's pained facial expressions suggested his ambitious dreams had not. When the scent veered far off the road and I signaled a stop, Jamshid let us off without asking what marker our fictional father had left behind for us to find him. Jiddi Muqbil nodded at us but still wouldn't meet Zakiyya's eyes.

A kid who knows too much is creepy.

"You empty vessels really do make more sound," Zakiyya muttered at me as she heard that last thought.

When we were far enough from the caravan not to be heard, Shaykh Nariman peered out of my pocket, and then gave each of us a slow glare he'd been saving since the bandit encounter. "Do not court death like that. The Prophet, peace be upon him, said to remember death, but that doesn't mean you should let it remember you."

We followed the scent of catnip in chastised silence , the irreverent giddiness of survival humbled by Shaykh Nariman's words. The minty flavor of the catnip stirred in well with the fresh aroma of the wilderness. We passed through tough bristles of brush and past a few tired trees that had missed Spring's memo. We worked our way over mild hills and a half-hearted stretch of woods. I skidded down the last hill, sliding into a spindly plant that saved me from colliding with a boulder, but the rescue came at the cost of several thorns.

The impact jolted Shaykh Nariman. "I wonder if you are cursed as well as blessed," he mumbled through his whiskers. "Your species' forefathers fell from heaven, but you *keep* falling."

We edged our way through the last outcropping of trees to a rocky mound. There was a gap in the stone, a cave which emitted an overpowering aroma of catnip.

We peered past the brown stalactites and stalagmites, the teeth at the mouth of the cave, and saw what should have been an alluring darkness disrupted by flickering light. We could see the shadow of a man sitting on a stone, rocking back and forth, the size of his form further distorted with every motion. His soft, rhythmic chant was magnified by the cascading echoes of the cave. I closed my eyes and listened to the man repeat the names of God. I pictured water dripping from a stalactite into a crystal pond, a delicate sound rippling outward endlessly.

"An *ascetic!* A man dedicating his life to contemplation of the divine, away from everything. It looks like we may have found a saint," Shaykh Nariman whispered excitedly.

Zakkiya and I both raised an eyebrow. After the cultic Khanqah and the demonic book we were more skeptical than before.

As if on cue, the meow of a cat broke the routine of the chant, and the chamber went deathly quiet. The man's shadow stopped moving.

"You damn cat. Shut up," he growled, his formerly holy rhythm now flaring with something less savory. We heard the thud of a rock hitting the floor and the scampering sound of paws.

Cruelty to animals? Definitely not a saint. But he could still have baraka .

"Wouldn't be the first time someone blessed is a jerk," Zakiyya whispered. I flinched.

We walked past the shadows and into the fire light. The man's hair was gray, his limbs weathered and emaciated. His beard was a wild combination of clumps and whisps. Even in the light's orange glow I could tell he was pale. *How long has he been in the cave?*

Zakiyya decided to voice my question and several others. Her words reverberated off the walls, multiplying the intensity of her inquisitiveness and lending it a spooky air.

The man glared at us and I felt my stomach sink. The smell of catnip was strong, so strong that I could almost see the colors of petals overlaid on my vision. Maybe the ascetic's annoyed attitude was due to hunger and not a lack of piety?

"For thirty years I have made this cave my haunt," he said. "It is not home, this world cannot be. But here my body resides. Few have bothered me in that time. I ask that you leave."

Zakiyya looked more disappointed than I did. His thoughts must not have been very pleasant.

"Sir, there is a great evil in the world," I interjected; he hadn't given us his name on account of 'names being binding ties to this world' or something. "There is a satanic darkness out there. We need those with God's blessings to confront it, to shine light in the dark—"

"That does not concern me," he growled. "I am in retreat from the world."

"But the world is in chaos!" I said in exasperation, the last word bouncing around the cavern.

"Yes, it is in chaos. And did not the Prophet, peace be upon him, say that a time will come when mischief is so great, the righteous shall escape to the mountains as shepherds?" The man demanded, his eyes boring into me so aggressively I nearly lost my balance.

"Well, where is your flock of sheep?" Zakiyya asked, her respectful pleading bleeding into a scowl. "Are you taking care of this cat?" She eyed the little furball that the ascetic had yelled at earlier. It was nearly invisible in the shadows, the camouflage of its pitch black fur marred only by its glowing ember-like eyes.

"The cat insists on being here from time to time. I toss stones at it, but it keeps coming back." His brow furrowed as if he was wondering whether tossing stones at us might work.

Before I could launch into a desperate tirade, Shaykh Nariman spoke up, glaring at the man. He stood on his tiny hindlegs. The cat eyed him curiously. "Have you heard the story of the pious man who left his people to live alone and never helped them? When destruction came for them because of their wrong-doings, he was destroyed by the avenging angel first because he could have done something to save others but never even bothered. Or what about the saying of the Prophet, peace be upon him, that you should plant a tree, even if the world is ending?"

"He's right!" I added. "We have a duty to do what is right, regardless of the outcome, regardless of the time. Didn't Imam Husayn stand up even when he knew destruction was coming?"

"Man is superior to jinn and still you try to preach at me?" The grim ascetic scoffed at Shaykh Nariman. "And where has your kind disappeared to? And you boy—don't lecture me. I'm here to reflect, not to argue." He turned away from us.

"Retreat for a time, but come back to the world!" Shaykh Nariman proclaimed. "The Prophet, peace be upon him, visited the heavens, but he returned to us!" The man didn't respond; for ten full minutes, he ignored our every argument.

"The Prophet, peace be upon him, said if you see an evil change it with your hands," I began. "If not with your hands, then with your words. And if not with either then at least detest it in your heart! You're not changing any evil. You're not even feeling something against it."

"YES!" he answered at last, yelling. "Because I don't see any evil! I am removed from it! Except for the evil of you filthy interlopers." He spat in our direction.

We retreated to about five meters from the entrance and perched on a boulder. "Someone who throws stones at a cat can't have baraka," Zakiyya said. "Wasn't there some story about a woman abusing a cat getting thrown into hell for that act?"

I shrugged. "That is so," Nariman said solemnly. "One must treat all animals well. And the Prophet, peace be upon him, loved cats."

"This guy is a hermit because he clearly doesn't get along with people, and not just for religious reasons. Maybe the cave itself has baraka?" Zakiyya mused. "We can bring back a stone. You couldn't sniff out an exact origin for the smell in the cavern?"

"It's too strong all over the place," I muttered. "I'll get used to it after a while and maybe then . . ."

I stopped speaking as I noticed the cat walking with elegant precision a few paces away. It was eyeing a fledgling chick on the ground. I hadn't noticed the chirping or whimpering as the creature tried and failed to flutter upwards, towards the nest from which it had fallen. The cat's muscles rippled beneath its lush black fur, and I stepped forward to intervene. After that conversation I wasn't in the mood to see a bird torn to bloody feathers.

Zakiyya put a hand before me to stop me and hushed me with a finger to her mouth. She was watching even more intently than I was. Rather than leap and lunge with claws and teeth, the cat continued to stalk towards the bird, its footsteps so silent and calculated that amidst its dazed struggle, the chick didn't notice the predator till it was right above it.

The cat opened its mouth and swiped up the bird in one swift, fluid motion—there was no fight, no chase, one moment the chick was screaming for the sky, and the next it was in the cat's jaws.

I wanted to dash forth, but Zakiyya gave me a meaningful look, and though I couldn't read her mind like she could mine, I knew what it meant: This is the cycle of life; Who are we to deprive the cat of its food? I was sullen, it wasn't right that an animal as cute as that cat could be so savage.

The cat didn't shake its teeth or swallow. The chick was perfectly still in its mouth. *Dead from the bite or frozen from the shock.* The cat sat back on its haunches, then leaped onto the tree, climbing with lithe efficiency. It sprinted onto a branch with the delicate balance and speed of a saint crossing the sirat on the day of reckoning. It reached the nest from which the bird had fallen. The other chicks had been chirping in a hysterical murmur after their sibling fell but now they quieted abruptly. *And that's it, death comes so easily.*

The cat ignored the chicks and deposited the fallen fledgling into its nest, unmolested. The cat hopped off the branch and landed with acrobatic expertise, glaring back at the nest as if commanding the chicks to remain there.

"SubhanAllah," Zakiyya whispered, releasing a held breath that matched my own. "The baraka . . . It's coming from the cat, isn't it?"

The cat turned to us and ambled over as if it knew it was the subject of discussion. Its yellow eyes met ours. Maybe it did know. It purred against Zakiyya's leg and then rubbed against my own. I reached my hand down to pet it. The smell of catnip was all over my fingers.

"Will you come with us?" Zakiyya lowered herself to the ground, kneeling as she asked the cat. It leapt onto her knee.

Shaykh Nariman poked his head out of my satchel, his pink paws resting on the Stories of the Prophets book cover as he strained to get a good look at the cat, forgetting that he was a mouse. The cat leapt over to him and the instincts of his form made him tremble.

"Hey remember: the Prophet, peace be upon him, loved cats," I said to the shaykh as he struggled not to shrink back into the satchel.

The cat reached out a claw toward Shaykh Nariman and petted him gently on the head before backing away shyly. Zakiyya snorted and I broke out into a laugh, of relief, joy, humor, everything really. Even Shaykh Nariman began to chuckle. The cat stared at us wide-eyed and then licked the back of its paw innocently, as if to pretend obliviousness to how impressed we were.

"Can you read the cat's mind?" I asked Zakiyya. "Does it have a name?"

"I can't really understand animal thoughts," she said. The pouting face she was giving the cat said that she wished she did. "They're too different. We'll have to come up with a name if the cat chooses to join us."

Zakiyya gave in to temptation and scratched it behind the ears.

Chapter 11

We decided on the name Kedi, which means "cat."

Shaykh Nariman was conflicted about the name. "It's simple, but faith is also simple. Yet there are so many historic cat names you young ones could have used. But naming one after the entire species makes the individual in question almost a platonic archetype . . ." He mumbled.

Kedi didn't share Shaykh Nariman's hang-ups. She purred deeply as Zakiyya and I took turns scratching the back of her neck.

We camped for the night near the cave, but not so near as to encounter the irritable ascetic.

I would have preferred his harsh words to what I encountered instead.

In my dream, I was still lying in my bundle. I could hear squelching, slithering sounds, and the padding of claws crunching twigs. The nine serpentine creatures crawled over me, crushing me beneath their weight, tenderizing the meat before the meal. Saliva dripped from their mouths, cool liquid that burned my skin with its touch.

I tried to shut my eyes, but they were already closed. One of the dream-creatures peeled away my eyelid like the rind off an orange and crawled into my pupil.

A growl froze the nine creatures. A lump of fur landed on my head, instantly ejecting the serpentine monster in my eye. It was Kedi.

She raised a paw and the creatures barreled toward her. They grappled in a bloody tangle of scales and fur.

I awoke to Kedi meowing energetically with the rising sun. She was so mature and saintly dealing with the chick the day before—and in my dream—but come morning she was jumping on my face like a kitten.

I recited the same old short supplication and turned to my left side to blow out three small puffs of air. I breathed in a new scent. A sharp spike of juniper smelling like the woods in northern winters; it pushed away the dredges of sleep that Kedi hadn't purged and then lingered long enough to pull us all along. It was coming from the southeast.

As we made our way back to the road, Kedi began to growl in protest and then mewl and whimper. "What's this about?" I asked Zakiyya. Kedi's fur was sleek, but now it seemed to be standing on end. She wasn't quite as brave as my dream suggested.

Zakiyya was as puzzled as I was. "There are people some-where on the road. But too far for me to hear thoughts distinctly . . ." She shrugged. "It couldn't hurt to stay off the road a little longer. Make Kedi comfortable."

It did hurt though. I tried to mimic Kedi prowling the wilderness gracefully and ended up scraping my knee for the millionth time after tripping on a loose root. When we tried to head towards the road again an hour later, Kedi raised no objection, but I would have ignored her had she done so. Or at least glared; it's hard to ignore a cat.

We settled into a routine on the road and didn't encounter

any trouble. Kedi alternated between running circles around us and yawning prettily in a not-so-subtle command to be carried. I was beginning to think she was more sultan than saint.

One morning, Kedi playfully tried to grab Shaykh Nariman mid-pontification. I chuckled as our scholarly mouse sought refuge in the satchel. I shook my finger at Kedi, who looked at it intently as if she'd leap for it. There was mischief in her eyes.

"Any cat might catch a mouse/But the devout would seize a lion," I recited at her. My mock sternness cracked into a smile, and Shaykh Nariman perked up out of the satchel, standing atop the Stories of the Prophets book with a wide-eyed look of wonder on his tiny face. It had been two months since I'd spouted any verses.

"Are you a poet?" Zakiyya asked. I'd forgotten she was listening. I cringed my way out of my reverie, though there wasn't any sarcasm in her tone.

"No, it's not my piece."

"Lines from Rumi which you paraphrased? Shaykh Nariman teach you those?" she asked.

"I've never been very good with poetry," Shaykh Nariman squeaked. "Too long-winded for such a precise use of a language. That's what the boy said, how many years ago now?"

My cheeks reddened at what a cheeky kid I'd been when I first met Shaykh Nariman. "My mom taught me. She would write poetry too; her parents were actually sponsored by a minor noble for their verses. My mom wasn't always a gardener, though my dad was. Poetry was how they met. She came to the garden looking for inspiration for some lines she was working on and the rest is history."

I'd started off just embarrassed, but by the end of the recollection, my eyes were wet. "My mom would always say I was the best couplet she ever wrote," I mumbled.

"I'm surprised that a gardener and a woman from a literary family got married. I'd imagine there was a class difference," Zakiyya said with a finger on her round chin and a thoughtful look on her face. She moved her hand to fiddle with a loose curl.

"My grandparents didn't object. They believed in the true love they'd write about. Plus, gardeners and poets both craft beauty," I said, wiping my face dry. "Don't you dare make fun of this," I warned.

"I won't," Zakiyya said calmly. She smiled. "I think it's cute." She stroked Kedi's back and earned a few purrs.

"They had these dumb nicknames they used to call each other," I said quietly. "My mom was *zaitun*, olive, and my dad was *tiin*, fig."

"Those aren't dumb," Shaykh Nariman scolded me softly. "God swears by both the fig and the olive in the same verse of the holy scripture. They were together—are together—as those words are together in divine speech."

I spotted a grove of date palms, fed by a tributary of one of the two great rivers. I climbed the prickly wood without putting too much weight on any one of its protruding pieces. I didn't want to hurt a plant, even if I'd never tended it. I shook off a couple of yellow dates.

We were still nibbling the last remnants when we arrived at Wasit, a medium-sized city whose name literally means 'middle.' "Perhaps it's the mid-point of our journey," Shaykh Nariman said as we approached. Pontification and puns were two sides of the same dirham.

We entered through a sandstone gate decorated with faded geometric carvings; the many strings of triangles had blurred into tangled lines. Inside, there were smatterings of mudbrick homes, aged mosques, and a few yawning markets, but it was the massive citadel which dominated the landscape. It wasn't any taller than the city walls, but its width and length took up at least a fourth of the city's area. A few ramparts were rubble on the ground, and only a couple archerer holes were manned. Like the rest of Wasit, it had seen better days.

The aroma of juniper was so strong it made me stagger. We did barely a half-circuit around the citadel before the scent resolved itself into a pretty unmistakable point of origin. "It's coming from the dungeon, there's no question about it," I said, digging my foot into the base of the stone wall. "The supposedly holy Khaniqah ended up being evil, so maybe a wicked dungeon will be relaxed?" I suggested hopefully. "There's probably a saint imprisoned there." Or maybe a Ghazi who'd resisted the regime. I'd almost given up hope of meeting a hero.

"How many times have we been burned by that thinking now?" Zakiyya asked. "The baraka probably isn't coming from a saint. Watch it be a rock or a cell key or something."

"Have faith," Shaykh Nariman piped up. "A few false friends of God do not disprove the existence of real ones."

Zakiyya sighed deeply. "So we have to get into the dungeon, figure out who the 'saint' is, and get them out . . . or find the magic rock." She talked about the prison break so matter-of-factly it made me wonder if she'd planned contingencies for getting caught while thieving before. She punched me lazily as she rifled through my speculation; of course she had developed back-up plans.

"I can split the walls with the staff," I said in an attempt to be helpful and avoid her ire. "We can have a real prison break!" Or a mining operation if it's a rock.

"No, that would attract too much attention." Zakiyya shook her head. "Plus who knows who you'd let out or crush by accident." Kedi meowed in assent and then promptly curled up against the dungeon wall to sleep without a care in the world.

I was warming to the challenge "Then we fake a crime! I get thrown in, I find the guy, and he and I fake death. There are some flowers that reduce the pulse. They throw our 'corpses' out, we revive in a few hours and are scot free." I emphatically clapped my hands together as I finished laying out my plan. One look at Zakiyya's face and my enthusiasm melted into chagrin.

"Faking death is risky," she shook her head bemused. "Also, it's not all that easy to get out of a grave if they bury you. There's an easier way though—we can bribe a guard."

"Do we have enough money for that?" I asked. *Money is always the answer for you, but are you okay letting it go?*

Zakiyya ignored my snide thoughts as she got caught up in her own ideas. "Shaykh Nariman can turn into a big bar of gold," she said, her eyes brighter than the metal she spoke of. "We can bribe the guard with it, and then Nariman can turn back and escape after the saint is free. We'll have to get out of town quickly afterwards to avoid the guard, but risks are pretty minimal unless he wants to melt the bar of gold or lock it up right away . . ."

"No idea is risk free," I said, scratching my barren chin. I shouldn't have been surprised that she wanted to rely on money without spending it. "I like that plan though. And melting the bar shouldn't hurt Shaykh Nariman if the book fire is any indication. Shaykh, what do you think?"

Shaykh Nariman had been fidgeting for our entire conversation. "You kids have too much energy," he said with a gravity that didn't match his high-pitched squeaking. "Just ask to visit 'the pious man' who was locked up; there is always someone with a positive reputation like that in prisons, you don't need to get thrown in to find him. Sometimes the easy path is the right one."

"And after we meet him—*if* they let us meet him?" I asked, crestfallen, that the obvious route might render our adventurous plans useless. "Or, what if he's not the one?"

"Then we can have your more . . . audacious plans on standby," Shaykh Nariman said with an indulgent squeak.

"Regardless, we need to talk about whether you can turn into gold," Zakiyya said, her green eyes alight like leaves caught in the sun.

***

We found out almost immediately that there was a pious man in the prison, just as Shaykh Nariman expected. People found him inspirational, and the regional government was worried about what he might inspire them to do. We got in to visit him so easily it seemed like divine intervention.

A guard led us down sets of heavy sandstone stairs into a dimly lit, cobble-stoned basement. The cells were thin rectangular chambers behind bars, with sloping ceilings that narrowed at the back.

The guard looked at the ground rather than at the cell. A raspy voice greeted him. It echoed in the close quarters, "Asalamualikum, how are you? Is your son better? And who are these young ones that you've brought?"

The guard gulped. "Fine, all fine," he muttered and stepped away.

We walked to the far end of the corridor, in front of the bars. We peered into the cell. The prisoner was a short, thin man, with dark skin, bony limbs, and a patchy gray beard. He wasn't much to look at.

But there was no question that he was the one we were looking for. The prison reeked of dried urine, perspiration, and hopelessness. But in this cell, all those other smells were gone. The scent of junipers was so overpowering that it was bleeding into my other senses. His presence was a wildfire and we were withering embers. Light literally oozed from his crinkled face, so much so that the dank dark stone of his prison chamber looked soft and warm. Zakiyya's mouth went slack-jawed upon seeing him. She rubbed at her eyes to prevent tears; whatever the pious man was thinking it moved her like nothing I'd ever seen.

"You have no suspicions?" I whispered to her. "No doubts? He didn't get imprisoned to increase his popularity or something?"

"There's no deceit in him whatsoever," she said, shutting her eyes tightly for a moment. "Most people are at least fooling themselves . . . But here there is only truth."

He was a bonafide saint, the sort so blessed and loved by God that reality warped around him. He smiled upon greeting us and it felt like the last few months had never happened. I was ready to bask in that smile till judgment day, but Shaykh Nariman nipped my finger. I didn't notice until afterwards, but the bite healed right away.

The saint listened to my entire explanation of The Servants and Zakiyya's recounting of our journey with a somber, thoughtful expression. "We need to get you out of here. We need your help stopping them," I finished, whispering so no guards could hear. I shook a fist towards the bars that separated us from him.

"I won't be able to leave here, my child," the saint said, turning his eyes away from us for the first time. The movement made it feel like the sun itself had set.

"We'll find a way to get you out. We have a lot of ideas," I said, rubbing my hands together and picturing myself stealing a guard's clothing. *New plan!* I thought mischievously; Zakiyya looked at the speckled smock I was wearing as if calculating.

"The means of getting out of here isn't the issue," the saint said, giving us a small appreciative smile that was so bright it nearly made me blind. "I won't be able to leave."

I answered him with childish petulance; I had to force it because his presence made me so calm. "So what . . You think you shouldn't help people? You think you should meditate in obscurity and that's what God wants?" I cringed even as I said it, there was no way that could be true.

"Never. Not at all," he said, shaking his head.

Zakiyya tried to pick up on my mean streak, but her heart was not in it, and the serenity of his thoughts had her distracted. "Are you going to say something like 'you can't leave now, but when you're needed, you will come'? We need you now. We haven't found any of the Servants yet, but even still we've encountered so many dangerous things. We need your help."

"I can't help my dear," he murmured. "Though I pray for your safety."

"Why not?" I demanded, ashamed to be speaking so aggressively to him.

Zakiyya's eyes widened as she finally read what he was

getting at in his thoughts. "Oh . . . Don't—" she began, but the saint shushed her with another small smile.

He sighed softly—not in frustration, but in comfortable resignation and mild amusement at our badgering. He looked past my shoulder toward the wall, and a full smile reached his face this time. "It seems it's time anyway. You'll see. There is no power except with God. There is no God but Him, and Muhammad is his messenger."

He walked through the bars of his cell. Not through a gap between bars, literally right through thick, physical bars that should have blocked his way, as if he were immaterial. Our mouths were agape in astonishment; Shaykh Nariman was the first to find his voice, he spoke without a care for guards passing by. "See what I told you all about the power of saints . . ."

The saint gave us a half-smile, then grimaced, clutching his chest with his left hand and raising one finger to the sky with his right. Pain outlined his mouth but a buoyant joy leaked from his eyes. He collapsed at our feet, tumbling to the floor. His limbs were lifeless but somehow he still landed neatly in prostration, the fundamental position of worship.

A guard came running, so consumed with the bureaucratic logistics of making sure the prisoner was dead that it took a couple seconds for him to notice that the cell was still locked. "May God forgive us," he whispered, lifting the light corpse like he would his own child. Tears streamed down his face as other guards came down and word began to spread.

We weren't even questioned by anyone. Some of the gaolers themselves were declaring that what the saint had done was a miracle and a rebuke to unjust imprisonment. "No cell can hold a friend of God," one guard declared, limbs shaking. "Did

we help the oppressors? Or were we the oppressors ourselves .
. ." he continued, trembling. Another burly guard slapped him
and barked out orders.

We were escorted out unceremoniously; the guard who was
attempting to take charge gave us a harsh warning to keep
what happened to ourselves; his voice was coarse and I didn't
need Zakiyya to know that he knew word was going to get out
within the hour regardless of our involvement. We stuck close
to the dungeon as we tried to make sense of what happened.
Kedi yawned her way out of her catnap, and stretched languidly
before rejoining us.

A guard caught between grief and guilt dashed out of the
prison gates proclaiming what had occurred as two of his fel-
lows half-heartedly went through the motions of attempting
to restrain him.

"When he said he wouldn't be able to leave, he meant he was
destined to die before he left," I said, poking at a stone with
my foot.

"That really was a miracle," Zakiyya said. "At the last
moment, he was thinking of the end, and he was so . . .
accepting. I could hear him say, 'I'm coming to meet you,
my friend, my creator, my purpose . . ." Tears leaked from her
eyes and she didn't bother to wipe them away.

A crowd began to form nearby; the sleepy, slowly decaying
city was walking up with a stormy vengeance. Zakiyya narrowed her eyes and rubbed her temples, trying to drown out
the cacophony of voices only she could hear.

"If that group finds out we were with him in his last moments, they might come for us and we will be trapped. It
already looks as if this may cause a local uprising," Shaykh Nariman squeaked amidst the din. All the houses were emptied,

and the markets were abandoned. Our location was a focal point for the whole of Wasit's population.

"Couldn't the governor spin it and say that the saint died because he was meant to be imprisoned and God punished him for disobeying or something?" I asked.

"He may try to spread such lies, but I doubt it will catch on. Hiding a miracle like this is as hard as hiding the sun," Shaykh Nariman answered in squeaky solemnity. "Clouds and night both fade away . . ."

"The funeral will happen soon, right? We should stick around for it." I paused as it hit me now that the awe had worn off; I looked at Zakiyya's teary face in a new light. "Are we responsible for him dying? We pushed him to what he knew would be his death . . . so it's our fault."

"You're guilty of asking for help, nothing more," Shaykh Nariman said softly. "One's time comes when it comes, and there is no changing that and no hastening of it."

"He was looking over your shoulder," Zakiyya said, shivering despite the heat. "I got a flash of an image at that point in the conversation. I couldn't make it out. A messy mix of light, a ram, and a friendly old man . . . I think he was seeing the angel of death. He knew what would happen when he left the cage."

A guard arrived and announced—or really, shouted, details of a funeral in an effort to disperse the crowd to send word. They would conduct the burial as soon as possible, to avoid a stream of outsiders adding to the unruly reaction to the death.

The scent of juniper from within the dungeon was dampened but not extinguished. When they lugged his body out an hour later, wrapped in white cloth, I smelled the weakened odor clinging to his corpse. "Baraka persists after we die," Shaykh

Nariman reminded me when I asked him about it.

We followed the procession to the closest mosque for the short, simple prayer, and regrouped to join it en route to the nearby graveyard. The body was lowered into a pre-dug ditch, and the imam tried to make his supplication louder than the anguished wailing of some of the attendees. Zakiyya rubbed her temples again, harder.

"No more funerals for a while, please," she said in exhaustion.

The body, in its plain white shroud, rested directly on dirt. It was tilted to its right side, head facing toward Mecca. The imam threw the first fistful of dirt into the grave, and a riot nearly broke out as people struggled and competed to throw in their own handfuls of soil, as they fought to be a part of the ceremony.

"Have some respect for the deceased," the imam bellowed. The people, feeling properly chastised, slowed their clamoring and more or less took turns approaching and dropping their handful.

I dipped my hand over the hole and let loose a clump of mud that plopped down carelessly. The scent of juniper remained with me during our speedy exit from the town and nibbled at my senses through Shaykh Nariman's repeated warnings not to get caught up in the possible riots. It accompanied me to sleep.

As soon as I closed my eyes, the nine serpentine creatures came at me from above and below, greeting me fang first.

I flinched—but neither the bites nor the end of my dream came.

The creatures had vanished in a puff of white smoke, the anger and hunger in their eyes blown away into nothingness by an ethereal wind.

I was dreaming and I was free.

I did backflips in empty space, unfettered by the pull of the Earth. I soared over the graveyard where the saint had just been buried; light leaked from the fresh soil and fueled my flight. I descended by the prison, only to find the walls broken to pieces, pounded to dust, chains shattered in the ruins, iron bars broken and rusted.

The saint sat cross-legged where his cell had once been. The blue sky danced as it reflected in his eyes, the breeze toyed with his curly beard. He smiled at me, the wrinkles of old age and hardship evaporated as a tranquil grin dominated his features. Twenty or thirty years were taken off him.

He stood this time, without creaking limbs, and walked over to greet me.

"Khurafa, this is your first true dream, is it not?" he said, his voice as soft as the gentlest waves of the sea.

"No," I answered. "I had one before, the one that started this journey. And I'm not sure, but maybe the ones I've had since . . ." He frowned ever so slightly and the whole dream flickered for a moment.

"I have not met the *Qutb*—the greatest saint of the time," he said, "but one of you has and will meet them again soon. I could see the mark of the Qutb's baraka upon you all. The powers that God has granted me pale in comparison to the Qutb's capabilities."

I woke to Shaykh Nariman sitting on my forehead peering down at my nose. "You snore so loud that the heavens themselves rumbled," he said with a snort. Zakiyya rubbed her eyes and muttered agreement.

I told them my dream, skipping over my aerial acrobatics.

Shaykh Nariman flinched when I mentioned the beginning of my conversation with the saint, his itsy-bitsy claws curling inwards. Like he was stifling a sneeze.

"I don't know who I've met who could have been the Qutb," I said, scratching my cheek.

Shaykh Nariman looked thoughtful while Zakiyya shrugged when she couldn't come up with a lead. "Guess I'm back to dreamless sleep," she said.

You feeling left out? Maybe he thought I was purer of heart or something.

Her punch rid me of any lingering desire to slumber.

Interlude

Khurafa tried to move a hand to the shoulder where he'd been playfully punched all that time ago. But he had no hand to help him touch the past, and his arm would not move.

His brow furrowed in thought but he spoke before the vultures reared their beaks. "It would have been nice if the saint could have just explained what he meant, in exact detail. Why do wise people have to be enigmatic?

"I guess, being a saint, and then being dead, he got a glimpse of the ghayb—the unseen, all the things that God alone fully knows. But what he saw—what he was allowed to see—wasn't very clear. Humans can't really know what the future holds, expect what God has told us.

"If I had known what the future held . . ."

III

Horrors

Chapter 12

Without a clear follow-up destination, we started moving north. For two days excitement built on Zakiyya's face. She really did want to visit her grandmother in Isfahan, I didn't need to read her mind to know that. I wondered what she would be like with the elderly woman around— she definitely wouldn't be able to hit me anymore. That's how grandmothers work, right?

I never got to find out. New fragrances in the air pulled us in the opposite direction the following morning.

For the first time, not one, but *three* distinct scents pulled us along. They were coming from the south, toward the marshland near the river. It took most of the day for the aromas to veer off-road. The herby fragrance of daisies, the warm orange smell of marigolds, and the oceanic scent of anemones wafted out of a dense thicket of green and yellow reeds and knobby trees.

It was late afternoon and my knees were shaking slightly. I'd heard too many childhood tales of jinn tormenting those caught out in the wilderness at night. Shaykh Nariman rustled with a yawn in my satchel and I reevaluated my fears. The only jinn I knew was a cute old mouse man.

"What even *is* an anemone?" Zakiyya asked. "I swear, if I

couldn't 'hear' you distinguish these smells, I'd believe you were making things up." I conjured an image of the flat, multi-layered flower and she yawned. Nature's beauty was boring apparently.

A swift merchant caravan trundled by just as we began to follow a trail into the marsh.

"I wouldn't do that!" a kindly old fellow said as he struggled to remain on horseback. "Nasty stories about the swamps in recent days. Nasty stories and a few bones."

"About what?" I asked, but he was already too far gone to hear me.

Kedi cringed as we made our way over to a twisted mix of roots, stones, and watery muck. She made a whining sound, plopped down, and refused to move. She growled into the thicket. Zakiyya picked Kedi up and cooed in an attempt to comfort her—the moment she turned away from the direction of the scents, the cat calmed down. As soon as Zakiyya turned back toward the trail, Kedi snarled. The further into the wilderness we went, swallowed by the reeds, the greater Kedi's discomfort grew.

"What's going on with her this time?" I asked. Kedi's patient determination was utterly unique for her kind. But now she was acting like . . . a cat. Kedi wasn't running away, so it wasn't like we were forcing her to come along, but I was starting to miss her kitten-like enthusiasm.

"I'm getting a strong feeling from Kedi, not a coherent thought. Hard to read animals, you know?" Zakiyya said. "But I think I can word it—" A hair-raising howl interrupted her.

A bulky man was thrown onto the mat of decaying leaves coating the trail. The blood on his hands dripped onto the ground as he tried to propel himself back up. A dark shape hurtled by, landing atop him with a thud. It was a monstrous creature, with sharp claws at the end of long, muscular arms and glistening fangs protruding from a mangled snout.

"Danger," Zakiyya finished.

This was the kind of monster Amir Hamza would fight. My attempt to leap into action and be like legends was stopped by a gnarly root. I ended up regaining my balance with my staff rather than swinging it. In the meantime, Zakiyya yelled at the predator. "Hey! Easier prey right here!"

The creature's lanky body was roughly human in shape; it settled most of its weight on two legs and its claws were equipped with opposable thumbs, though its entire body was covered with matted brown fur. There was nothing human about its face. The closest approximation for its features would be a wolf, from the yellow, hungry eyes to the raised ears quivering at the slightest indication of movement. The beast turned its bruised snout in Zakiyya's direction and sniffed like it was identifying food.

That was all the distraction the lumbering man beneath it needed to knee it right in its gut. The blow created the space for him to lance a crystalline dagger into its chest and flip the creature over, below him. He stabbed the creature again, and this time the dagger seemed to glow white hot. The creature howled again—now in agony. The man didn't let that howl turn into a snarl; he hammered its head with his free hand over and over until the howl became a whimper, and then silence.

The man rose shakily to his feet, panting while stepping towards us. He had a wide forehead, framed by his scraggly hair, a heavy brow, a crooked nose, and cauliflower ears. He wore a close-cropped brown beard, and had gray, unflinching eyes, like the moon at midnight.

Even if I hadn't seen him take out that monster, I would have known he was a fighter, though the yellow sheen on his chalky skin made him look sick. He was enormous, as tall as the trees that grew in the unstable soil here, and probably twice as wide. The leather tunic covering him was thick, but even so, his muscles bulged through. A Ghazi. A holy warrior. Finally!

"Salam!" I said, my forced bright tone drowning out the beast's final pained yelp. There was no mistaking the scent of daisies clinging to the man. The aroma of anemones leaked from the drawstring bag fastened to the belt on his waist, and the smell of marigold came from somewhere behind him. "We've been looking for you—"

He raised a massive hand to quiet me. "The *borz* always hunt in packs," he practically whispered. "This is the third I've killed. But there were tracks for one more . . . "

Zakiyya and I followed his lead, going silent, listening for a rustle of leaves, a squishing step in the swampy mud, a sudden breeze—anything that would indicate an approaching threat.

Kedi however did not get the memo. She turned her head and made vehement hissing noises to the right. *Get anything from that?* I thought to Zakiyya. When nothing struck from the direction Kedi indicated, Zakiyya shrugged.

The man turned towards Kedi. "It's warning us about something from the east?"

"She's just freaking out, I don't know if she's actually saying anything," I said.

He didn't answer, but instead walked in the direction that troubled Kedi. We followed, and a quarter of a mile away there it was—another bestial humanoid, bent over a porcupine it had brutalized, feeding in a frenzied bliss without a care in the world for the quills piercing its snout.

The man tensed, his unblinking gray gaze measuring the creature up and down, waiting for a moment to pounce. I was confused as to who the real predator was.

The creature—a borz is what the man had called it— sniffed the air and Kedi whined. Before anyone else moved, I sprinted to its exposed back, staff flailing in the air. There were no gnarly roots to mess me up on this muddy patch of earth. I could be a gazi too. I landed a clean hit on its back, expecting it to be rent apart, spine split clean in two. Instead the staff bounced off harmlessly.

"What," I wondered dumbly as the creature made a swipe at me. I fell backward in an effort to dodge it and bumped the ground hard with the bottom tip of the staff.

The wet earth split open, a five-meter-long crevice snaking out before me. The creature and its half-devoured prey fell right in, while my legs dangled out into the depths as I balanced precariously on the edge.

I dug one hand behind me through the layer of detritus into the mud, wrapped the other holding the staff around a sturdy reed, and pulled myself away. The creature leapt from the bottom of the crevice, jaw open wide and ready to devour my right foot which still stuck out in the open air.

The man rushed out and caught the beast's snout in the anemone-scented black cloth sack which had been tied to his waste. I expected him to muzzle the creature, and hack at it, but instead I saw the impossible.

The creature vanished, consumed by the bag.

"What— what was that . . ." I mumbled, my foot still dangling free.

"That was foolish of you." The man said. "The staff of Moses does not divide living things."

I nodded dumbly. The staff of Moses. Of *course*. A staff which could split even the Red Sea. Could it turn into a snake too, like when Moses faced the sorcerers? Why had I never made the connection? The staff tingled in my palms.

"You really should have reviewed that *Stories of the Prophets* book," Zakiyya muttered to me.

"Now then," the man said, peering at the exposed roots in the crevice I'd made. "You said you were searching for me? Who sent you?"

"Wait!" Zakiyya interjected. "The bag—what is it?" She didn't ask how it did what it did. It seemed pretty obvious that baraka was the cause.

"This is the bag of Khidr, the wandering immortal," the man said softly. "It's called the *zambil*. It can fit multitudes."

"What happens to things inside?" Zakiyya asked curiously. She might as well have asked, 'are there treasures inside?'

The man shrugged his log-like shoulder. "Perhaps it shrinks them or takes them to another dimension. I've never taken anything out, so I can't be sure."

"Are you Khidr?!" I asked; I'd always imagined the legendary and mysterious mystic would be green somehow like his name suggested. If we'd found Khidr then the journey might be over. He always found heroes. Khidr was also known for pronouncements of wisdom that would put even Shaykh Nariman to shame.

The man tsk-ed quietly. I was beginning to realize he didn't whisper before solely for stealth. His large frame belied a soft, perpetually quiet voice. "No," he answered. "Though I pray to meet him one day. I'm Shahid of the Five Pillars. Now, it's my turn to ask questions."

As if our lives hadn't been threatened by monsters only

moments ago— or perhaps because we survived, Zakiyya and I launched into an especially enthusiastic explanation about our quest and capabilities.

"I see," he said softly once we ran out of words and breath. "So there is a jinn amongst you? Who has acted as your chaperone?"

"Yes," Shaykh Nariman squeaked. "That would be me. Tell me, why is it that something about you feels . . . familiar?"

"Familiar?" the man—Shahid—asked in a whisper. "I don't believe we've ever met. Perhaps you knew an ancestor of mine?"

"That may well be," Shaykh Nariman said, the uncertainty in his voice making it sound like he was whimpering. "All of this has not come as a shock to you."

"There has been more darkness in the world during these past few months. And your story about the Servants might be part of the answer to a mystery I have been unable to solve."

"And what is that mystery?" I asked, noticing the hope buried in his stoney expression.

"I am of the Five Pillars, as I mentioned. We are five baraka-laden warriors—ghazis—tasked by our late master with handling manifestations of *fisq*—mischief, malignancy, evil. Each of us is trained in martial and spiritual arts, each of us handle blessed objects that have been handed down for generations. The Five Pillars have been operating with generational shifts in membership for nearly 400 years. The story of the Servants is one our master mentioned once." He paused, looking a little uncomfortable. His lips quivered as if he hadn't spoken this much in a very long time. Or ever.

Meanwhile, my jaw dropped; this was the exact order of supernatural evil-vanquishing heroes that Shaykh Nariman heard of. It was all way too good to be true.

And, apparently, it was. "Usually the five of us travel together or at least in pairs," he said. "Some months back, we were hunting a filshad, a creature rampaging far into the east."

"What is that?" Zakiyya and I asked in unison.

"It is like an elephant, if you have ever seen one. But bigger, hairier, and more violent," he said. I had seen elephants once, tributes given to the Caliph before the Mongols came. They were giant gray beasts with long noses and floppy ears. Zakiyya gasped at the mental image of the creatures I conjured.

"We were hunting the filshad, working to save a village," he paused, as if stringing together so many sentences was awkward for him. "We drove it off into an isolated area and camped, waiting to attack. Then a messenger from the village came with news. That Baghdad had been ransacked." His stoic demeanor broke for the briefest second.

"We fight monsters and sometimes sorcerers. We seek them in the far reaches of the land. We weren't around to help Baghdad, we were not to blame . . . But we had many friends who would have defended the city. Who must have died before the gates were breached." He breathed deeply and continued. "I'm not entirely sure what occurred after we received the news. There was grief, the filshad struck. And the next thing I remembered, I was lying on the ruins of our encampment completely alone, neither friends nor monster in sight."

"Not to blame," Zakiyya mumbled, her eyes unfocused.

"Wha—what happened?" I asked.

"I've been trying to figure that out," he admitted. "Our master passed away some years ago, but he was a true saint. Once, he showed us *Tayy al-ard*. Folding the earth."

"Instantaneous travel across long distances," Shaykh Nariman interjected for us.

"Before he passed, he prayed for us, that in our worst moment—when near to death's door—the same miracle would come to our aid," he said solemnly. "I assume that restraining the filshad got out of hand and the others were transported away. But I don't know where to . . . we agreed on a meeting place to be used if we were ever separated, but though I spent over a month there, none of them ever showed up. Their disappearance happened right when you say the Servants became active. So there is a chance the two events are connected. Such monsters would desire the loss of those with so much baraka."

He finished his story and gave me a grave look. "You have a highly refined ability to detect baraka. My own senses are not so keen."

"I haven't detected a group of five scents," I said truthfully. "Though I'd imagine there would be even more scents if they're all carrying blessed items like you. But that doesn't mean they aren't out there . . . instantaneous travel—that means they could have ended up in the far reaches of the world." And in that case, I'd still find them. I found one, so I could find the others.

"That's what I tell myself," Shahid agreed, speaking more to himself than to us. "Better distant than gone."

We sat in silence for a moment, until Zakiyya broke it with the 'what next' questions. "So you've been hunting evil alone for some time now?"

"Better to move than to wallow," Shahid said, standing up and eying our cat curiously. "But I think you have provided an advantage in that regard that makes this work easier."

Both of us raised an eyebrow as he continued to look at Kedi. "I believe this feline can detect *fisq*. The way she anticipated the borz was beyond what I've seen any animal or human do."

"Wow," Zakiyya said, elbowing me, "that would mean she's just like you but inverted." I wasn't sure how I felt being put on the same level as a cat, but I already loved Kedi so I bit back a retort. The way Kedi held herself, I should consider the comparison an honor.

"And," Shahid said, "it seems she is sensing something even now. So we must make a move." Kedi was hissing, staring into the shadows of trees towards the southeast.

"Now?" I asked, my limbs still not recovered from the recent exertion.

"Every moment a creature of *fisq* is out there is a moment people are in danger." His soft tone shifted to one of quiet intensity. It seemed monster-hunting was more than his job— it was his coping mechanism.

"You'll join us in finding further allies to fight the Servants?" Zakiyya asked, raising an eyebrow. More saints and the rest of his group of ghazis.

"First we must deal with what is in front of us," he answered. "But yes. I have a feeling it will help with the search for my comrades too." He plucked up Kedi in one arm despite her squirming and began walking at a relentless pace toward her fears. He moved as if we were on the road and not a misshapen trail.

"He's thinking about duty," Zakiyya whispered as she eyed the ground to avoid wayward roots. "He wants to find his friends, but feels fighting evil and stopping monsters is what he's supposed to do. He hopes that the Servants are connected to what happens to his friends, but he'd help us regardless."

"Well that's admirable!" I exclaimed. Zakiyya shot me a dirty look but my volume didn't catch Shahid's attention or break his focus on the path before us.

"You would say that," she said, shaking her head. "It's similar for you. Always duty, duty, duty."

"What's wrong with that?"

"What about doing things because you want to do them?" She stomped on the muddy ground to emphasize her point. If she wasn't careful, Shaykh Nariman would launch into a lecture about treading lightly on the earth.

"If we all just did what we want, we'd be slaves of our desire. We have to do good." I scowled.

"Yes yes, but what about wanting to do good?"

"If you do what's right even when you don't want to, that's righteousness," I countered.

"Sure," she acknowledged, "but have you ever heard about the Saint, Rabia Al-Adawiyya?"

Shaykh Nariman chimed in at that point. "Stories say she used to wander with a torch in one hand and a bucket of water in the other. When asked, she said she wanted to burn down paradise with the torch, and extinguish hell with the water. She believed we shouldn't act out of fear of hell or hope for heaven, but solely out of love for God."

"Exactly," Zakiyya said in triumph, "Acting out of love. Wanting to do good, not just doing good because 'we have to.'"

"Whatever," I muttered. But she'd hit on something even if I couldn't pick it out. Whether it was duty to the garden, duty to this quest; the sense of responsibility was all the same.

Chapter 13

"I can't believe his group is called the 'five pillars.' Like, its named after the five ritual actions of faith? That's so cheesy." Zakiyya said hours later, as her eyes bore into Shahid's expansive back.

"It is cheesy," I agreed. "But if they're all as powerful and put together as he is, it'll be hard to laugh at the name. I'm surprised you're telling me this though and not just teasing him!"

"He's bummed about being unable to find his friends. A jibe feels wrong." Zakiyya shrugged.

We paused our march to watch the sunset from a clearing on a hill; the red-orange glow of a dying flame receded before the dark turquoise palace of the sky. Zakiyya rolled her eyes at the poetic description swirling in my sleep-deprived thoughts.

As the last embers of the sun disappeared and the stars took their place in the sky, Kedi stood high and yapped into the distance like a dog, before retreating to Shahid's arms for refuge. Shahid was built like one of those heroes from the epics—a Rustam or a Sohrab—but there he was dealing with the ball of fur awkwardly, changing his position constantly to provide her with optimal comfort but failing every time.

"We should keep moving," he said in a low voice, looking

out toward the direction Kedi had shrieked in.

"We don't know how far away it is," I mumbled, rubbing my eyes.

"It's dangerous out at this hour," Shaykh Nariman added.

"If there is something there, it's better to go and confront it, than to sleep and let it catch us unaware," Shahid said softly. He swaddled Kedi under one arm and tightened his sword belt with the other. "You two can rest. I'll take the cat and go hunting alone."

"That may be wise," Shaykh Nariman squeaked, "and safer."

"You'd leave two kids in the wilderness alone?" Zakiyya challenged them; neither came up with an adequate response.

We moved in every direction Kedi tried to squirm away from. Each of her frightened meows felt like a gut punch. We made our way out of the forest and onto trade roads. Dawn came around and Kedi stopped squirming, whimpered, and fell asleep.

"What do we do now," I asked, scratching at the black circles under my eyes. Who would carry me if I fell asleep? I wished I was a cat.

"We find a place to camp, watch, and wait. Whatever is out there must be inactive now, if not gone." Shahid said, without even a hint of a yawn. His voice was so soft I almost nodded off while standing.

Our zombie-like search for a place to topple onto the ground, yielded a result so pleasant it felt like I was already dreaming.

Zakiyya caught sight of the beige stone bricks of a caravanserai. It looked like a square fortress. Horses bolted out of the massive gate upon our arrival and wagons careened onto the road. We were ending our day when others began it.

The caravanserai caretaker took a long, sympathetic look at our haggard expressions—well, mine and Zakiyya's, although Shahid's ever-so-slight look of disappointment at not finding anything to fight could have been mistaken for exhaustion. "There's breakfast being served if you're hungry; and there should be some place free to nap if you want . . ." the caretaker said.

We thanked him without any energy. He looked at my brown skin and straight black hair, Zakiyya's olive complexion and curls, and Shahid's yellow-tinged paleness and brown hair. "A family, is it?" he asked.

"Traveling with our uncle to visit our grandparents. Thinking of 'prenticing with him too," Zakiyya responded on instinct; her eyes were so bleary there's no way her lies were conscious.

"He shouldn't have pushed you like that at night," the caretaker said with friendly concern and more than a little admonishment.

"Any idea how long you'll be staying?" he asked.

"Forever," I mumbled.

For once, Shahid was louder than I was. "We may stay the night, it remains to be seen. Long journey to recover from." Not that *he* needed the rest.

"Fair enough," the caretaker said. "You know the rules— we welcome all travelers, provide for them, and protect them. The gate is closed at dusk; I wouldn't open it for the Caliph himself. Well, the Caliph has passed now, God rest him, but even if those Mongol hordes were banging on the door and threatening heads, it wouldn't budge. Stay a maximum of three days, no pay. The financial endowment for this spot is still going strong despite it all, but. . . " There was an expectant glint in his eyes.

Shahid fumbled at a pouch and the caretaker accepted the payment with a warm smile. "My name is Uzayr," he added, "and my wife is Asma. Holler at us if you need anything."

I tumbled into a cot in the first open room we found. The classic smells of travel and hospitality—horsedung, and warm, freshly baked bread, lulled me to sleep instantly.

All I needed was rest, but that came at a cost. My nightmare was claustrophobic—I was covered in oppressive darkness. I pushed against the substance pressing down on me and found mud between my fingers. I tasted soil on my tongue and detritus in my lungs.

I was buried alive.

Before I could hyperventilate, the soil was pierced—one hole, two, three. Nine in all. Light didn't shine through the holes, fresh air didn't rush in. Instead nine hungry maws bit down. The dirt clogged my throat as I tried and failed to scream.

I woke up in a cold sweat; unlike the mud in my nightmare, the blanket came off me without resistance. And there were no holes in it.

Shahid was towering over me as my eyes fluttered open, his lips curled into the ghost of a smile. "We thought you were going to sleep all day," he said.

Zakiyya added, "There was still someone in the cot when you plopped down on it! He yelped—but you were out cold and didn't even notice."

"I was sleepy," I said, gritting my teeth; embarrassment was more effective than cold water in waking me up. The vestiges of my stifling nightmare were smothered by their playful poking.

"So what're we doing today? Kedi pointing anything out?" I asked, bouncing to my feet. It was both a let down and freeing not to be the guide anymore.

"Kedi slept almost as long as you," Zakiyya said. "She's relaxed, but Shahid says the way she was acting last night, there is definitely something in this area."

Shahid didn't want us to go too far out if there was something lurking around—he was adopting the overprotectiveness of his fictive uncle-status. He would prowl the wilderness for signs of any malevolent presence, while Zakiyya and I would interview guests and staff.

Shaykh Nariman chose to stick with Shahid for the day. I wasn't jealous or anything, but it did make me feel a little lonelier.

We worked our way around the caravanserai in a circuit. Zakiyya charmed an onslaught of cheek-pinching out of the matronly cleaning lady. "Have I seen any strange things? Well, a small family traveling all night and arriving at dawn is strange," she said playfully. Zakiyya gave her a winning smile and went off skipping toward the small garden in the corner that was the caretaker, Uncle Uzayr's pet project. His plantings were uneven, there was no symmetry or clear theme in the small floral patch, but the stems were all strong and the petals vibrant—he had a green heart if not a green thumb.

"So, you got something . . .?" I asked Zakiyya.

"When I asked about strange things she was thinking about how her grandkids are not much older than we are—but another thought slipped in," she said. "A traveler died a couple days ago. He arrived ill. Nobody else has gotten sick though."

We chewed on that, then left the caravanserai and hopped around nearby shops and a smattering of homes. We got a couple juicy kabobs to eat but no notable news. One aunty heard a rumor about something preying on passersby in a forest a day's trek away. Or a night's trek. Zakiyya grimaced and flexed her toes.

Shahid made it back right before sunset; Kedi was curled up in his arms purring. We gave him our brief account while leaning against a new stack of crates in the caravanserai's courtyard. He frowned at the mention of the sick traveler, but otherwise his expressions were pretty blank. When we finished, he muttered his own findings, or rather, lack thereof. "No tracks, no markings, no reaction from the cat. We'll move on tomorrow, it seems like the cat made a mistake. Or perhaps whatever it sensed was killed."

We listened to the clang of the gate's closure as the sun dipped into dusk. As if on cue, Kedi began to spaz, slipping from Shahid's arms with a feral shriek. He rushed to grab her, but she hurled herself toward the gate, tearing through the small remaining gap, out toward the road and the wilderness. Shahid just missed her fleeting tail; his hand banged against the shut gate. He didn't strike it again in frustration.

Whatever evil was lurking about, it had made a scaredy cat out of Kedi. Baraka didn't mean a lack of fear.

"Can you open it please?" Zakiyya asked Uncle Uzayr.

"No can do; the rule is more iron-clad than the gate. It's night, you'd better rest up!" Uncle Uzayr answered jovially.

"Please," Zakiyya said, affecting a pout. "Our cat is out there. It's not safe for her, she's not used to being alone like that . . ."

"Dear girl, this is a cat you're talking about. I fear for the rest of the wild, not her. I can help you search for her in the morning if you're worried, but she'll be fine. Come along now," Uncle Uzayr said. His kindly voice brokered no compromise.

Zakiyya cast a glance at Shahid who was opening and closing

his fist. Thinking.

"I can find Kedi tomorrow," I said, smiling reassuringly. "I can smell her, remember?"

Zakiyya nodded; that wasn't what she was worried about.

"Whatever it is, is in here. And it's active only at night, which is why the cat reacted as it did." Shahid said in his usual whisper, which now sounded ominous.

"I'll help search," Shaykh Nariman proffered when the caretaker was out of ear shot. "Don't let the two of them go alone, Shahid."

"What's with the protectiveness?" I asked. "We were all alone just a day or two back."

"We were looking for baraka then, not hunting the darkness." Shaykh Nariman scurried off to search. Or run from his guilt at seeing us in danger?

The caravansarai's layout was more or less square, with a courtyard containing the misshapen garden in a back corner, and an elevated prayer room in the very center. Around the courtyard, lined against the walls, were sleeping chambers, stables, a kitchen and a cafeteria. The walls were high to prevent bandits from breaking in, with guard stations positioned along their length. Uncle Uzayr was acting as look out, yawning at the top of the stairs above the gate.

I darted stealthily up the stairs on the other side of the courtyard before Shahid could protest. I crouched into a ball at the peak so that Uncle Uzayr wouldn't notice me while I observed any movement in the courtyard beneath the combination of orange torchlight and the white glitter of the stars.

The wind rustled against the crates in the corner of the courtyard. Crickets in the distance started their orchestral performance. A bloated merchant left his chamber to find the bathroom. Shahid and Zakiyya weaved in and out of rooms all night. There was a tiny scurrying mass of darkness I made out once or twice—probably Shaykh Nariman doing his own rodent reconnaissance.

It began to get chilly up on my ledge, without the full towering protection of the wall. I hugged my legs and jutted my head out above them, now watching and looking like an owl.

The cold and several self-inflicted slaps kept me awake as dawn approached. Zakiyya would chide me for taking the lazy approach to monster hunting, unless I found whatever creature haunted these grounds before she did. I kept my eyes peeled, but there were shadowed areas by the walls that I couldn't make out perfectly.

A scream tore through the last sliver of night, right before the advent of the sun. Shouting followed; Uncle Uzayr shook away his grogginess and stumbled down the stairs to the chamber that was the source. Zakiyya and Shahid leapt out of another chamber and hurried over, and I took three stairs at a time so I wouldn't be left behind.

In our shared room, beneath Uncle Uzayr's torch, we saw a man sleeping in a cot. Well, his position suggested sleeping— one hand under his cheek, one leg stretched out more than the other. The problem was that the hand was desiccated and frail, and his exposed calves were deathly pale. Based on his companions' desperate attempts to shake him awake, he hadn't looked like that when he'd gone to bed.

Two holes in his neck glistened red.

"He's been drained of blood," I said, mouth agape.

Uncle Uzayr turned on our group. "How could you do this?"

he asked, lunging for us.

Chapter 14

"What—" I began.

The caretaker ignored me and grabbed Shahid by the throat. He looked like an elderly David trying to wrestle Goliath. "You were moving around the courtyard late at night. I didn't think anything of it, but then this happens. Only you and the girl were wandering about."

"What about the other residents of this room?" Shahid asked—his ever soft tone sounded suspicious, and his sickly yellow complexion didn't help.

Uncle Uzayr started rifling through Shahid's possessions. The ancient crystal knife and well-worn sword were not points in his favor. "The blood isn't here. And only someone who left the room could have disposed of it."

"Not necessarily," Shahid countered matter-of-factly. "They could have drunk it."

The macabre claim only made him look more guilty. Uncle Uzayr seized him. For a moment Shahid tensed, as if he would break free, but by this point all the other guests had gathered at the door. I don't think they could've stopped him if he really tried to resist, but he reserved his fighting for monsters.

Uncle Uzayr reached a hand toward Zakiyya and I, ire knitting his brows.

Zakiyya's worried face abruptly became a fountain. "My uncle Shahid! What's happening with my uncle? Whyyyyy—I couldn't sl-sleep, I m-miss my mom and—and he took me for a walk. And then—and then—I dropped my necklace and looked for it." She elbowed me while pretending to sniffle.

Thankfully no one noticed my "ouch." After the second elbowing, I faked my own sobs as best I could. They made me sound like I was dying and probably should have earned repulsion rather than sympathy. Fortunately Zakiyya's act was more than enough for the both of us to receive warm, caring glances.

Shahid almost ruined our escape. He sniffled and attempted a sob that sounded more like a choking noise. A whining sound came from his throat—it resembled a horse undergoing a seizure. "My niece and nephew. Don't take me away from them! We are just passing through. What a horrible thing— "

His terrible acting caused a few bulky visitors to the caravanserai to join the caretaker in swarming him. "We'll lock you up in one of the rooms until we can get a Qadi to come by. These cute kids are unlucky to have a suspicious 'uncle.' Wouldn't be surprised if the man kidnapped them. They can go free."

The forced desperation on Shahid's face instantly transformed to creepy calm as he resigned himself to imprisonment. He glanced at Zakiyya. She frowned at his implacable expression—the thoughts of the curious crowd were clouding her receipt of his silent instructions.

Just then, a ragged, frail breath disturbed the tension in the room. It came from the near-bloodless corpse. An unseeing eye flickered open, then shut.

"He's alive!" Uncle Uzayr shouted, more in shock than joy.

A couple temporary inhabitants of the caravanserai shuffled forward to haul the dying man over to a doctor in a neighboring settlement. They were merchants selling dried leather; the parched body fit in a little too well with the goods on the back of their cart.

Four men pulled Shahid to a chamber in a corner of the Caravanserai at the caretaker's direction. They moved gingerly, as if afraid he would fight them all off and gobble them up, but he might as well have been meditating. The chamber had probably been a study or storehouse at some point, but its heavy wooden-door suggested that Uncle Uzayr moonlighted as a bounty hunter. There were thin slits on the door from which we could see Shahid's still-stoic expression.

Uncle Uzayr's wife, Aunty Asma, came by and fussed over Zakiyya and I. "Is he your mother's brother or your father's? Every family has a black sheep. My own cousin did something terrible once. It's so awful. You poor things."

"Our uncle is innocent," Zakiyya said, feigned tears welling up in her eyes. A single drop rolled down her hooked nose.

Aunty Asma patted Zakiyya on the head. "Well, I'm sure they'll check things thoroughly when the Qadi gets here. In the meantime, you two could use a home-cooked meal. I can't imagine what that horrible man made you eat."

Better not to think on an empty stomach, I thought. *Is eating while our companion is imprisoned wrong though?*

Zakiyya clutched her stomach. "Food sounds good." She did not share my compunctions.

We joined the kindly woman for breakfast and Zakiyya engaged in preoccupied small talk. After the meal, which included some especially sweet chunks of watermelon, Zakiyya adopted her saddest, most exaggerated pout. "Can we play outside?" she asked Aunty Asma.

"Of course, young lady," the woman said with an apologetic smile. "I can have one of my sons keep watch for you all—it could be dangerous still . . . "

"No, no, it's alright," I said, attempting to puff out my chest, "I'll take care of my little sister." Zakiyya's eyes were daggers.

"That's a good big brother." Aunty Asma pinched my cheek.

We left her and returned to the courtyard of the caravanserai.

"Big brother?" she muttered. "You'd definitely be the younger sibling. But honestly, having a sibling as annoying as you would be insufferable."

"You can be the older sister this time—actually, we can say you're the aunt next time. Or great-aunt. You have an authentic hag vibe," I snorted.

Zakiyya caught my gaze with murder in her eyes, but a glimpse of Shahid's prison at the far end of the courtyard sobered her. "I got some details from reading Shahid, but I'm missing pieces because of all the interference—too many scared people around. I know he doesn't want us to break him out, so forget grabbing the staff. That'll cause an uproar . . . "

A sharp pain came from my shin; I cupped the source, and there was a familiar furry lump.

"Apologies for the scratch, you were quite focused, and I needed your attention," Shaykh Nariman said. He did not like infighting. "I slipped into Shahid's chamber. There was a suitable gap under the door. I do not know if the caretaker overheard him whispering, but that would help a madness legal defense."

"What are we looking for?" I asked.

"He said the creature is called an *obur*," Shaykh Nariman recited. "They're from the west. His band encountered one once in a remote village in the Caucasuses. On occasion, the recently deceased in that part of the world awaken from apparent death as horrific obur. At first they are only active at night; during the day they appear as a corpse. They suck the blood out of their first victim, then hide away as long as the sun is up. Unless they are killed before sunset comes again, the victim will die. If an obur survives until nightfall after its first kill, it can become active during the day and feed at will."

"So we need to find a hidden corpse before dusk, or that man will die and the obur will go wild . . ." Zakiyya summarized. "This explains why Kedi can only sense it at night. During the day there's no danger for her to register."

"Precisely."

"There are some terrible things living in the dark. But all the way from the Caucasus mountains?" I said in wonder. "Monsters are pretty adventurous."

"I doubt the corpse was brought that far," Zakiyya said. "Maybe it was someone from that area who traveled this far and died here."

My eyes lit up. "The traveler who was sick and died!"

We spotted Kedi curled up on a barrel en route, but let her rest. It didn't take long to find the small, sleepy graveyard near the settlement. It was a conglomeration of a few unmarked stone slabs with various degrees of patchy weathering. We went to the least aged rocks. I didn't have to prod the soil to tell that one grave had recently been dug up.

"So is this it?" Zakiyya said. She kicked the dirt but made no motion to dig.

"They said the man died a couple days ago. This grave fits with their reckoning." I pinched a little dirt and lifted it, rubbing my fingers together as it fell. "If anything it could be more recent. No need for us to dig though." I was having flashbacks to my dream of being buried alive. Mud on my fingers was usually so comforting, but not this time.

"No, we need to check." There was sympathy in Zakiyya's voice, but not enough to help me. "It could've been something Shahid hasn't seen before. An obur is a being inhabiting a recent corpse, so if the corpse is missing, we can confirm what we're dealing with and act accordingly."

Shaykh Nariman's whistling voice piped up, "And if it is an obur, we must find out how it got into the caravanserai."

"What'dyu mean? It's a monster—it could have climbed the wall," I said.

"Before it feeds, it's unlikely to do any preternatural physical feats," he lectured. "Shahid explained that it gains strength from blood."

"Alright, you two look for ways it might have gotten inside from here," I said, then muttered sourly, "and the gardener will dig."

Prying free recently-dug soil is a lot easier than digging a new hole. And I'm a professional at clawing through the earth, even if seeds and bodies are different, even if I'm feeling revulsion. There was nothing at the bottom of the grave. Well, not quite nothing. A corpse is usually wrapped in a couple of pieces of cloth. One such piece was loose in the soil.

"If we had a well-trained dog, it could sniff this and find the missing corpse. Instead we have a sleeping cat," I sighed and called out to Zakiyya. "The corpse is gone- its an Obur and I dug for no reason."

"Good that we have confirmation," she said, "because I figured out how it got into the caravanserai." She had the easy job, and now she could gloat.

I poked Shaykh Nariman with a question as we headed towards Zakiyya's discovery. "Why did the Obur go to the caravanserai? There are people in nearby houses too. People less defended."

"Shahid said that obur instinct is to first feed where it died, not where it was buried," he answered. "I imagine it may be to get rid of witnesses from when it was alive." Would the Servants want to get rid of witnesses too? Get rid of us?

"What kind of childhood did Shahid have, stuffing himself with knowledge about monsters?" Zakiyya asked the air.

What childhood do we have chasing them?

She led me a quarter mile away from the graveyard to row upon row of watermelon vines, the green leaves lush and drooping. Several open wooden crates lay amidst the rows, heavy piles of nearly ripe oblong fruit peeking out from within.

"Recognize the crates?" she asked.

They were made of light criss-crossed wood, heavy duty enough to fit dozens of watermelons, and maybe even a contoured body.

"The crates in the caravanserai!"

"Exactly. My guess is they move the crates there for some merchant to pick up. If the obur hid beneath the watermelons, it could've easily gotten into the caravanserai without exerting itself," she said in triumph.

My excitement at her find was turning to horror. "Then the watermelon we ate this morning . . . I think I'm going to be sick."

I struggled not to retch as we worked our way back to the caravanserai and went straight to the crates in the courtyard. All the crates but one were closed tight. I pried the loose cover halfway off the shoddily closed box, moved my hand around the pile, shoving aside heavy melons. After a lot of fiddling, I felt a mud-flecked fabric. I pulled it out and showed my find to Zakiyya—it was a perfect match for the funeral shroud.

"It was in here. It was right here. We missed it. If we hadn't—"

"Do you all want some more watermelon?" Aunty Asma asked. I almost fell into the crate in surprise at her sudden presence.

"Umm—" I started to think of what to say. The thought of eating a watermelon that had been smothering an undead creature made my stomach twist. Rationally I knew watermelon rinds are thick, but still . . .

Zakiyya put a hand on her belly. "Sorry. We smelled something really good and wanted to see what it was!"

"These melons don't belong to us. Old Rashid is supposed to come by and pick them up in a couple days. But I have more in the kitchen, like you had earlier. They're ripe and scrumptious! You have to pay attention to the discolored patch near one of the ends. If it's white, the fruit isn't ready. If it's yellow, you're in for a treat."

I felt my queasiness evaporate—what I'd eaten that morning had been from a separate, clean batch! Aunty Asma grabbed us both by the wrist and dragged us along.

Zakiyya whispered, "We can check the kitchen this way at least."

A few minutes later we were sitting at the counter and sugary pink liquid was trickling down my chin again. Delicious. Is this what blood tasted like to the obur?

Zakiyya swayed and knocked over a glass of water. It shattered into a half dozen shards on the floor. My thought was messed up but not enough for her to react that way.

"Oh, I'm sorry, I'm sorry! I'll clean that up!" Zakiyya cried, clasping her hands together in mock anxiety. This wasn't on me. She was planning something.

"No need, young miss. I left my broom in the other room, give me a minute. Be careful not to step anywhere!" Aunty Asma ruffled her hair, all concern and no reprimand.

Aunty Asma hopped over the shards with an agility that belied her years. No sooner had she turned her back than Zakiyya plopped down onto the floor, twisting in her own show of acrobatics to explore the room. I tried to join her but she put up a hand to stop me. "There's no way you can tiptoe over glass without slipping somehow," she said. That fall would hurt.

Zakiyya conducted a quick but thorough check of the cupboards, clay oven, and even the meat salting closet. She found nothing.

Zakiyya hardly made it back to her seat before the matronly hostess returned. "Didn't finish your watermelon? You didn't like it?" Aunty Asma asked as she swept up the glass.

"No I love it, I just . . . I feel bad eating when you're doing work!" Zakiyya batted her eyelashes.

"Oh honey, it's alright. What a responsible girl you are."

I thought I got away with rolling my eyes and scoffing, but Zakiyya punched me as soon as we left the Aunty. I was getting used to the strength of her jabs though and barely winced.

"I'll have to start hitting harder, huh?"

I clutched my shoulder pretending to be in great pain. "Please don't."

"Remember, I always know what you're thinking," she warned. There was no safe mental response.

"Kitchen clear, crates clear. Now, what? We check under

beds and in crevices?" I asked, stretching my arms. Monster-hunting was a lot like looking for lost items. Failing wouldn't result in my mom's playful reprimand though. Lives were at stake.

"Yes, but if we're scavenging around everywhere, we'll look really suspicious, especially with Shahid being accused," Zakiyya said.

"That's true. How do we get access and search without seeming suspicious?" I wondered. "Wait! I've got it." I ran back toward the kitchen, Zakiyya following close behind. "Excuse me ma'am! We were wondering, is it ok—"

"If we play hide and seek?" Zakiyya finished. Always stealing my thunder and not just my thoughts.

We said it so eagerly that the kind-hearted woman acqui-esced right away. "Don't tell my husband though, he won't approve. If he sees you poking around, tell him you're looking for a mouse. That'll shut him up." Shaykh Nariman shuffled uncomfortably within my pocket. Caravansarai are safe for travelers, but not rodent hitchhikers. They were probably worried about disease, though I think Shaykh Nariman could only infect people with endless information.

I counted against the wall while Zakiyya ran off to find a place to hide. In reality we both used the opportunity to search. I caught myself wondering about what a real game would be like, with friends. Maybe it was best we were only pretending to play; Zakiya would definitely beat me if it were real.

The obur was clearly better at this game than either of us though. An hour of fiddling through nooks and crannies and misleading the confused guests of the caravanserai with childish grins yielded nothing.

We climbed the steps of the wall and peered out over the

courtyard, trying to brainstorm any place in the building we'd missed.

"You know, at this rate, the obur will win and attack someone else in the night," I said in despair.

"At least then they'll know Shahid wasn't the perpetrator," Zakiyya muttered.

"Yeah, but someone will get hurt—or die. And maybe they'll think we did it. Or we could be the next victims," I let fear get the better of me. I'd dry dead flowers. They were pretty, even without moisture. I'm not sure I'd like the same way.

"I'm going to go to Uncle Uzayr's garden. It needs some tending to," I said, trying to salvage some dignity and reorganize my thoughts.

Zakiyya followed me to the patch of flowers "Huh," Zakiyya said. "Looks like it needs a lot of work. The flowers aren't evenly organized at all."

"Wait—you're right. It's worse than yesterday," I said. She could take my thoughts, but not gardening, please. Even if the burial dream made me queasy.

"It's in the soil!" Zakiyya whispered excitedly. "It burrowed itself into the ground. The soil is fresh and easy to move. There are plants all around that could cover it. When everyone ran to see the victim—it must have happened then."

I took an instinctive step away from the flowers. That was the first time I could remember doing that.

"Well," Zakiyya said with an air of command. "It looks like you'll definitely get to tend to a garden." I braced myself, swallowing the bile in the back of my throat.

It wasn't hard to find a shovel. A little rummaging under the cover of our game and I had a hefty piece. I found a knife for good measure, to take care of the monster as soon as I uncovered it. What was challenging was digging without Uncle Uzayr getting angry. I figured that I could explain away my antics as helpful weeding. Zakiyya agreed to act as a lookout just in case.

What did us in was another sneezing fit. Zakiyya had failed to mention that she was sensitive to pollen. She sneezed seven times in succession, which didn't just obscure her vision for a few seconds but actually brought Uncle Uzayr close in concern. Her olive skin was red, and her nose looked like a tomato.

I dropped the shovel as soon as he towered over her. The clang drew his eyes. I smiled innocently, readying my explanation. When the shovel fell, the head flung up a large wad of dirt, exposing what looked like a large, dead gray larva. The caretaker and I did a double take at the same time. It was a finger—the obur's finger.

"What have you done?" Uncle Uzayr asked, abandoning Zakiyya and yanking me away from the soil.

"What do you mean? Oh, what—what is that?" I asked, pretending to only just notice the finger.

"You know damn well what it is!" Uncle Uzayr roared. "Don't move."

He picked up the shovel while glancing back and forth between the patch of the garden and me. A few scoops revealed the body.

"I'd heard that you two were seen playing around the graveyard," he said, anger mixed with disbelief. He dusted away dirt with his hands until he could recognize the corpse of the traveler. "What kind of perverse satanic joke is this?" Uncle Uzayr swore under his breath.

"What, what is that?" I tried again to feign childish fear. It wasn't all acting—the body was terrifying enough for me to look away.

"You both come with me," he said, pulling Zakiyya and I along. Zakiyya squirmed. There was a good chance we wouldn't be able to explain this, in which case the caretaker and everyone else in the space would be at risk. We needed to kill the obur before it could rise.

Zakiyya heard my message; his grip on her was loose. She jerked free, and intentionally 'tripped' toward the body, reaching for the discarded shovel. Uncle Uzayr didn't miss a beat—he caught her mid fall without letting go of my wrist.

"What were you planning to do?" he asked, yanking the shovel away from her.

"I—I fell. I was trying to get my balance—" she extemporized.

"I'm locking you two up with your uncle. That fact that you acted so calm around a body. . . I don't know what you three are doing, but I know it's a danger to us all."

Shaykh Nariman slipped out of my pocket; he'd find it distasteful, but a rodent's nibbling seemed to be our last hope, and not for the first time.

"The danger is that thing," I yelled. "We didn't do anything, it moved here itself. There's something evil in it. You have to stab it in the heart and it won't get up and the other man will be saved too. I swear—"

He looked at me like I was mad. "What wicked things is that man teaching you. Making games of desecrating a corpse," he caught sight of Shaykh Nariman and kicked the shaykh away before he could bite the sleeping obur. I held a breath, but Shaykh Nariman skittered off with speed belying his ancientness. He was okay.

"Habibti!"Uncle Uzayr called out to his wife. "There's a

mouse here."

"We're not crazy." He ignored my protests and brought us to the chamber where Shahid was being kept. I screamed a warning, but Shahid was squatting in the corner. He jumped from the distant ground toward the door in one enormous leap, it was shut before he landed.

I looked down at what he'd been squatting over. A piece of yellow parchment, a small opened bottle of ink, and an aged yellow-dyed reed pen lay beside the case he'd been keeping tied to his waist. On the parchment was a list of the names of God, written in an elegant calligraphic script. Shahid lifted it up before talking to us; leaving God's names on the floor was bad practice, and even in tense circumstances he wasn't going to let that slide.

"The marigold scent I've been smelling—it's coming from the reed pen?" I asked. "What is it? What can it do?" Hope and curiosity blotted out my fear. Shaykh Nariman would be giddy if he knew we could write our way out of problems.

"It was the pen of a great calligrapher called Ibn Muqla. He devised Arabic scripts that are used to this day. God blessed the tool, perhaps because wrote with it. Whatever is written with it comes out with a beauty beyond the user's skill," he said in his soft voice. "I was practicing."

"So it's useless," I deflated. Art, stories, what was the point?

"Beauty is never useless. But it won't break down the door."

Chapter 15

Zakiyya and I called out, over and over, "Stab the corpse! If you don't, it'll wake up soon and attack! Please!"

Our cries led only to grimaces of disgust in the faces of the few who heard. Our possessions were back in our room, including my staff, so the easy method of breaking out wasn't an option.

Shahid took our failures in stride. It was enough for him that we'd found the obur. He rammed the door. "At this point, it's better to be condemned as a criminal than let a bloodbath happen," he said in his calm way.

He made the door shake, but he was unable to dislodge it despite his immense bulk and his best efforts. The doorframe was metal and the door itself was incredibly thick lumber. The caravanserai was too well-constructed. Once the main gate was closed after sunset, everyone would be completely trapped inside with a monster, and no one would be able to break out.

Shaykh Nariman slipped through the crack at the bottom of the door, huffing and puffing. "There was no opportunity to steal the door key or strike at the obur. Asma, Uzayr's wife, is looking to kill a mouse. And she might succeed." How many humans could kill a jinn?

"We're glad you're okay," I rasped, my throat hoarse from

all the shouting, "Can you change into a key?"

"I've only ever mastered animate transformations. That is why your gold bar plan would never have worked either," he said gently. He'd been sparing Zakiyya that later disappointment for a while, but now it seemed inconsequential.

My frown deepened in worry, but Zakiyya worked furiously. She tore out a wire that held up some decorations and twisted it into her best approximation of a lockpick. Then she jammed it into the keyhole and contorted it as best she could to garner a click. Try as she might, she couldn't quite get it to work. I thrummed my foot on the floor in urgency. Some thief she was.

She glared at me.

"What are you doing in there?" Uncle Uzayr shouted. He probably saw the doorknob jittering.

Zakiyya backed away from the door and hid the lockpick.

"No—nothing," she said. She bit her lip in desperation. "Wait, I really, really have to use the bathroom."

"Go in there!" Uncle Uzayr snarled.

"There are men in here, doesn't matter if they're related," Zakiyya pleaded.

"Tell them to turn around. There's a bucket in the corner."

Zakiyya affected her most dramatic sobs. "Please, just let me go to the bathroom without shame. I'm a girl."

"Shame? You play with a dead body and talk about shame!" He spoke with fury, but his determination was wavering.

"I—I—" Zakiyya let her eyes glisten. She knew she had him.

"Let the girl go to the bathroom!" Aunty Asma commanded. "For the love of God. I'll supervise her and you can stand back a distance. She won't be able to do anything."

"These maniac-types though, you can't be too careful,"

Uncle Uzayr said.

"She's a girl with a bad influence. Not irredeemable. We're not monsters," the matronly lady said.

The caretaker sighed as the last remnants of his stubbornness faded.

"Break out this time," Zakiyya whispered to Shahid as Uncle Uzayr approached.

"Wait!" Uncle Uzayr said as he fumbled with the keys.

"I want the big man back against the far wall where I can see him before I open this door. Don't want you trying anything funny."

Zakiyya cursed under a particularly venomous breath. Shahid shuffled to the back wall, his eyes dull and unfocused. He was whispering so I could barely hear, but I knew Zakiyya would be able to read his mind. "Stab the obur. Slip away from them—whatever it takes." She touched the lockpick tucked in her sleeve; it would make do as a shiv.

Zakiyya slipped out, with Aunty Asma clutching her wrist and Uncle Uzayr looming over her shoulder.

Her footsteps faded off into the distance and we waited, with bated breath.

A shout echoed from the courtyard, followed by the reverberation of a cascade of furious steps. Did she do it?

A minute later, Zakiyya was thrown into the room. Shahid made a mad rush for the door, but a sword poked out from the opening crevice.

Shahid stopped his dash inches before impaling himself, but I've gotta admit—heroic-types are built differently. He grabbed the sword with his bare hands, palms against the flat sides of the blade, and tore it out of Uncle Uzayr's grip.

Shahid tried to flip the blade so he could hold the hilt, while bulldozing his shoulder into the opening. Midway through the maneuver, Uncle Uzayr knocked him on the head with a back-up cudgel he kept at his belt waist. Shahid was driven back from the door only for a brief moment, but that was enough for the caretaker to catch the sword and slam the door shut.

Shahid banged his fist against the door, demanding it to open.

"You're insane!" Uncle Uzayr shouted. "I have half a mind to carry out a punishment without waiting for the Qadi. I wish I could shackle you but this isn't a prison . . . though we have some horse restraints."

"Honey," Aunty Asma said in a dead tone, eyes boring into Zakiyya like acid. "If you enter that room alone, he'll overpower you."

"Lock the corpse up tonight at least. It'll come to life and try to attack. You'll see," Shahid said, his voice still soft and calm, as if he hadn't tried to steal a sword moments ago.

"Madness. Are you heretics maybe? The way the world is right now, I shouldn't be surprised," Uncle Uzayr said, moving back a few paces, and lowering himself out of sight.

"He plans on staying there, watching the door all night," Zakiyya said with a depressed sigh. For once our thief had failed. She didn't even glare at me for that thought.

"What . . . what happened?" I asked gently.

"I got away from them and made it to the garden, but they'd already moved the obur, and I couldn't get a read on where—" She looked from me to Shahid, the same thought on everyone's mind: If they'd reburied it, if it was outside the Caravanserai, it could escape to anywhere. A killing spree could plague the countryside and haunt the cities.

Shahid placed a palm against the door and closed his eyes

in concentration. He was leaning toward the door, but his muscles were not flexed and he was making no attempt to push it. The pale white and yellow back of his hand slowly tinged pink. After a few minutes, it reddened. Meanwhile his free hand looked clammy and gray, trembling as if he was shivering.

"What're you doing?" Zakiyya and I both asked. A sliver of smoke wafted from his hand.

"Trying to burn the door down. It's hot enough but it's not even starting to smolder. The wood has been coated with something to make it less flammable," he said with quiet intensity.

"You're trying to burn it with your hand?" I asked; if anything, it looked like his hand would start to smolder rather than the door.

He was panting slightly as he explained, hand still against the door, the skin starting to peel off. "It's a technique some of the Five Pillars have. Based in Unani medicine, humoral theory. I'm transferring heat from my surroundings and most of my body into one focal point, raising it to blistering temperatures. I'm more skilled in it usually, but for the past few months I've had trouble."

"How does it work?" Zakiyya asked.

"Manipulating the classic humors allows for imbalance which enables the transference of heat. The details are rather complicated." Sweat leaked from his arm and evaporated while he suppressed a shiver.

"I see," Zakiyya said, tracing a diagram in the air as she read his thoughts. It looked complicated, but Shaykh Nariman had lectured me about the humors long ago. Can't say I remembered much.

"If you're transferring so much heat, then one hand will roast, and the rest of your body will get frostbite—or hypothermia," I said shakily. The room around me became frigid; I could see the ghost of my breath. If this was him having trouble, I was worried about seeing what he could do on a good day. I remembered the way his knife had glowed with heat when he'd attacked the borz.

"I have a high cold threshold," Shahid said. He let out a sigh and dropped from his crouch to a sitting position, cradling the blistering, almost boiling hand with the other. "Though unfortunately a weak heat tolerance. The wood won't catch fire. It must have a flame-resistant coating."

"If that coating is removed, will it burn?" Zakiyya asked; she was already moving close to the door, flexing her fingernails.

"It could, though I imagine the wood was soaked in the substance for some time before use. Even without the coating, it might not work," he cautioned.

"Hey, let's not suspect the worst without giving it our best," I said, forcing an encouraging smile.

"Failure isn't losing, despairing of hope is," Shaykh Nariman added with a solemn squeak. I was starting to sound like him.

Zakiyya rolled her eyes at our pronouncements. She broke her nails against the wood and produced a hideous scratching noise. The sound crawled into my ears and ripped at my brain.

Uncle Uzayr heard the sound from his post. "What is it now?" he demanded. "Can't you people just be still?"

Zakiyya didn't bother to answer. She only scratched more furiously. The tips of all her nails broke off, but she managed to scrape off a thin layer of the wood's crust from a space the size of a sheet of paper.

Shahid placed his palm on the spot, not wincing despite the twisted splinters that rammed into his already blistered and pinkened flesh. Nothing happened, but he kept heating his hand as Uncle Uzayr yammered at us.

The trail of light that leaked through the slit in the door trickled away, and the outside world went gray. It was sunset, and the last flashes of sun were behind us, out of view.

The wood scorched ever so slightly. All of us held our breath, as if the slightest change in the air would whiff out faltering embers. The pallor of Shahid's skin made him look like the corpses we saw earlier, while the concentration written on his face made him seem to be stone.

The scorching quivered, and the sliver of smoke faded away.

"It's not working." Shahid said softly, in apology to Zakiyya's bleeding fingers. "The wood was soaked too thoroughly."

"God asks of us effort, not results," Shaykh Nariman squeaked. "We—"

His words were cut off by echoing screams.

The caretaker's yammering broke off. We could see him through the slits in the door, turning his head to the left and right to locate the source of the scream. "What is this?" he asked in confusion.

"The obur!" I shouted. "That corpse is attacking out there! Let us out and we can help." That meant the dried-out man was dead. Because we hadn't been effective enough. Some monster hunters we were.

Uncle Uzayr clutched his sword and oriented himself in the direction of a second set of screams.

"Let us out first!" Zakiyya joined in my shouting.

Shahid lifted a hand to silence us. "Cut off the head or aim for the heart," he told Uncle Uzayr in a steady voice. "Don't be shocked by what you see, just act."

Uncle Uzayr charged into the distance. We listened to the fluctuation in the symphony of screams; the caretaker's nearby roar, the sudden quiet of a gasp or death.

Uncle Uzayr staggered back into view, blood leaking like the ink from Shahid's calligraphy case.

A gray blur swerved after him. It was the corpse we'd uncovered earlier. Its cheeks were bloated with the blood it had feasted on. The rest of its face was gaunt, the upper and lower lips torn away along with the gums behind them, so the teeth and their roots were visible. The body's every feature was elongated, and thick blue veins peaked out from below the skin. Its nails were ten times longer than normal, as if all the growth that would have occurred in the rest of his life had the man not died, happened all at once. The nails were dense and mangled, but the edges were sharp like claws.

The eyes reflected the serene glow of sunset and laced it with the darkest malice. Terror made time move slow for me—being frozen in fear took on a new meaning. I saw the creature's lightning leap, and its animalistic descent, teeth barred like fangs. I saw its nostrils flare, I smelled its putrid saliva dripping in anticipation of another feeding. And I caught sight of the flurry whir that saved the caretaker, even if only for another minute.

Kedi bounded onto the obur's face and scratched at it in a ferocious feline frenzy. Every instinct of our little mascot screamed "run away," but she held firm.

The obur landed half on top of the caretaker; it screeched as it tried to tear Kedi away from its eyes, its intended victim temporarily forgotten.

Uncle Uzayr wormed out from under the creature and crawled toward our door as blood gurgled from his mouth. Meanwhile, the creature seized our fluffy friend, but cringed and cowered on contact, as if it had touched an open flame. Kedi was amazing.

Uncle Uzayr shoved a heavy bronze key forward with a raw, mangled hand. The pulpy sinews in his palm tore from the strain of trying to work the lock.

The obur shrieked and the caretaker fumbled the key, catching it in an oozing open wound. His whole body shuddered, but he tried again to open the door.

The lock clicked and he threw himself inside the room. He barricaded the door with his slumped back. Zakiyya looked above him, through the slits as the creature tossed Kedi away. Our feline hero landed on her feet and proceeded to snarl as she clawed at the creature's bony feet. She was a true gazi.

Shahid put a raw, pink finger to his chin and said in wonder, "Legends say obur are somehow related to bats. Bats are like mice with wings. Perhaps a residual instinct makes cats scary . . ."

He turned his attention to the caretaker. Blood dyed the older man's tan tunic, his unfocused eyes swivered aimlessly. "You're in shock," Shahid said.

Uncle Uzayr's response was even softer than Shahid's normal tone. "You were right. You were right. My wife is dead, and I imprisoned the only ones who could have saved her . . ."

"You couldn't have known. We seemed suspicious," I said, lifting his shirt to check the depth of the wound. My knees shook and my stomach turned. Aunty Asma was dead, that kind woman who stuffed us with watermelon. Her husband wasn't far from joining her.

"Where did you leave your sword?" Shahid asked. He already unlatched Uncle Uzayr's cudgel and tested its weight and feel.

"Dropped it while running. Not far from the door."

Shahid nodded. "Stay in the room until I get you, and if I don't come back in fifteen minutes, don't open it until morning."

"Let me go and get our things. The staff and your bag could help." I addressed Shahid but looked imploringly at the caretaker for a hint of where he'd stored them. He pointed the general direction out, letting his hand drop limp to his side. Zakiyya mind-read the specifics.

"Fine," Shahid said, "I'll distract the creature and you bolt for our things." No time for arguments. No time for safety.

He turned the doorknob before I could get another word in and lunged toward the creature. It dodged Shahid's attempts to ram it with the cudgel, swiveling by each swing. Their movements looked like a dance between a bear and a snake. Shahid's footwork, though slower than the obur's, was not random. He waltzed his way over to the sword and ducked suddenly, scooping it up in one barrel-sized fist. The obur hopped above the dual-wielded attack.

I was transfixed by the fight. Shahid bit his lip and gave me a glare mid-swing which jolted me back to my task. I dashed off towards the closet where our stuff was stored, and found them with the help of their floral smells floating past the blood.

When I returned to Shahid, he was breathing audibly but not heavily. The monster was gone.

"It ran off," he said before I could ask. "It realized that it might lose to me, so it escaped—leapt over the wall in the darkness." Shahid was what the terrors in the night feared.

"We can track it with Kedi," Zakiyya said, running a hand

down the cat's agitated flank.

Shahid wielded our terrified little heroine like a torch, aiming to shed light on where the creature went. "We follow it on horseback," he said. "That will give us an advantage in speed. And I know the exact moment when it's at its weakest."

"When?" I asked.

Zakiyya went to unhitch some restless horses that didn't belong to us. Shahid didn't answer me until we were saddled, supplies at the ready. "The obur is capable of superhuman feats, but it has low stamina. It makes up for this by constantly refueling. It ate well here, but it will be hungry again soon. It will stop."

"We have to find it before it next feeds then," I said. Shahid made a slight "hmm" noise, but otherwise didn't respond. Zakiyya looked like she was biting back heated words.

The caretaker hobbled out of the room. "Kill the fiend," he said groggily. Despite his wound, he mustered up enough strength to crank open the gate for us to ride out in pursuit.

"I'll take care of the survivors," Uncle Uzayr said. He staggered. Two guests emerged from a locked room now that the immediate danger was gone. I noticed that their pants were wet, and not with red. Before they could regain enough feeling in their legs to run, Zakiyya commanded them "Make sure everyone is okay." The taller of the two guests scurried off anyway, but the other stayed and helped the caretaker.

"We'll never get a good night's sleep, will we?" I said; my chuckle sounded deranged.

"When evil is awake, justice cannot sleep," Shahid declared with a heat that defied his usual softness.

"It is good to know you five pillars aren't made of stone," Shaykh Nariman noted, as we put distance between ourselves and the caravanserai. The pun barely made me smile.

Kedi guided us south and east, but looked sick the whole while. Our horses were sluggish at first. They'd been roused from sleep unwillingly in the chaos. Shahid's presence seemed to galvanize them, however, and they picked up speed. Another miraculous effect of baraka, I figured.

We skirted through and past a village, and Shahid raised his still-blistered hand to keep us quiet. He slowed his horse down to a trot. He handed Kedi over to me, and I put a hand over her mouth to prevent her cries from ringing out into the night. Zakkiya scratched her behind the ears.

Shahid slipped off his horse and crept towards an isolated shack-like house on the village's far fringe, which had an unhinged door, swinging in the wind. He took a deep, almost audible breath, unsheathed his knife, and crept inside. We followed despite his silent, overly calm attempt at a glare.

A man and a woman lay on a straw pallet. The obur was above them, tearing into both at once, alternating between ripping out flesh and dipping in for a bloody drink. A child was paralyzed in the corner, too frozen in fear to cry or whimper.

Shahid drove his knife through the back of the obur, just as it dropped the globs of flesh in its hands. Zakiyya scooped up the kid, hugging him tightly.

I edged close to Shahid looming over the three corpses, and he finally answered my earlier question.

"The best time to attack an obur is when it's feeding." he said; his voice cold, quiet, and now ravaged. "It has great difficulty stopping mid-meal."

"You—you planned for it to be this way?" I asked, horrified. I flinched as the obur suddenly fidgeted above the dead couple, twisting free of the knife and throwing it out of Shahid's grip.

The obur bore its fangs as it rounded on Shahid, who then reached for his waist, instantly skewering it again—with the reed pen. This time he drove the obur to the floor, impaling the pen all the way into the inkwell of the creature's flesh. He put his knee on its stretched, leathery back, pinning it down.

"I didn't plan for it. But I prepared for it."

The obur wriggled once more and shrieked, trying in vain to run.

"Obur are feral at first, but after a few feedings, they gain increased sentience. Can you speak?" Shahid asked the creature beneath him. It strained against his knee furiously. "If not, I'll impale you again, this time without missing the heart." There was no hitch in his voice.

I took one look at the red remnants of the couple, then picked up the knife and handed it to him.

Zakiyya plopped the child down on the ground. His dam had broken, and tears streamed down his chubby cheeks. Kedi languidly leaned against the kid, her soft fur and purring dulling his cries. She could fight a monster and comfort a child all in the same night. Zakiyya let the cat take over and approached the obur.

The obur snarled and flailed. Shahid plucked the reed pen out and immediately jabbed the knife into the creature's back, directly behind the heart. Zakiyya put a hand on his wrist to stop him before he pierced the organ.

"It's screaming no," she said. "I couldn't hear it when it was hiding and dormant, but I'm catching it now. It can talk, though the words are dark . . . and garbled. It's like the gurgling speech of a drowned man."

"Why are you this far east?" Shahid asked. It hissed rather than respond, but Zakiyya rummaged through its inadvertent thoughts.

"A message. There was a message seeking allies received in a village of its kind. A meat slab—that's a human, I suppose. A meat slab volunteered to be infected and travel the whole way undetected, but it died and turned too early." She shuddered, putting her fingers in her ears as if to block out the disturbing sound of the creature's thoughts.

"Volunteered to be infected?" I said, confused. Who would volunteer to become a monster?

"When an obur is . . . made," Shahid explained, "a new creature comes into being, but some of the residual memories and personality of the human who it was before remain. The degree to which that's true varies. Oburs live indefinitely unless killed. Even deprived of blood and flesh for months, they'll go into a coma rather than die. Some people are willing to trade the hereafter for that twisted version of eternity."

"This meat slab is regretting it though," the Obur said hoarsely, venom in its voice. "Its remaining speck of consciousness is aware of all we've done this night and is crying out." It hacked and snarled at the same time.

"That's a laugh," Zakiyya interpreted.

"Who invited you?" Shahid demanded, inching the knife closer to the obur's heart.

The creature coughed violently, and spoke, its voice a screech in the night, "I tell you, and you'll still kill me . . ." It eyed Zakiyya and me. "I wonder what these kids taste like."

"We taste like your death, you monster, " Zakiyya said. "He doesn't know who invited him, except that the obur elders knew of the figure from long ago and were afraid of him—and were surprised that he was back."

"One of the Servants," Shaykh Nariman said.

The obur sniffed like a dog. "A rodent?" It asked. "No, this smell is older. But we know you. I've been told your kind tastes exquisite."

Shaykh Nariman ignored the obur's peculiar provocation. "One of The Servants has contact with the obur. He was sent, maybe as a messenger. That means one of The Servants is in this area, somewhere. He was heading south. But what was his destination?"

"You heard him," Shahid said, steel in his quiet. "Well?" He looked at Zakiyya rather than the obur. She closed her eyes to listen, and the obur suddenly thrashed against Shahid's hold.

"That's useless," Shahid said, "you know that—" He let go of the knife and stared down at the obur. Its blood-stained teeth were bared, but frozen.

"It's dead," Zakiyya said. "Moved till the knife hit its heart. I got nothing, only the direction. South and east."

"Even a beast can be loyal and protect secrets." Shahid's forehead wrinkled ever so slightly. "Why southeast? Toward Basra?"

"And then maybe across the sea," Shaykh Nariman murmured. "It would make sense that the Servants might travel there, considering which civilizations ended there. According to Tabari—"

There was an approaching sound of several footsteps. Shaykh Nariman bolted back into the satchel, curling up against the Stories of the Prophets book.

"Took long enough for the villagers to wake up," I said. "Do we run for it?" I wasn't sure I could. My knees buckled as a wave of exhaustion hit me.

"There's blood on the creature's teeth. And eventually the

kid will be able to talk. Better to hand them the perpetrator than leave as if we're criminals," Zakiyya said. "I'll do the talking."

"After we're hailed as heroes, can you get them to give us a place to sleep?" I requested, joining her with a yawn. I was glad I was sleepy. Wakefulness would make me think of the bodies left behind.

No one had ever told me adventuring and heroic quests meant perpetual drowsiness. I didn't anticipate the fear either.

Chapter 16

Shahid washed the reed pen clean of the obur's dark, muckish blood; the coagulated lumps bubbled. I'd worried that he would write macabre calligraphy with the obur's insides as ink, but he wasn't weird like that. Though he was still weird.

The abundance of real life nightmares was making me imagine terrifying things.

Shahid burned the obur's body in a forest clearing and buried the ashes in a shallow grave. His silence throughout was smoldering.

I didn't help Shahid. After dreaming of being buried, and digging up the Obur, the sight of soil unsettled me queasy. If I was going to return to gardening after our journey, I couldn't afford this aversion. I hadn't thought that far in the future in a while. There was no guarantee I'd find another garden to tend, and I certainly wouldn't be the same kid any more. But if a bloodsucking corpse slaughtering the inhabitants of a peaceful caravanserai taught me anything, it was that there is no guarantee anyone or anything would be around at any moment. One has to make due with uncertainty—and hope for survival.

I was glad that Zakiyya didn't hear those drowsy thoughts percolating. She would have mocked me for pondering a sedentary life after so much travel. But she was like the wind while I'm a plant at heart.

She busied herself with the villagers, who woke from peaceful dreams into a world of bloody nightmares. She explained the circumstance to them; a vicious animal attacked the family, and we, a hunter and his apprentices, tracked it down and saved a child. It wasn't exactly a lie. There was too much flesh missing for them to think we did the killings. There was too much flesh missing for them to look at the corpses at all without retching. Maybe they noticed the beast's humanoid appearance, but they said nothing. There are many strange horrors in God's green earth.

The villager's offered us a place to sleep. Kedi went off with the traumatized kid, who clutched her like a lifeline. Both had witnessed far too much already. Those soft creatures deserved cuddling, not violence. I found myself praying we wouldn't take Kedi along any farther, though I would miss her.

I didn't dream this time. No serpentine beasts came to haunt me. The emptiness scared me more.

I woke up to the smell of fertilizer, muffled by the earthy flavor of grains in the fields.

Zakiyya offered to help around the house that hosted us while I yawned. The couple whose home it was, declined the offer and fussed over us instead. They thought Zakiyya and I were as traumatized by the killings as the child. The trembling in my limbs meant they weren't entirely wrong.

Shahid murmured apologies and thanks to the couple. Zakiyya's face darkened.

"What's up?" I asked.

"Let's talk outside," Shahid said.

No sooner had we exited that Zakiyya burst out. "No!" she

hissed, "you're not leaving us behind! We're the ones who brought you into this, not the other way around."

My jaw dropped. I gave Shahid a searching look, hoping that Zakiyya's reading was wrong for once. But he shook his head. "I was too zealous in looking for the obur. One of the Servants is close. If it brought that creature here, imagine how much more terrible it could be. Shaykh Nariman and I will go with Kedi. It's not safe for you."

"Are you kidding?" I asked. "We had the prophetic dreams! Shaykh Nariman came to us, and we're the ones who found Kedi. You can't just take them. *We* are meant to fight The Servants."

"Shaykh Nariman is already willing to go. We spoke last night," Shahid said. Despite the soft voice they were delivered in, his words punched me in the gut and knocked the wind out of me.

"We're helpful!" Zakiyya said. "We're the ones who found the obur! Fighting a cunning enemy will be easier with me around to read them." She pointed at me. "And he can find more allies on the way. And the staff— "

"You're not. Helpful, that is. I'm grateful you apprised me of this situation. I'm grateful that you care so much, but you're children. Every moment I worry over you is a moment an enemy gets ahead," Shahid said, his tone gentle, as if he were talking to kids. Which I suppose he was. "You can't hold your own in a fight, and you know nothing about what we're dealing with."

"Oh yeah?" I asked angrily. "And what if your weird silence gets you imprisoned again? Who's going to help then? You haven't seen Zakiyya fight—she'd whoop you. And how do you expect to find your friends without me?"

"I made mistakes because I was distracted. I spoke with this family. They'll host you for a while. And perhaps you can look for my friends eventually. I'm counting on you," he said.

"Will you come back for us?" Zakiyya asked. He didn't answer. He wasn't the sort to lie.

"Shaykh Nariman!" I growled. "How could you agree to this? "

"My dear boy," he squeaked, emphasizing the last word. "Your job was always to get this information to those who could deal with it. To gather allies, not join the fight. And you've done that. I'm proud of you. You can't be asked to do more. But don't worry, *I* will come back for you."

"You're abandoning me," I shrieked. "Everyone leaves."

"You can find more allies." Shaykh Nariman nodded his snout. "Or another garden. You have the choice now. Either way, follow the smell of flowers. You have no idea how proud I am of you."

I clenched my fists in frustration, then opened them and breathed in deep. I plopped myself down on the ground, legs-crossed. When angry, change your position to calm yourself. Shaykh Nariman had said that many times.

I gave Zakiyya a weak, pained smile. "Maybe we can go to your grandmother at last. These detours have been pretty wild, huh?"

"Yeah," she muttered.

Shahid plucked a small pouch from his waistband. and plopped it into Zakiyya's outstretched hand. The coins inside jingled to the tune of his guilt. "I'm not abandoning you. I'm looking out for you. It hasn't been long, but intense days say more about a person than dreary decades. You're good kids. Now live and get the chance to grow up to be great adults." He ruffled my hair and took my staff.

Shaykh Nariman hopped out of my satchel. "Don't try anything crazy," he squeaked. And then, they were off. The moans of our reluctant cat were muffled by the wind.

I turned to Zakiyya. "You were right to always be skeptical of them," I said. "Anyone can betray you. There's always been something off about Shahid, the quiet—"

"No—they're doing this to protect us," Zakiyya said. "That doesn't mean they're right."

She cleared her throat. "With the dreams we both had, I can't believe that we are meant to sit on the sidelines. And honestly, I don't care about the dream. I know I can make a difference. They left, but you can track them, Khurafa. Shahid's baraka."

"You really think we'll be helpful?" I asked. "They said we aren't needed."

"That doesn't matter," she answered. "We don't act because we think we'll succeed, we act because to do so is right. And we don't do right because we have to."

"Well, they said to find allies and I can't sense any new baraka. They didn't say they had to be new allies. So I'll follow that familiar scent," I reasoned.

"Whatever you want to tell yourself," she muttered. "As long as we're still doing this."

Getting away wasn't as easy as we'd hoped. We rushed over to where we'd tied our horses the previous night, but they were gone. Shahid had paid a villager to return them to the caravansarai.

"If we walk while he rides, we can't catch up," I said.

"I'd say 'don't say the obvious,' but you'll think it and I'll hear it anyway. Give me a second." She walked deliberately by each home, dodging villagers who rushed to plow their fields.

"There," she said at last. She knocked on a rickety door and a sour-faced, middle-aged man opened it.

"How may I help you?" He yawned.

"I understand your crop hasn't been growing this year," Zakiyya said briskly.

"What of it?" the man mumbled.

"I believe I know why. I'm wondering if that information might be worth making a deal—oh, I'm sorry—I'm mistaken." She took several sudden steps back.

"What? You know why?" His face livened. "A deal? I'll trade anything, anything at all!"

"N—no, I'm sorry, my mistake," Zakiyya said, flustered. She shuffled off while the man kept calling after her.

"What was that?" I whispered to her. The man stumbled into the road in pursuit—he reached a hand out towards Zakiyya but she swatted it away.

I glared at him. "My sister gets premonitions sometimes," I fibbed. "She saw that you—hadn't been praying enough and that's why your field wasn't growing. But upon seeing you she realized she might be wrong. Now please, back off." I was not as good at this as Zakiyya, but she wasn't speaking.

The man ignored me and reached for her again. "That look says you know something. Now girl tell me—"

Zakiyya screamed; the sound split my eardrums. Other villagers rushed to the scene and the desperate man backed away while we slipped off, dismissing their concern.

"What was that?" I asked.

"I picked up some thoughts around town. I knew how his field was made barren, but I didn't listen long enough to know why. I was rushing too much to trade info for a horse," she said.

"What did you learn?" I asked. She opened her mouth to answer when a stout woman whose lined face and callous hands shouted solidity, butted in.

"Excuse me, young miss," she said. "My brother-in-law mentioned that you knew something about his field?" Her eyes bore into Zakiyya.

Zakiyya's cheeks reddened, and she didn't meet the woman's gaze. "I don't know anything," she said, and then added more softly, "What you're doing is right though."

The woman's face was etched with shock. "What is it that I am doing?" she asked. She regained control of her features. "Come with me for a moment."

"There's no need," Zakiyya said. But the lady was already walking ahead, leading the way. Outside her house a younger woman was sitting on the porch and basking in the sun, barefoot. A smile spread over her hallowed face.

"I am Rafat and this is my sister, Amal," the stout woman said. She stared at Zakiyya for a long moment. "Amal stays with me because her husband can't support her. The field being barren and all. I get the feeling his fortunes will change once he finalizes the divorce. He's been thinking so too."

"Do you want sherbet?" Amal said with buoyant brightness.

"That's alright," Zakiyya answered. "Honestly, we're trying to get a move on. We're looking to buy a horse, you see."

"A horse," Rafat said blankly. "You're the kids of that hunter? Are you trying to catch up with him?"

"N—no," I began to interject, but Zakiyya put up a hand and stopped me.

"Yes," she said. "He's our stupid uncle who thinks that he doesn't need help. But family members need each other."

Rafat gave her a searching glance and nodded. "I suppose

that I might be able to persuade my brother-in-law to sell his horse cheap. He squandered her dowry, you know. Might be a good way to recover it and get proceedings moving."

Zakiyya lit up. "That would be . . . thank you."

"No, thank you miss," Rafat said. "I don't know how you figured it all out, but thank you for not . . ."

Zakiyya handed her our entire pouch of coins. "The more we can keep from this, the better," she told Rafat. The stout lady nodded and walked off. My mouth was agape—had *she* really let the whole bag go?

"Sherbet in the meantime?" Amal asked radiantly.

We gave in and sipped the sweet rosy concoction while lounging on the porch. "What happened?" I whispered after a pleasant slurp. "What's going on?"

"We don't have enough coin to buy a horse fair and square," she said. "I thought if we help someone out, we'd be able to do it. I overheard the thoughts of Rafat. I saw that she was purposefully pouring acid into a field every few nights. I didn't understand why, but when I heard the thoughts of the guy whose field was suffering, I figured I could tell him and get a horse in exchange."

"Wait, Rafat is poisoning her brother-in-law's field?" I whispered furiously. "That's terrible—"

"Yes, he is," the sister said, stepping in at that moment. How much had she overheard? She touched a spot on her arm absentmindedly, and picked up the narrative where Zakiyya left off.

"My . . . husband was—is—an abusive man. I told my sister of course, but my husband hardly let me out of the home and he was doing well. He had a lot of sway in the village. I couldn't get out if I wanted to. So my sister . . . changed my husband's fortunes. Made him a pauper so he had to let me go," she said.

"What a gift you have to be able to figure that out," she said to Zakiyya. "And what a soul you have not to use it to your advantage."

"I—I almost— Zakiyya began, shivering. Whatever memories she'd seen when talking to the husband had left a mark. "I almost put the picture together too late."

The woman pinched Zakiyya's cheek playfully. "How's the sherbet?" she asked.

"Sweet," Zakiyya said, with a weak smile.

"A taste of paradise," I chimed in.

The older sister came back half an hour later with a horse in tow. Her fist was bloody but not bruised. She handed Zakiyya the reins and tossed the coin pouch to Amal, who caught it without dropping her own sugary glass. "The start of the dowry," Rafat said. "He'll hand over most of the furniture and the dishes too, and that'll be the divorce. Then I'll see about giving him some farming advice."

Amal looked to the ground. "Well, maybe. I'm forgetful and there are so many things that can go wrong in the field," Rafat finished.

The animal she brought over was more plow horse than stallion, but even riding together, Zakiyya and I were a lighter load than Shahid. We'd make good time—I had multiple scents to guide us.

We thanked the siblings—Zakiyya hugged the younger sister fiercely. "Congratulations," Zakiyya whispered in Amal's ears while casting a glance toward her belly. Tears stemming from a jumble of emotions leaked from the younger sister's face.

"Don't do too much of that," Rafat scolded. "It'll fall in the cup and you'll have salty sherbet." She gave me a strong handshake. "You siblings take care of each other, ok?" she said.

"We will," I nodded, inadvertently puffing up my chest. This time Zakiyya did not roll her eyes.

We rode off, the intermingled floral scents of Kedi, Shahid, and the various items pulling us through another farming village and well on our way beyond .

Chapter 17

Our mighty steed tired before it got dark. But I knew Shahid with his horse-whispering would find a way to travel through the night.

"We use the same strategy he used for the obur," Zakiyya said. "He'll stop and slow when he's hunting. That's when we'll catch up—and that's when he'll need us."

"He didn't do a very good job of stopping us from following," I said. "No one in the village really prevented us from leaving, though he probably told them too."

"They thought he was strange, trying to abandon his 'family' like that," Zakiyya snorted.

He was strange. A soft-spoken hero who seemed perpetually covered in beeswax, who'd nabbed our mission and tried to run away with it. I fell asleep thinking about how much stranger it was that two kids were following him, thinking they could do something. I patted my satchel out of habit before I drifted off; my hand hit only the Stories of the Prophets leather cover beneath the cloth. Shaykh Nariman was not there.

I was alone again in my empty dreams.

***

We set off bright and early.

The scents grew strong as we approached a hamlet, just past

midday. I caught a view from uphill: Clutches of thatched mud houses lingering in the half-shadows, a stone well in the village square, and a small square building with a pointed hat-like dome and a little 't' carved from wood on top.

I could make out a small garden by the square building. It was dotted with a crop of poppies. I squinted. The green stems and red flowers didn't match up. Petals were scattered, roots covered leaves. They were ripped apart.

A crowd of wary people eyed us as we arrived. I waved, getting ready to ask if they'd seen a dour giant.

The people scampered over like squirrels. I was about to dismount to greet them, to shake hands. "Wait, stop." Zakiyya held me in place with a grip so hard her fingers turned white. She twisted the reins. "WE HAVE TO RUN!"

Our horse teetered. The crowd had leapt onto our steed. Zakiyya and I jumped off. Without the staff, I couldn't even poke at them.

We fell hard but landed well. Our horse was not so lucky. There was a cracking sound as it stumbled, and it's right legs collapsed. It struggled to rise on the broken limbs, whimpering as the people dug into it. Actually *dug*, with fingers and mouths as shovels, looks of hatred emblazoned on their faces and rabid, pink foam on their lips. There was a heavy smell on them. The hormonal odor of a predator about to attack. Filth mixed with fury.

"What's wrong with them? Why are they—"

My voice died as the mad folk turned their attention to us. A doddering old woman whose eyes were a carnivorous yellow bellowed as she charged. Her mouth held more blobs of coagulated blood than teeth. No wonder Zakiyya wanted to visit her grandma; the anger of elderly women is fearsome.

Zakiyya pulled me into a run. "Where is Shahid?"

"Th—this way!" I said, scrambling off toward the back of a sturdy house.

There was a small horde clawing at the cellar door.

"Of course he's there," Zakiyya muttered.

Shahid was pinned down inside. *Didn't need our help, indeed!* Vindication overcame what should have been mind-numbing terror. Heroes need help too. As Shaykh Nariman would say, only God is independent.

We swerved to avoid another frenzied villager. Being small helped with slipping away, but we'd have trouble breaking free.

"Predict their movements, dance a little, and create some space?" I asked Zakiyya between ragged, panting breaths. This game of tag was draining and home base was too well guarded.

"Their thoughts don't tell me enough to predict," Zakiyya grumbled. "It's like listening to a storm. 'Anger, anger! Attack, attack!'"

"So Shahid did something stupid and made everyone angry." I dodged another villager as I ran farther away.

The door of a different house peaked open. A hand beckoned us over.

"Let's grab that hand," Zakiyya said, wiping away sweat as she sprinted over. I dashed after her. The door flung wide open right before I got to it, and I flew over the threshold, toppling into a shaking, spidery thin man wearing a tiny skullcap.

Zakiyya shut the door and leaned her back against it as a mob rammed into it. "Thank you," she said and helped the spidery man to his feet. He introduced himself as Yaqub.

I rose unaided and surveyed the space. A few families huddled together in the corner, knots of children were embraced by their mothers, and a father paced aimlessly. Red and gold dyed cushions were strewn about the room, and half-finished cups of a brown liquid sat on a low round table. There were hints of black pepper and frankincense in the air.

"What's happening out there?" I asked.

"We don't know what's going on," Yaqub said when the door stopped jolting. "Nothing ever happens here. But today, people started going wild. Wantonly destroying things and attacking people. Not talking, not thinking, just rampaging. I saw parents pull at their own—" he stopped, eying a kid hunched on his knees and wrapped in a blanket. He continued in a whisper, "The kid was attacked by his own parents. They would have ripped him apart if I hadn't snatched him."

Zakiyya processed what we knew. "Villagers started going on rampages this morning. Hmm . . ." She turned to Yaqub again. "Did you see a really big man come through recently? A stranger carrying a cat?"

"Aye, I saw him get stormed. He was asking someone a question, the cat went ballistic, and three, four people were grabbing at his limbs. I swear, this is normally a hospitable place."

"Yup," I said. "People wanting to feed us becoming people wanting to eat us isn't that big a shift." His face paled at the terrible joke, and Zakiyya elbowed me hard.

She surveyed the room. "A couple kitchen knives. . . that's not enough. We could break legs off the table and use them as cudgels so we're not completely defenseless."

"You'll hurt them? Those are our friends and family!" a woman clutching her daughter shouted. Her tan face reddened, and the cross around her neck shook as she spoke.

"We don't want to kill anyone," Zakiyya said. "Still, we can't let ourselves be killed."

"Mama, I'm thirsty!" The daughter cried, her black braids bouncing. She pulled at her mom's sleeve, preventing her from responding.

"Sister Mariya, I'm afraid I haven't drawn anything up from the well," Yaqub apologized. "Ran out yesterday and fasting today, you see" he said, putting a hand on his thin belly. No food, all stress. No wonder his limbs were quivering.

"That's alright, I had a water pouch when we fled my husb— when we escaped the frenzy," Mariya, the mother, said. She produced it from under her shawl and her daughter took a long, deep sip.

"Thanks mommy," the girl said with a smile that dispelled some of the stress in the room. Dimples formed in her soft cheeks. Her father had gone berserk—she'd witnessed it and now here she was, smiling at the smallest thing. Her mother ruffled her hair and I was all smiles too. There's no comfort like a mom when the world goes to hell.

"HOLD HER DOWN!" Zakiyya screamed, shattering the peaceful moment. The girl bit down on her mother's forearm, the baby teeth failing to penetrate her skin. Mariya wore a look of confusion like nothing I'd ever seen. Her daughter began to ram her head into her mother's chest.

Zakiyya ran over and ripped the girl off her mother. "The water!" Zakiyya said, as she struggled to restrain the girl who was now frothing at the mouth. "It must be the water. Has anyone drunk from the well today?"

"N—no, I didn't," Yaqub rasped as he helped Zakiyya hold the child down. We already knew that he was fasting. Others shook their heads or explained: "I drew water two days back", "I was heading to the well when this happened."

"Did anything happen to the well?" Zakiyya asked.

Mariya, staring in desperation at her raging daughter, answered, "Someone from out of town came by to draw water for himself and his animals . . . he took a long time."

"Did he leave town?" Zakiyya demanded.

"I—I don't remember. I went home with the water I'd fetched . . ." Mariya's voice trailed off as her daughter screamed.

"Then that was . . ." I began with a chill.

"One of The Servants," Zakiyya finished. "He did something to the water and the water is doing something to the villagers." She bit her lower lip.

The banging outside the room had subsided enough that we risked taking a peek. The door wasn't open a foot before one of the 'frenzied' attacked. Still, we saw enough to know the cellar was still surrounded.

"Why are they going after Shahid so persistently?" I asked in frustration. Are heroes all danger magnets? How were we supposed to save him?

"They're . . . normal people," Zakiyya said slowly.

"What's normal about wrecking their own town?"

"They're just acting . . . berserk. Like anger and hate and all those mad emotions have been turned on one-hundred percent and they've lost the ability to think. Everything they're doing is within normal human capacity. There's nothing supernatural about their speed or strength. So that goes for their perception too. It's human. They react based on normal hearing and sight." Zakiyya twirled her hair in thought.

"That explains their pattern of attacking us, but why won't they let up on the cellar?" I asked.

"I think . . . Look, you said I have baraka, right? And you can sense it. But it's not the sort or the amount that anyone but the most perceptive could pick up on. But Shahid is different. You found him, but even I got a sense of something. I think the average person can tell subconsciously. It could be that they're targeting him because of that."

"Then why doesn't he run away to draw them out of town?" Shahid left to handle things on his own and this was the result. I was looking forward to letting him have it, but he'd be unfazed as always.

"The problem started here. It would be hard to fix it if he runs from the source," Zakiyya said. She raised her voice to address everyone. "My brother and I are going to go out there. At night."

"At night?" I whispered. But then it dawned on me. They were normal people gone berserk. They couldn't see any better in the dark than I could. But Zakiyya could hear their anger. So she could figure out their locations.

"I want you two to come with us," Zakiyya said to Mariya, who had bound her daughter and muzzled her using scraps she tore from her own dress. "The person we are trying to meet up with may be able to help her."

Mariya removed a hand from her daughter and placed it for a split second on her cross. She nodded, determination overwriting the worry on her face. There's no force like a mom when the world goes to hell.

"I—I don't like the idea of you all going alone," Yaqub said, wringing his hands anxiously. A group with three children—one of whom would do anything to kill the others—wasn't exactly the dream team for dangerous missions.

"We'll attract less notice than you would," Zakiyya said. Not everyone needs to brave the dark. Sometimes a helping hand

and warm rest spot is plenty.

By the time it was night, we were all thirsty. A few fractional peaks out the door revealed that storm clouds were blotting out the stars and moon, giving us the perfect amount of darkness for our plan. I wished the rain would pour and wash the troubles away.

The four—well, three—of us crept out the door. The fourth, the daughter, was manhandled by her mother. Despite Mariya's angry protest, we managed to convince her to give her daughter a powerful sleeping draught Yaqub concocted. Otherwise she'd make too much noise. Whatever nightmares Yaqub usually used that draught to counter would have plenty of fuel if we all survived this.

We made swift, silent progress toward the cellar, relying on memory, floral scents of baraka, and the varying gradients of darkness to locate the safest path. The frenzied still crowded around it. Zakiyya hurled a ceramic pot she'd borrowed from Yaqub. It crashed some dozen feet away; the sound of it shattering was followed by grunts and frantic movement in the dark.

There were fewer shadows by the cellar and it looked like we might be in the clear. But then a heavy wave of dark closed in on our momentary opening.

A yell echoed from far behind us to the left. "I'M HERE YOU WACKJOBS. YOU WANNA TEAR AT SOMEONE, I'M RIGHT HERE!" Yaqub hollered in spite of his dry throat and parched lips. A helping hand wasn't enough for him. His announcement was met with a flurry of footsteps and incoherent, primal roars. He bellowed his own battle cry, "RAK CHAZAK AMATS!"

He bounded off with his long, shaking legs, yelling all the while. "DON'T WORRY ABOUT ME! THEy DON'T ATTACK

THEIR OWN KIND! I'LL DRINK THE WATER BEFORE THEY CATCH ME SO YOU'D BETTER CURE ME!"

Only two desperate figures stayed back scratching at the door and shrieking. Zakiyya and I lifted our makeshift cudgels while Mariya cradled her daughter protectively.

"Now!" Zakiyya whispered fiercely. We knocked the figures out with simultaneous blows. My combat skills had come a long way. But there wasn't time to feel pride.

The sound of our strikes would draw more in moments.

"SHAHID! SHAYKH NARIMAN!" I shouted. "The cellar door is clear. Open up! Quick!"

For a split second nothing happened and blobs hurtled towards us. If Shahid were actually asleep at night for once . . .

The door hurtled open and his bear-like arms dragged us all inside. He'd left us behind, and yet his presence still made it feel like the danger was past.

The stairs collapsed beneath our combined weight, but Shahid landed solidly and set us down away from the splinters. He secured the door and turned to us under the orange glow of his lantern.

"What are you doing here?" we asked each other at the same time. Kedi jumped on my face and then Zakiyya's, meowing joyously.

"You answer questions first," I said to Shahid, jabbing a finger at his pale yellowish face. I recollected my annoyance, but couldn't help stroking our fluffy friend.

Shahid went off on his own and spent the whole day locked up? After the obur situation, I was beginning to think he got trapped behind closed doors a little too much. That wouldn't happen to Rustam or Sohrab.

His story went much as we'd figured: The village went

haywire when he arrived. He was pursued by a horde too large to restrain without killing. He'd holed up in the cellar waiting for them to fall asleep so he could investigate.

"And you thought you didn't need us!" Zakiyya said in triumph.

"The plan hasn't changed. They're riled up now but I'll be able to check things out soon. Unless you know anything . . ." he said quietly. Zakiyya had a smirk on her face which loudly proclaimed she knew everything.

When she didn't say anything, Shahid sighed, and spoke with a tender softness. "I've lost everyone. The other members of the five pillars disappeared, and I haven't been able to find them. I couldn't risk losing people in another hunt. I'd enjoyed the company of all of you—it reminded me of what it was like, what I was missing, but then I was also reminded of the danger that comes with traveling with a group. I don't regret leaving you behind, but I am sorry for how it made you feel. I'm impressed by your resolve, but also worried about it. Don't be hurt by Shaykh Nariman's actions—I gave him an ultimatum; my help and your safety or me leaving the task completely." That utterance took more out of him than any combat I'd seen.

His honesty thawed our icy retorts. "The people outside aren't going to fall asleep tonight," Zakiyya said. "The way their minds read; they're exhausted but there is no desire for sleep. Adrenaline and sheer emotion can keep one up for a few nights. And if we wait that long, they might all die from the overexhaustion before they can be saved."

Shahid's statuesque serenity fluctuated. He put his head in hands, but abandoned the pose almost immediately.

"Did Shaykh Nariman find anything out?" I asked. Kedi migrated to the mother and daughter. Always comforting those most distressed.

"I'm here," Shaykh Nariman said, poking his head out from under a table. Mariya was too distracted by her daughter and our cat to notice him. "I'm glad you understood what I meant about following the flowers. Following the scent of Shahid and the objects."

Zakiyya and I shared a glance—if that's what he'd meant, it took away some of the sting of him leaving.

"You don't get to decide when we start or stop our journey," Zakiyya said, but his pronouncement deflated the angst she'd been saving.

Shaykh Nariman nodded. "Of course, of course. Now then. The mad people, they'll target anything living and they are quite aware of their surroundings. I was going to check things out alone at night—which is now . . . "

"There's no need!" Zakiyya said confidently. "It's the water—the well water was corrupted and it's driving them all crazy."

"The water?" Shahid murmured.

Zakiyya continued, gesturing toward the sleeping girl. "We brought her so you can figure out how to fix it."

"I don't have many medicinal supplies," Shahid said, "but . . . there is something I wanted to try. Everyone was moving around too much for me to attempt it." He put a hand on the girl's forehead and concentrated. His palm slowly began to glow, white tendrils of lazy light wafting off it. The girl woke and screeched.

"You're going to burn her!" I yelped. Zakiyya shushed me.

The smell of daisies was overpowering. "It's Baraka," I said, shocked that I could actually see it. I imagined this was what intoxication felt like. "You're concentrating your baraka and trying to overload her."

Shahid closed his eyes. The girl's struggles stopped—and she began to snore. That's what a Rustam or Sohrab is supposed to do. Make a world where kids can sleep peacefully.

Mariya's grasp on her daughter's clawing hands relaxed. She embraced the sleeping child, crying. "Is it over?"

"Whatever polluted her is neutralized," Shahid said, the tiniest hint of exhaustion in his deadpan voice.

"So we need to restrain them one by one and purify them," Zakiyya said, working out the calculations.

The grim but determined look in Shahid's eyes told me he'd die trying. "Or . . . we go for the well," I said, scratching my chin as an idea came to me. A beard—or at least some scruff—would be nice for these eureka moments.

I plucked out a small waterskin I'd confiscated from one of Yaqub's guests. It contained a tiny portion of the corrupted water. "I'm going to drink half of this," I said. "Purify the other half—imbue it with baraka if you can, then pour the water on me. The problem is that it takes time for your baraka to cure the fisq, yeah? Maybe this way you don't have to make physical contact."

"That's not a bad idea but it's risk—hey!" Zakiyya's concern transformed to fear as I swallowed my dose of poison before she could finish. No thoughts, just action.

Chapter 18

I felt it all at once. Anger at my parents for dying. Anger at Shahid for leaving. Anger at the Servants for poisoning people. Anger at myself for not saving Aunty Asma. Anger at everything and everyone, for moving, breathing, for daring to feel anything different.

I was fire incarnate. My insides lighted up, my mind exploded, everything burned away but the rage.

Destroy, tear, kill, ignite.

Drops of cool water plopped onto my skin and into my consciousness. The fire sizzled and turned to smoke. My thoughts gathered themselves in the ruined wreckage.

So tired. I drifted away, pleasant dreams beckoning to my singed soul . . .

A slap on the cheek knocked away the possibility of restful recovery. "Wake up, idiot!" Zakiyya's nagging brought me back to the nightmare of reality.

She knew what I was thinking, so I got another, harder slap.

"It worked," I croaked.

"Yes, but how can we purify all of them?" Shahid asked. Was his constant commitment to what came next hiding relief?

"I have an idea for that," I said. "But we need to get to the well, and you need time there."

"Leave that to me," Mariya said, gently patting her snoring daughter's cheek. "My husband is still out there. After what you've done for my little girl . . ."

I was about to object but Zakiyya stopped me. "If you get hurt, what about your daughter? What's she to do?"

"If I don't do something to help our home, how can I ever face her? And if they aren't stopped out there, she won't be safe," Mariya countered. She put a hand to her forehead, the center of her chest, then each shoulder.

Zakiyya nodded. "What do you have in mind?"

Mariya gestured to the materials in the cellar—worn barrels, cloth, scraps of wood. "I'll draw them away with a torch. I used to win all the footraces in the village before I gave birth to this one," she pinched her daughter's cheek. "I reckon I'm still faster than most. And I need the practice if I'm going to keep outrunning her when she grows up. Light and sound should be more than enough to lure them away."

"The luring is only part of the plan," I interjected. "We want to gather all the infected and get them close to the well. Within a dozen meters."

"I can do that," Mariya stroked her daughter's hair one final time. She assembled her makeshift torch. I gave her the final pinch of corrupted water as a final resort if she got cornered. If you can't beat them, join them.

"Promise you'll find a home for my girl if I don't make it," Mariya said.

"If you don't make it, we probably won't either," I admitted.

"Now, we need to figure out how to get out of here," Zakiyya said. The animalistic snarls outside suggested that at least a dozen frenzied were waiting.

Kedi nuzzled against my staff. It clattered to the ground. I retrieved it. Less than a day apart, but I'd really missed that stick. I didn't need it to walk, but it kept me upright.

"I—I couldn't use it," Shahid said softly. "I tried when I was first swarmed but it didn't work. I assume it's become keyed to you after so many uses. It resonates only with your baraka."

"So it likes me!" I grinned. I had the loyalty of Moses's staff. That was an honor beyond what I could process.

"I can't read the mind of sticks," Zakiyya said, "but I still think I heard it snort a 'no.' Sounded like splinters."

"You're just jealous that the staff likes me," I said. "You can read all the minds in the world, know everybody intimately, but nobody really knows you—" My words died when Shahid, of all people, glared at me. A real glare this time.

"You know her, it's been brief, but we all know her," Shahid said with quiet intensity. "Blessings can be burdens. Don't mock the weight others carry."

Shaykh Nariman murmured his agreement while Zakiyya stuck out her tongue. My words were uncalled for but she knew what I'd *actually* been thinking at the time. That I knew her. That the staff might not be keyed to her baraka, but I was. I had a new garden, at least, it smelled like one to me. I even let a mouse roam this one.

Some things are embarrassing enough they need to be masked with meanness.

We stowed the little girl in a barrel with Kedi, who hardly scratched at the wood. Mariya lit her torch. I took a deep breath, reared back with the staff in hand, and slammed it into the wall farthest from the barrel. Mortar split with a thunderous crack and earth crumbled into the room. My aim was a lot better than the last time I used the staff to find an exit from a basement. The ceiling didn't collapse on us now.

Mariya wadded through the dirt faster than it fell, lifting the torch high. Her determination blazed bright as she reached the surface.

I rammed the staff again, this time into the cellar entrance. The crowd of frenzied, already divided and confused by the earlier sound of stones splitting, lost their balance in the new landslide. I knew what that was like. But not this time!

Shahid stepped over them like they were stairs on his way out. We followed suit. They roared, but the tangle of limbs and Shahid's massive weight slowed them. The last frenzied of the group recovered enough to grab at Shahid's ankle, but he broke the grip with a savage jerk of his leg, and bolted toward the square.

We scampered after him, Zakiyya murmuring the locations of enemies hidden by the dark. In the meantime, Mariya dashed in the distance, dangling the flaring torch, taunting the frenzied into pursuit. Most took the bait, chasing after her like kids leaping to catch a firefly. To squash a firefly. The rest rushed us.

Zakiyya clipped one frenzied in the face with a dislodged cellar brick. I slammed the staff into another, pushing it off its feet. I didn't have time to bask in the satisfaction of seeing someone else fall.

The woman ran from house to house so smoothly that it looked like she was dancing.The light from her torch streaked across the town as she hollered, "Come after me! Come after me, you sorry louts!" She called her mad neighbors by name, spewing out every invective she stored up over the years. Small towns aren't really more polite than cities.

When we made it to the well, no more frenzied followed us.Mariya's antics attracted a crowd circling the well from a safe distance, like it was the kaaba. She gradually guided them closer. A familiar thin shadow trailed her. Yaqub had survived by switching sides.

"Shahid! Can you fit in the well?" I asked. I'd forgotten how huge he was.

"What? Yes, why?" he asked.

"I want you to dive down there. Purify the water with your whole body and imbue it completely with baraka."

He climbed in nimbly for a swim, no hesitation. A glow soon followed, as if the moon shone from the well.

"When the water is imbued with baraka, I want you to do that heat trick you did before!" My voice echoed into the well. "The humoral manipulation, or whatever you called it. Get the water to become fumes with your body, but put the cold into one hand as high as you can so it condenses a little on the way out. It's humid enough today that we can make mist!"

The water bubbled as Shahid carried out my instructions. All was well and good. I turned to gloat to Zakiyya.

Then Mariya's torch went out, caught by a resilient gust of wind.

Uh oh.

"Don't stop you wild wackos!" she shrieked. "After me!" I was convinced that she could outrun mongol horses and not just this village. She kept much of the crowd, but many came for us.

I readied the staff.

"I got you," Zakiyya guided me in the direction of incoming frenzied. "You're not alone. No falling."

I rent holes in the ground under Zakiyya's direction. Light taps meant less earth splitting.

"Hurry up, Shahid!" I screamed. A wave of bodies approached. A staff blow strong enough to sink the crowd would sink us all

Something rammed into the wave.

"I'm still here you lumbering idiots!" Mariya screeched. The crowd consumed her. She was going to be torn apart.

"Drink the water!" I shouted. "HEY! COME FOR US INSTEAD!" It was still too early to face the frenzied, but I didn't want her daughter waking up in that barrel, alone in the world.

They flooded toward us.

"Into the well!" I screamed at Zakiyya.

We edged inside, back to back, feet pushing against the wall. Shahid's acrobatics were beyond us.

The horde crowded around the edge, spit flying from their mouths.

Two toppled in, crumpling our delicate formation. The four of us fell into open air, weightless.

Shahid caught us and continued his work, undeterred. Steam oozed around him and above us, his cold hand over our heads slowing its ascent.

The two frenzied were unconscious.

"Why aren't we burning?" Zakiyya asked. "The steam, even his body, we should be in pain, why—" she read my mind. "The baraka in the water. You thought the baraka in the water would protect us from the heat?"

"Burning in fire is punishment from God. I figured baraka as a blessing would counter it."

"Like the cool fire in the story of Abraham," Zakiyya murmured. That was yet another 'Story of the Prophets' I should have reviewed in our baraka-endowed book.

The mist built up at the mouth of the well, sluggishly embracing the crowd of frenzied. I raised the staff with one hand as high as I could, and poked the condensed air above me. The mist split into two waves that burst out and washed over the crowd.

They raged and roared. The mist mingled amongst them. Blanketed them.

The roars cut off one by one, replaced with a sea of snores.

"Hold on tight," Shahid said. He carried all four of us out without losing his grip. No discomfort at his clothes being soaking wet.

The clouds cleared as if on cue, rays of moonlight lit the square. Piles of people in tattered clothes were sleeping soundly. Doors creaked in the distance and a few uninfected folk crept out to see what had happened.

"Go gather everyone," Zakiyya said. "We need to make sure everyone in town is cured. We have to account for everyone to make sure none of the frenzied made it out of town." The bewildered spectators ran to obey.

"It worked!" Mariya said, hurling a lumbering, drooling neighbor off her. She was bruised and scratched up, but stood without help. "Hey you," she said, tapping one of the drowsy villagers. "Wake up, you oaf."

"Huh? Honey? What happened . . ." her husband said, the exhaustion of a whole day berserking settling in on him.

"You caused me a lot of trouble. Now come on, we need to retrieve our child," she said, dragging him to his feet. "We're going for run later this like. Like when we first started talking . . ."

Zakiyya followed them. "We need Kedi and our supplies," she said.

Yaqub was the first of the townfolk to stir without intervention. "You did it!" he rasped, rising shakily to his feet. I got him a cup of water from what was left of the well.

I eyed Shahid's flagging form. Finally. So even heroes are human. "Should we wake them or let them sleep?" I asked Yaqub. "Actually, I'll leave that decision to you. Any place we can crash?"

"Not yet," Shahid said as he steadied himself. "We need to make sure everyone is accounted for." Always duty.

Over the course of the next hour, together with the villagers we managed to find everyone. No one had left the village except for the stranger who infected the well. Several of the uninfected had been injured before finding refuge, and a few infected were wounded from efforts to pry open doors. Half the village's livestock was dead, and six people had been killed.

"Not a good result, but better than we hoped. God is merciful," Shahid said. "We need to pursue the stranger. If someone could describe him that would be helpful . . ." He staggered.

"First you need to sleep," I said, grabbing his hand. "Catch some shut-eye before you catch one of the Servants or you'll lose." I didn't believe that. No way he could lose. I was as tired as him, but I wanted to be the responsible one. It was better vengeance than scolding him.

"So much violence. And for what?" he murmured, as he let himself be dragged to Yaqub's place.

"An experiment," Shaykh Nariman piped up when we were alone. "This member of The Servants is testing techniques of turning humans toward his ends. Pursuit is critical."

Zakiyya stroked a sleeping Kedi who flailed away from the south as if caught in a nightmare.

"Our feline friend has some ideas about where to head next." Shaykh Nariman said, lowered his snout to Kedi in deference.

"Tomorrow." I nodded off, praying for a night of nothing-ness.

Instead, I was in the well, gazing up at endless stars.

A massive scaled head obscured my view. A serpentine beast, fully grown.

It dived into the well, fangs and foul breath first. The cobblestones buckled while the water at my feet began to steam.

Chapter 19

Kedi led us reluctantly in the morning.

We were passing by cows nibbling greens when I asked Shahid, "Why does your skin have that yellow sheen to it? Are you secretly ill?"

"It's beeswax," Shahid said in his paper thin voice. "I was born in the far north, where the people are pale as snow, and the sun burns them. Beeswax protects me."

Shahid looked down at me. "Why do you fall so often?"

"He's just clumsy," Shaykh Nariman interjected from the satchel. "It's gotten much worse since, well, umm, since what happened to Baghdad . . ."

"No," Shahid said. "That's not all of it. You might drop things, but it's the falling that is beyond normal."

"I . . ." I gulped. "It has gotten worse, but it's always been more than normal. My parents asked a doctor. He thought maybe my humors or whatever were out of order and that was affecting my balance. Nothing he did worked though."

"I've heard of that—sometimes it's beyond galenic medicine. There is no visible limp so people think you are simply clumsy. But impairments can't always be seen." Shahid grew more quiet, if that were possible. If it hadn't been for the past two days, I wouldn't have imagined he knew anything about impairments.

"It is what it is," I said. "It's not convenient, but I can't control everything."

"You're right about that," Zakkiya muttered. She didn't mean it as a jibe at me. I think.

"Perhaps . . ." Shahid said. "Perhaps many with balance difficulties have trouble because they are meant to be walking in paradise. This world is too uneven." There were wrinkles in his face when he smiled. For a moment the great hero looked more like a cuddly bear.

"I like that," I said, taking extra long, exaggerated steps. "I'm meant to be walking in Heaven!"

"We all belong with God, but don't be so quick to presume your destination, " Shaykh Nariman laughed. "Hope for paradise but never self-congratulate."

He went quiet as we spotted the village at the foot of a hill. Small buildings made from thatch and mossy wood were sprawled around a rectangular, mudbrick mosque in the center. Rows of jagged stones covered nearby fields.

"I know this place," Shaykh Nariman said softly. "Although it's changed. The village is new, but this . . . this is Mudhar."

"What's that?" I asked. A burly man in the road gave an exaggerated wave up ahead. I lagged behind the others so Shaykh Nariman could speak.

"It was the site of a battle centuries ago, during the time of The Servants, though they were only peripherally involved. It should never have happened. So many sides seeking pointless power." He nestled in my stachel.

I sniffed: a few old incense smells came from the graveyards. I was about to mention that to Shaykh Nariman when the large, welcoming man approached. "Are you travelers in need of anything?" His grin was wider than his face.

"Actually, some water would be great," I said. The last proper drink I had drove me crazy. I was parched.

" I have a fresh waterskin on me," the man said, gesturing to a bulging pack looped to his belt. He took one glance at my dry, cracked lips, and ripped the knot holding the waterskin to his waist. "Here." He uncapped it.

He shoved it toward me, but when it was within my grasp, he continued pushing, forcibly fitting the opening into my mouth and slamming my head back so the water drained down my throat. He squeezed the bag so the flow increased, and pinched my nose shut.

I sputtered and failed to cough; my esophagus clogged with water. I was drowning while standing on dry land.

Is this it? I'm going to be killed by kindness gone wrong? His grip was like iron. "Drink up! Drink up!" he said amiably.

Shahid was ten meters ahead and totally ignorant of my impending death until Kedi growled and turned back. I was glad to know our cat, at least, cared about me.

"We have to save him!" Zakiyya yelled. "His dying thoughts are too dumb. "

She tried to rip the man's hand away. When that failed, she tore her nails into the immense waterskin. Shaykh Nariman nibbled the man's fingers, but the bleeding didn't stop him.

Shahid barrelled back. Several villagers appeared behind him. It took their combined effort to pull the burly man off me.

The waterskin slipped from his grasp. Its remaining contents sloshed into the parched earth. First the corrupted well water now this. I was not having good experiences with waterskins.

I couldn't cheer in relief. I couldn't breath. Zakiyya slammed her palm into my chest and I spewed and spat.

"Thanks," I croaked.

"We're so sorry," a burly woman among the townsfolk said. "We didn't realize my brother had gone crazy too. He's not a bad man, I promise." She held him to the ground as she spoke. Another townsperson grabbed a shovel and thwapped the man's head hard enough to knock him out—but not crack his thick skull. The shovel-bearer dragged my assailant away.

I coughed. "What's going on here?"

"It began yesterday," the woman said, eyes trailing after her brother. "He—

"Harris is an angel, it makes no sense—" a villager interjected.

"This is a friendly place—"

"Jinn possession, it has to be jinn possession—"

The villagers talked over each other and we couldn't make sense of anything.

I cleared my throat but didn't have the strength in my lungs to quiet them. Shahid spoke but his timid voice was drowned out.

Zakiyya clapped her hands together and bellowed, "Please, one at a time!"

Zakiyya sobered the crowd a little too much. She made them realize they were telling outsiders all about their troubles. Everyone was speaking and now everyone was silent.

"My poor little brother was a victim of that man, and we'd like an explanation," she coaxed them. I tried to complain at being called the younger sibling again, but a cough foiled me.

"We're not here by accident," Zakiyya continued. "There were attacks in a nearby village and we came from there, worried that they might have spread."

"What kind of attacks?" the heavily muscled woman asked, turning toward where they were heaving her brother.

"You first," Zakiyya said.

The woman faced us, took a deep breath, and glared at other villages before they could interrupt.

"My name is Ayesha. I'm sorry that this happened to you. And I apologize on behalf of my brother.

First of all, you should know that we're a friendly people. A battle happened here a long time ago—and nothing has happened since! Attacking outsiders is not something we would do—ever. There's a madness here. A sudden madness. And we don't know where it's coming from.

It started yesterday, as far as I can tell. Harris is the town head. He's not old, and he won't accept any title, but we all give him that respect. He's the sort who would give an arm and a leg for a stranger, let alone for his neighbors. His wife Summayyah said he brought food to a few of the sick elderly folk in the morning, then went out to feed the livestock of a friend who was out of town. He came into the mosque after, before noon prayer, acting as if there wasn't copious amounts of blood dripping from his clothes onto the carpet.

When the imam asked him if he was alright, Harris said yes with his cheerful smile, and offered to help the imam with plugging leaks in the roof. The imam tried to say no, to tell Harris to wash up and see his family. He couldn't see any wound on Harris, but the blood was everywhere. Harris ignored him and plucked out his hammer, nails, and plywood from the usual spot, and when the imam attempted to pull him outside . . . Harris hammered the plywood into the imam's hand.

My brother Jawad and I, along with a few others—we heard the imam's scream. By the time we tore Harris off of him, he'd punctured the imam with at least four or five nails. 'All fixed!' he said, over and over, a beatific smile plastered on his face. It's the freakiest thing I've ever seen.

Before passing out, the imam managed to explain what happened, to tell us some of the blood on Harris wasn't his.

My brother and I wanted to find out where that blood came from. Sumayyah is a strong woman. She suggested checking the friend's livestock which her husband looked after. We found all the animals butchered, the carcasses lying on the barn's floor split into red, raw chunks.

We locked Harris up in his house. He kept crying out, asking for the opportunity to help. Questions about his actions didn't register with him at all, and the imam wasn't in a state to do an exorcism.

A couple hours later, when Harris' voice finally went hoarse from all the shouting, we got another shock.

Sarah is a righteous young woman. I've known her since she was little, and it's been a pleasure to see her grow up. She was a kind girl, who never hurt a fly. I mean that—she accidentally squashed a bug once and brought it to us cupped in her hands asking if we could heal it.

She isn't much different as an adult; she took in two orphans after their parents passed away and showers those kids with love. She works as a midwife with a perfect record delivering live babies, and she does extra healing around town without asking for any pay.

She was going on her rounds yesterday, checking up on a pregnant friend, overseeing the elderly, and then quietly treating the imam. Afterward, she tended to Yaseen the Tailor, whose leg had been fractured in a fall. Then she offered a remedy to an aunty with a rickety cough, and went home. The pregnant friend came by Sarah's place to drop off sweets in gratitude.

She ran inside when she heard the screams. Sarah was supposed to be cutting her kids' hair, but instead she was tearing every follicle out. Their scalps were leaking red. Had we not arrived in time, she might have drilled into their skulls. We couldn't grab her because of the knife in her hand, but my brother threw a vase at her, and it knocked her out.

Jawad and I went to check on the imam, and it turned out his throat was slit. By Sarah.

Yaseen, the tailor, had passed out when she bent his leg until the bone showed, and the aunty with the cough never woke up after drinking that remedy.

My brother retraced all her remaining steps to check and make sure that the elderly folk she'd visited weren't harmed. I don't know why, but I had a bad feeling about it. Jawad is a responsible enough guy, but he has a tendency to overdo things—to bite off more than he can chew. But he was alright when he came home; he went straight to sleep.

We prayed at home rather than in the mosque this morning—the blood stains on the carpet were still too fresh. After we finished, I asked him to clean the kitchen—it was his turn. We'd stuck to a schedule since we were kids. I went back to sleep, but there were noises that bled into my dreams. When I got up, I found the kitchen was smashed apart. Pots and pans cracked, cupboards splintered, grain coating everything. I figured that the madness had seized my brother too.

He hadn't stepped into our mother's room, thank God.

I went out to find him, rounding up others to help. And that was when I saw this little boy drowning." She concluded her account breathlessly, gesturing at me.

The situation was too somber for Zakiyya to quip about me being a little boy.

Shahid tried to reassure her in the barest whisper, "I am trained to do an exorcism."

Shaykh Nariman wiggled in my satchel, banging his paws against the Stories of the Prophets book, so I spoke up, my voice still froggy. "It's probably sihr-dark magic. I don't think it involves jinn . . ."

"We specialize in this sort of thing," Zakiyya said. "Tell me, did anyone strange visit town yesterday? And do you have a well?"

Ayesha turned toward the other members of the crowd. "We can't say anything about a strange visitor," Ayesha said, "but we get our water from the stream, it draws from the Tigris. Why? Is that important?"

"The well was poisoned in the last town we visited," Zakiyya said. "But poisoning a moving body of water would be hard. Let's take a look at the people driven mad. Harris, Sarah, and Jawad, right?"

Ayesha inclined her head and led us toward Harris' house. The village had no prison.

"It's possible that 'The Servant' poisoned them directly," Zakiyya whispered as we walked. "I mean, this incident is different from the last one. People aren't going on an animalistic, violent rampage. They're normally good people who seem to think they're still doing good . . . while doing evil."

"So a typical human rampage then," I suggested.

Zakiyya shrugged. Ayesha ushered us into the receiving

chamber with the three berserk folk. "Make sure to stand back," she said. "They scratched up the last person who got too close. Said they wanted to get rid of his wart or something, and took off a lot of skin instead."

Two young men stood guard within the chamber, cudgels in their hands. Harris, Sarah, and Jawad were chained up to posts driven into the ground, through the floorboards and into the dirt.

My throat went dry seeing the man who shoved water down my throat. He was seated, unconscious, his head slumped forward.

"You're new to Madhar, darling. Can I show you around?" Sarah yelled, making me jump. She had a white-toothed smile plastered on her face and big eyes which bore into Zakiyya. "You're not too much older than my little munchkins. I can introduce you and you can have some fun together!" she strained against her bonds.

"If you're looking for work, I could use a man of your strength to help with new construction," Harris said, reaching a hand out to grasp Shahid's shoulder.

"So their desire to help has intensified to the point of obsession, and instead of helping, they try to destroy." I edged back toward the door and away from the ecstatic, leering faces.

Shahid walked close to the maniacs; the guards rushed forward to stop him but he lifted a hand in the air and gestured for them to back off. They listened—his silence was more commanding than his speech.

He touched the prisoners one by one, praying softly as he dodged their attempt to grab him.

After half an hour of standing there, virtually dancing in place. Shahid spoke up. He was quiet as leaves rustling in a faint breeze. "I can't purify them for some reason. Whatever is affecting them is stronger than in the last case . . ."

The guards slouched in disappointment. They were herders, not prison keepers.

"We have to find the source," Zakiyya said. "Maybe that will help with curing them.They all started going wild at different times, so it doesn't seem like the poisoner went to each of them. He infected something and it infected them. And it probably wasn't the stream . . ."

"Can I get a list of all the places you know they visited?" she asked Ayesha, who was staring at her brother, her lips set in a thin line.

"Oh, I can tell you where everyone went!" Sarah screeched gleefully. "Hell, the bottom of the sea, over the edge of a cliff, under the butcher's knife . . ."

"Oh," Ayesha stumbled out of her reverie. "The places they visited . . . I can show you. Let's see—"

"Don't worry about it anymore," Zakiyya said. Ayesha's thoughts were sufficient. "You keep an eye on Jawad. I know what it's like to worry about your brother." She rolled her eyes in my direction. That earned her a pained smile on Ayesha's face.

We started with the mosque. We pushed through the pseudo-sandalwood doors and caught a whiff of lyme. The imam's bereaved wife was on all fours, scrubbing the turquoise carpet by the mihrab—the prayer niche . Her eyes were puffy and dry, her tears mingled with the water she used to wash out the blood.

Kedi hopped out of Shahid's arms. We waited with bated breath for her to start growling; instead, she rubbed against the woman and meowed. The woman dropped the bucket and cloth, and clutched our warm lump of fur for dear life.

Zakiyya ran over to the woman. They spoke in hushed voices.

Zakiyya recapped the conversation when we left; her face shadowed by the woman's anguish. "Everyone in town wants to do things for her, but she wants the mosque clean so people can pray here again, right away. Pray for her husband . . ."

We headed to Harris' friend's barn. We passed through leafy green pastures and hopped on smooth stepping stones across a crystalline stream.

There were red handprints on the barn door.

The butchered animals were gone, cleared away by the villagers. Red streaks crisscrossed the walls of the barn, telling the story of what happened. The leftover smell of iron and putrefaction was overpowering. Kedi took a lap without reacting, taking care to avoid the sickening puddles. Shahid retrieved her and cradled her in one arm, more at ease than when he first held her. He didn't have to readjust his grip once. She fell asleep.

We trekked back across the stream and my right foot slipped on a wet stepping stone. I plummeted backward toward the water. Before I could drown in minimal water yet again, Shahid caught me with his free hand.

"Walking in paradise, are you?" he whispered.

I regained my feet. "Should we check out the old graveyard? Shaykh Nariman said a battle happened there during the lives of The Servants, maybe—"

Shaykh Nariman interrupted me with a squeak. "There won't be anything of interest there. I can't imagine the Servants returning to such a site and the townsfolk would not visit enough for an infection to spread."

"If not the graveyard, then there's a chance something is

the source of infection in the home of one of the old people in the village," Zakiyya said. "Harris brought them food, Sarah visited their homes. And Jawad, the one who attacked you, retraced her visits. The home of one of them could be the spot that all of the mad, infected people have in common."

Zakiyya made a few inquiries, and then led us to the homes of the elderly. They all had that traditional old people smell, a complex aroma of warmth, nostalgia, home, and worry. We were greeted with pastries and sherbets that we turned down for the sake of time.

At the fourth house, the residence of the oldest man in town, Kedi growled.

"Everyone, stay back," Shahid mumbled. He went to the door alone and knocked three times, then stepped back half as far as the rest of us.

"Achoo!" Zakiyya sneezed while we waited. She rubbed the bottom of her hooked nose.

"Can you stop?" she asked, her lime green eyes boring into me.

"Stop what?"

"You keep thinking that my nose is hooked," She said. "Where I can hear you. I'm kind of . . . well, I've heard thoughts about it my whole life. And a lot of remarks too."

"Really?" I asked. "You're actually telling me how you feel? I would have expected you to have hit me because of it earlier."

"That would have just drawn more attention—" she stopped as the door creaked open.

We were hailed by a wizened man with decrepit limbs and sagging skin, his scraggly white beard swaying in the breeze. Kedi began to squirm and popped out of Shahid's arms, snarling with bared teeth. More tiger than kitten.

"So many visitors these days," the old man said. "Welcome, how may I help you?"

"So many visitors?" Zakiyya asked. "Who? Sarah? Harris?"

The old man looked at her blankly. "Names don't stick too well anymore. But there was a man checking how I was doing yesterday, a woman who helped me with walking exercises, a man who brought food, and a merchant who didn't sell anything."

"He was visited by everyone," Zakiyya whispered. Out loud she said, "What's this about a merchant?"

"Man came to my door, early, early morning yesterday. He had loose, flowing clothes. Though he might have been a sailor, a merchant come from down south. Don't think I'd ever seen him before, but not too good with faces anymore. Said he wanted to sell something. Asked if folk visit me often to help out. I said yes, more or less. Then he shook my hand real, real tight, and walked away without saying what he wanted to sell."

"That's him," Zakiyya whispered. "One of The Servants. And I can see him! His thoughts are murky, but I caught a face." She asked Shahid to borrow his parchment and baraka-laden quill and left us to continue the conversation while she doodled what she'd seen.

"Did you feel different after that man left?" I asked.

"Not particularly," the old man said. "Do you want to come inside? My knees are starting to hurt from standing so long."

"I—can't come inside, sorry," I began, but Shahid put a hand up to stop me.

"I'll come inside," he said, his voice barely audible beneath Kedi's snarling. The closer he got to the old man, the more furiously Kedi strained against his grasp. When he was within arm's reach, the cat burst out of his arms.

"I think you may have been infected by the merchant," Shahid said calmly. He clasped the old man's fragile hands. "Yes . . ." he murmured. "Did the other visitors touch you at all?

"The men shook my hand, the woman helped me flex my knee . . . What's this about being infected? I'm sick?"

"No. I don't think you're sick. But you're contagious," Shahid said. "Give me a moment."

Shahid prayed as he held the man's hands. I could make out a soft white light, as gentle as Shahid himself, glimmering from his palms.

Kedi sought refuge behind Zakiyya's squatting form. I peaked over her shoulder—baraka quill or not, she was not a good artist. The face she was scrawling looked more like an elephant than a person. She blushed and started over.

I plucked Kedi up by the collar. Kedi didn't exactly purr when we approached the old man this time, but she didn't try to escape either. She looked up at him and then Shahid with hesitant feline curiosity.

"He's cured?" I asked.

"I think so," Shahid said gently. "And I think . . . With him purified, whatever curse is on the victims should be easier to remove. I have an idea." He ran off ahead of us.

I muttered apologies to the old man, and Zakiyya abandoned her art project with a sigh. Kedi protested the rapid movement as she jostled in my arms. "I promise, I'll let you nap after this is done." She kept squirming and mewled.

Shahid barged into the room where the infected were being held, startling the guards. "I've figured out how to treat them, don't worry," Shahid waved away their concern. This time his words were commanding enough.

Shahid grabbed something from his waist and moved from patient to patient, chanting loudly. Zakiyya and I panted as we crossed the threshold. I failed to figure out the verses as I caught my breath.

Zakiyya followed Shahid while I went to examine the first infected Shahid had treated. The patient, Harris, was silent after the treatment, except for a slight gurgling noise. It took me a long second to process the neat, red streak at his neck, and locate the crystalline knife in Shahid's hand, tearing into Sarah's exposed throat.

"What're you—" Zakiyya angled to get a better view.

"Get away from him!" I shouted, dropping Kedi and drawing the staff like a sword.

Shahid turned to Zakiyya

"Ah yes," he said, "You're sick too, aren't you?"

She dodged his first swipe on instinct. Droplets of glistening blood from the knife splashed onto her.

I leapt through the air after them, and tripped on a loose tileupon landing. I dug the staff into the ground to regain my balance.

Zakiyya dodged the second swipe, then a third, but Shahid was more skilled than any bandit or thug. The fourth strike was a feint. It didn't matter if she could read it; the follow-up took her in the chest. She froze, staring at the hilt buried into her, sagging to her knees.

He ripped out the gleaming blade. Her blood welled up, soaking her clothes, dripping to the floor. Dripping, leaking, pouring.

"He wasn't thinking of violence . . ." she whispered as I bowled into Shahid with the staff. This could not be happening.

This could not be happening. This could not be—

The blow did nothing beyond ripping his shirt. He looked at me curiously, his head tilted. Like I was a new kind of insect.

The guards stormed the room. I swung the staff again, scoring a blow on his elbow, but he ignored it and stomped toward the entrance.

He bumped into my satchel as he brushed by me. His step faltered.

"Wha—what—" he said, eyeing the blood on his hands, dropping his knife.

"He got infected too!" the guards yelled, seizing him by the shoulders..

"Wait, what happened—" he sputtered, looking down at Zakiyya, bleeding out. Her mouth was moving furiously—whether she was trying to get out one final quip or prayer, I don't know.

Kedi nuzzled against her, meowing desperately. She'd been trying to warn us since we left the old man.

"What have I done . . ." Shahid stammered, despair etched into his very being. The blessed fragrance of daisies that always clung to him faded as his cries intensified.

"Stop her bleeding!" Shaykh Nariman squealed without regard for the guards hearing him.

I grabbed a piece of Shahid's torn shirt and wrapped it around her wound, pulling tight.

"Don't die, don't die." The blood seeped through my makeshift bandage. "God, please don't let her die. I'll do anything."

Zakiyya's breathing slowed. I expected her to stand up, to brush off the wound like she did the wicked book's fire. To laugh at me for worrying.

Her breathing stopped.

Shahid's cries ended abruptly. He turned to me. There was fear in his eyes, guilt. And then the emotions were gone. All that remained was a cold emptiness. Not a soft quiet like his voice, but something hard, sharp.

The gray in his irises looked like gravestones.

"I didn't expect to be back *here*," he said, his voice at a normal volume for once. A twisted grin contorted his face. "It's good to see you, Nariman."

Shahid surged forward, pushing at the guards, flinging them away like they were toys. He launched himself at me.

This could not be happening.

I grabbed the staff, ready for an attack.

No blow came. Instead, he unlatched the zambil, that bag of Khidr with a seemingly infinite storage capacity, and released its drawstring. He caught my staff in the bag's mouth and it went right through, into the dark depths. The opening widened as it got closer, until it consumed me too.

My eyes swept around the floor of the bloody room one last time as I was drawn into the bag, but Zakiyya and Kedi were gone.

Then the room disappeared altogether and I sailed into two voids.

Interlude

Khurafa's voice tapered off.

The large vulture stayed still, watching with cold eyes, but its smaller companion spread its wings, engulfing Khurafa in shadow.

Khurafa sighed. "Bite, strike. It hurt more then, you know. And talking about it . . . "

The vulture leaned in. Khurafa didn't blink. It wasn't the vulture he was seeing.

"I fell into the darkness. But this was the second time. I remember the first. For two months, in every waking moment, I relived it.

My parents wouldn't leave. They knew the city might fall, knew the hordes were at our doors. But they wouldn't give up on the flowers.

'We can't just let them wither and die,' they said, the day the siege began.

When the situation didn't change, when my father heard that the Abbasid soldiers melted in the fields, he tried to send me and my mother away. But there was nowhere to send us anymore, no safe route out.

And my mom wouldn't go anyway. 'When the end of the world comes,' she quoted the Prophet, peace be upon him, 'and you're planting a tree, finish planting that tree.'

She planted a sapling right by the entrance the morning the siege broke. The horseman trampled it the moment he charged in.

The thundering of hooves made it seem like the earth was shaking. I lost my balance, and by the time I got up again, the flowers were bathed in blood.

The horseman had dropped his sword. His mouth was agape and his eyes glistened. He wasn't looking at my parents' bodies, still embracing one another protectively, crumpled on the ground. He was seeing the flowers, and the orange tree, all the beautiful things they'd made and nurtured over the years. It took his breath away, and he turned his horse and left. Not noticing me claw to my feet.

If he'd paid attention to the flowers a few moments earlier, how different would things have been? Would I have had that dream in the first place?

Would Zakiyya have been stabbed? Would I have fallen into the bag at all?"

IV

Falling

Chapter 20

I slammed into the wrecked remnants of a vase. Ceramic shards crumpled beneath my back; few broke skin. Pain was welcome. Beneath the fragments, the ground was soft, almost velvet. I pushed myself up with a groan and stared.

I was in a cavern, but instead of subterranean stone, every surface was dark fabric. The sky was black cloth, the floor was black cloth, the world was endless stitching. Dim light permeated through the threading. On the outside the zambil's opening was a small hole closed by a drawstring. From within it was wider than a castle's gate. But it was shut tight.

The strangeness of the supernatural space should have left me in silent awe or excited laughter. I should have run to explore its every nook and cranny, plotted mischievously on how to escape. But instead the cloth suffocated me.

I choked on loss.

The image played before my eyes again and again, a ghostly apparition against the black canvas. Zakiyya, bleeding out. Zakiyya and Kedi, gone.

My sobbing brought me to my knees. *But what if she fell into the bag too? What if she's here? Maybe she can hear my thoughts, hear my mourning and is snickering at it. But no, she'd been stabbed, she needs care, she needs—*

With the desperation of a wounded animal I searched. There was no sign of her arrival—not even a drop of blood. I found rubble and clean bones from a massive creature; the femur was as tall as me, and the rib cage could have been a house. I was too focused to even wonder what killed it.

Nothing, nothing, nothing.

The fabric void muffled my screams.

I'd never been mad at God before. Not when my parents had died, not when the Mongols had torn my world away. On our journey all I ultimately found—even in the worst times—was hope. A reason, a purpose, finally, to exist. A duty. Something that made sense. But there I was. My journey at an end. Not just because I was trapped but because my companion—my *sister*—was gone.

Shaykh Nariman moaned. I hadn't heard him earlier, hadn't remembered to check if he'd been hurt on impact.

"It's going to be alright," He said through clenched teeth. "It's going to be alright, my boy. You'll see. After difficulty comes ease."

I wanted to yell again, to scream once more. But I didn't have the energy for it. I looked toward the crack of light streaming from the opening, from the entrance to my prison. Maybe I could open it. Maybe I'd find Zakiyya staring down at the zambil with a look of amusement masking her concern. Kedi would be scratching at the bag trying to get us out. And Shahid—I couldn't think about Shahid.

Nothing I did worked. I pulled, tugged, tore, but none of my actions had any effect. I hammered my hands into oblivion.

Despair dug its claws in deep. I knew what was happening, knew it was irrational to be so defeatist so fast. I should've slapped myself and called myself pathetic. *There's always a way out. There's always a way if we think cleverly enough, work hard enough, pray and plead with God enough.* I just didn't have the will to do so anymore. Every horror that I'd bottled up with tasteless humor leaked out. I'd seen too much death, too much blood. What happened to Zakiyya was the breaking point.

"What about the staff?" Shaykh Nariman asked. It took a moment for his words to pierce my storm cloud. *The staff.* I could split the entrance open.

I scrambled through the rubble and found the end sticking out from beneath driftwood and an enormous, elongated skull. I pulled out the staff, ready to tear cloth apart, when I heard a footstep. Even against the fabric floor, it was heavy.

I barely avoided the borz's claw. The air whistled where my head had been.

I slipped on one of the driftwood pieces and landed on my butt. The borz howled above. The wolf-headed, hairy humanoid that Shahid had trapped in the bag, dove in for the kill.

I'd gone through too many emotions in too short a time. Grief, desperation, and now a profound numbness at the sight of the nightmarish creature. Did I have it in me to fight?

I didn't have to find out.

There was a twang and the air sang. The borz toppled backwards. In the time it took me to blink, someone had shot an arrow into the creature's brain.

"If you were going to use that to break out of here, I wouldn't," a woman's voice said. It was rich and even, heavy but not sultry.

"You were using him as bait Sajda?" a man's voice interjected. It was nasally but good-natured, more amused than chastising.

"I was about to apologize to him and explain where he is. Though I'm curious as to how he got here," the woman, Sajda, said.

"He was traveling with Shahid," a third voice interjected. This one was fierce and passionate, raw fire made into spoken word.

They stepped into the dim light. The woman was dark skinned and lithe, with high cheekbones. Her gray eyes shone in the distance. The first man was short and stocky, his brown skin speckled with thick black hair. He had dimples when he smiled. The second man was tall and bony with a flat face and thin brows. His right hand was open, raised in welcome.

"Who are you?" I asked. But I'd already figured it out—I could smell them now; shock had made me forget to use my nose earlier. The gentle sugary scent of violets, the rough leathery odor of saffron, and the earthen aroma of chrysanthemums, mixed with other weaker smells. I also caught a whiff of the spicy stack flower, but its flavor was faded.

"I'm Sajda. This is Zawar," the woman said, pointing to the jovial, stocky brown man, "and that's Saim," she said, gesturing towards the bony man with the fiery personality. "We are members of the Five Pillars."

"I imagine you've been looking for us," Saim said.

***

A bout of concentrated sniffing confirmed that neither Zakiyya nor Kedi were in the bag—no catnip, and no honey-suckles. Finding out that the people Shahid had been looking for were right by him, inside the zambil the whole time was a shock, but I had no time to process. I knew there was no way Zakiyya could have survived that wound for this long—and she'd vanished from my vision even before I'd been sucked into the bag—but I had to reach her. I moved to slam my staff into the fabric.

The tip struck a shaft of wood which instantly splintered.

"I told you to wait," Sajda said, her smile dangerous, her bow loose in her hands.

"You slam that staff into the ground now and you'll end up killing a lot of people," Saim exclaimed.

"I can't wait—" I began.

It was Shaykh Nariman who shut me up. "Listen to them, son."

I glared at the group, refusing to let my frustration be worn away by the warm intensity of their fragrant baraka.

"I presume you have control over the staff," Saim said, edging closer cautiously. "But this isn't normal cloth. If we were shrunk to fit in the actual, physical bag, we'd feel it move. But we don't. Somehow this is another realm, another dimension. If you successfully split the 'cloth,' it might tear the whole dimension apart. And everything in the zambil will be unleashed into the world."

"What do you mean everything?" I scowled.

"Monsters. Dozens of dangerous creatures trapped here, waiting to feed," she said.

I weighed the deaths the monsters could cause against Zakiyya's life, which was almost certainly over already. I had a duty to keep people safe, not to endanger them . . .

But screw duty. There were too many ashes, too much death. I slammed the staff toward the ground a second time, ready for the world to burn as long as my world, for once, was intact.

The staff was wrenched from my grasp before it struck the ground. Saim held it with his left hand and wrapped his right arm around me. I hadn't seen him move.

I wrestled against his grip futilely. He may have been bony, but he was strong.

"Shh, it'll be okay," he whispered as if I were a baby having a tantrum. I struggled, thinking of the blood leaking out of Zakiyya. Why hadn't I seen her when I was sucked in?

"What was she risking her life for? Do you want to dishonor that?" Shaykh Nariman demanded as I tired myself out.

I stopped resisting only when my muscles gave out. "How did you all end up here? And how can all those monsters be alive?" I asked the three pillars.

Their baraka allured me, urged me toward ease, but I'd been taken in before. By their friend. Shahid.

"Second question first," Zawar said with his perpetual smile. "The zambil was used for storage long ago. Things were organized in here and preserved. Somehow. Several generations ago, one of the first incarnations of the Five Pillars inherited the zambil. Over time, the skills of succeeding generations . . . lessened in comparison to their predecessors. The zambil offered a way to trap creatures when they couldn't be easily defeated. The bag can't be opened from the inside and the user has to willingly take something out—we can't just slip out the opening. Since the monster trapping began, no one has tried to remove anything."

My interest was piqued despite my restless anger, but I tapped my foot in impatient protest.

"Whatever preserved items also preserves *living* things," Zawar continued. "The creatures trapped here still needed sustenance, though less than they would outside. And what do you know—ample food from generations past was stored here. Or at least, it used to be ample. Since we ended up here, we've been working on eliminating the monsters—partly to survive, partly because it's what we do, but I won't lie, sometimes it boils down to competition for food."

It occurred to me that they probably had martial and mystical skills to match Shahid's. Sajda's skill with the bow was proof. The meaning of their earlier conversation hit me. "You used me as bait," I accused them. "You knew the borz was around, you knew I'd entered after you heard my screams. And you figured it would attack me and expose itself . . ."

"You're a sharp one." Sajda gave me a toothy grin. "Seems you have some experience hunting—or being hunted."

"He does," Saim said, raising an affirming fist.

"How do you know?" I asked. Zakiyya would be mad she wasn't the only mind reader. But Zakiyya was no longer around

. . .

"I can hear through the entrance crack," he explained. "I have a firsat that allows for an enhanced perception of sounds. I caught snippets of your journey and learned about the staff."

"So you've been watching me—listening to us. Then tell me, why is Shahid pretending to look for you? What's his motive? Why did he trap me here—and why are you here?" I burst out.

"We don't know," Sajda said, her grin dying.

"Are you going to act ignorant like he did, then attack me?" The accusation felt stupid even before it was off my tongue. Sajda had just slain a monster. None of them were in the bag voluntarily. "And wasn't there supposed to be one more of you?" I asked. The weaker aroma of stack bothered me.

"There used to be." Saim's fiery tone cooled.

Zawar reached over to pat him on the back. "We were hunting a filshad—it's a creature that—"

"I know what a filshad is," I interrupted, finally making

sense of the massive bones scattered around, recalling how Shahid had described it: a giant, hairy, elephant-like creature.

"Well then," Zawar said amiably, "that makes this easier. I always find it difficult to explain monsters. We were hunting a filshad, and while making camp we got news about the fall of Baghdad. We were all shaken by the news and then the filshad struck. Shahid caught its trunk in the zambil in one try—he moved faster than I'd ever seen. Before we could cheer, he turned on us."

Zawar's eagerness went from stale. "He caught Sadeeqa—the remaining pillar—with the zambil first. We paused longer than we should have. It seemed like an accident. But then he leapt at Saim and Sajda . . . " He broke off with a deep breath.

"We landed in the bag like you did," Sajda said, "except there was a raging filshad waiting for us. It thrashed around when it landed, its gigantic trunk, its mountainous body flailing—and Sadeeqa was struck before she hit the ground. She didn't make it." Sajda's eyes twitched.

"Since then we've been trapped here, killing monsters, wondering what the hell happened to Shahid," Saim chimed in. "Every time I checked the entrance, it seemed like he didn't know what he'd done, like he was as confused as the rest of us. Until now, apparently."

The three of them gave me a meaningful look and I summarized what had happened in the past few days. My grunts were expanded by Shaykh Nariman's interjections; the sight of a talking jinn-mouse didn't phase them, though I can't imagine many things would after spending months in a baraka-laden bag's pocket dimension.

"The Servants' poisoning affected Shahid," Sajda thought aloud after Shaykh Nariman and I finished. "We need to be out there doing something, and we now have the means to get out—but we have to make sure nothing escapes with us first." She glanced at my staff resting in Saim's palm then plucked the arrow from the borz's head.

She rubbed the gray mush on the arrowhead against the fabric floor.

Chapter 21

"Let's go hunt monsters," I said. My back stung from the ceramic shards, but I ignored it.

The three pillars looked at me: Sajda raising a finely arched brow, Zawar squinting hard, and Saim squirming in discomfort.

"We've trained to fight since youth. Each of us is an expert with multiple weapons and has our own specialty," Zawar said, his friendly demeanor becoming serious. "Some of us have firsats which are useful in combat, others have tools that are baraka-imbued."

He unsheathed his sword. I caught a whiff of polygonatum. The blade was the total opposite of its humble abode, a jewel encrusted line of gold highlighting its dull silver edge.

"This is khurmehr." He admired the blade. "The sword of Solomon. Items can be invested with baraka by use. But a blade usually can't contain blessings. Swords are designed for violence. When wielded by righteous men to implement justice and protect the innocent, on rare occasions they can—"

Sajda interrupted, "That's off topic, Zawar."

"Oh right." His excitement dampened. "I'll tell you about the sacred swords later. We have skills, weapons, tools, training in using the medical sciences—knowledge of the humors—to enhance our abilities. You have the staff but it can't be wielded to fight here because you might accidentally rip the zambil open too early. I'm sorry my young friend, but you're useless here."

"I don't want to be useless!" I said, too deflated to muster a counterargument this time.

He was right. I hadn't been able to do anything when Zakiyya was attacked.

Sajda tapped a finger against her chin. "We don't have the time or conditions to train you fully in the humors, but I can give you a crash course."

"That could kill the boy! And we don't have the appropriate supplies—" Saim huffed.

"You doubt my caution?" Sajda asked, a smile ruining her mock affront.

After her stunt with the borz, I did doubt her caution, but I wasn't going to cripple a gift horse.

She continued. "Remember what our Master would say—to make someone feel useless, to destroy their pride, is as bad as attacking them. Besides, we *could* use the help." Seems everyone had a teacher spouting unsolicited wisdom.

Zawar shrugged but there was a wry smile on his lips. "Let me know when you want to give a demonstration."

Saim shook his head and muttered something about tracking prey and not wanting to be part of a child's death. He stalked off with my staff.

Sajda turned to me. She could see the pain etched on my face. "Action is a great way through grief," she said. "But talking helps too."

"I want to get out of here . . ." I said. I wanted to hurt something, and monsters seemed like the right target. "Teach me now, please."

Sajda ruffled my hair then bent her knees so we were face to face. "That's not how we do things. There is no baraka in unbounded anger or revenge. Think of why you embarked on this journey in the first place. You wished to protect people, for the sake of God. And now you know firsthand how at risk the world is. Fight to carry on your friend's will, not get revenge for her."

Zakiyya's will? To do what is right because we want what is right? To steal? To pick on me? To roll her eyes at—

I didn't say anything, couldn't say anything. The possibility of fighting reanimated me, but suddenly I couldn't stop the tears. *I'm a mess, aren't I? I almost endangered how many innocents? At least no one can hear my idiotic ramblings anymore . . .*

Sajda wrapped me in her wiry arms and let me sob myself into silence. I wiped my eyes and eased myself out of her clumsy embrace.

"Teach me," I said.

***

"You're familiar with the four humors?" Sajda asked.

"I learned about them once . . . Phlegm, bile . . ." I mumbled, trying to reconstruct what Shaykh Nariman taught me ages ago.

"The four humors are four vital substances in our bodies: blood, yellow bile, black bile, and phlegm. Most medicine involves putting them into balance. When there is too much of one and not enough of another, a person gets sick," she said. "You're a gardener, correct?"

"How do you know that?" I tensed.

"Because of your hands," she said. "The shape of the

calluses suggest planting and pruning tools. Despite the rough work, you cut your nails clean—to avoid dirt accumulating. You know that gardening is also about balance—not too much water, but not too little. The perfect amount of fertilizer. The proper amount of sunlight. People are the same way, balance the humors and their associated states—wet and dry, cold and hot—and you maintain health." Clearly Shahid was not the smart one in the Five pillars.

"Associated states?" I asked. What was that?

"Ah yeah . . . That's going to be too much for you to remember right now. It might be easier if I draw a diagram for you." She pulled out aged parchment, a pen, and dried ink. "You can find anything in the zambil." She gestured to the dark fabric sky.

She drew a diamond and cut it into four quadrants. She wrote 'blood' on the left corner and 'black bile' on the right. 'Phlegm' on the bottom, 'yellow bile' on the top. She drew symbols for the elements—a curl for wind under blood, a series of rocks for black bile, drops of water for phlegm, and a small flame for yellow bile. On the upper left side of the diamond, she scribbled the word 'hot,' on the upper right the word 'dry,' on the lower left the word 'wet,' and on the lower right, the word 'cold.'

"Everything is about balance," she started over. "Blood is connected to air, it's hot, and wet, black bile is connected to earth, it's cold and dry. Phlegm is associated with water, it's wet and cold. Yellow bile is associated with fire—hot and dry. The vital substances need to be balanced for us to live healthy lives and maintain emotional stability. Imbalance is dangerous, and if sustained, leads to death."

"So what, you're a doctor? You'll teach me to heal?" I

scoffed.That knowledge had come too late.

"I am a healer, in addition to many other things," Sajda said, "but that's not what I'm going to teach you. Imbalance—too much of one substance, is dangerous, but it can also give preternatural powers. Boundless energy and speed, immense strength, impenetrable defense, genius-level intellect. With imbalance you can burn things with your bare hands or freeze them, you can dry and age a plant, or renew its lease on life. The challenge is two-fold—causing imbalance, but mastering the control not to go too far."

So that's was what Shahid was doing when he manipulated the heat in his body to boil the well water. I clenched my fists."How do I master this?"

"Master is too strong a word for what I can teach," Sajda said. "Usually, we manipulate humors through the ingestion of foods and medicine that have properties relating to them. We meditate to develop a hyper awareness of our body. Slowly, steadily, we learn to simulate what the substances can do—causing rapid imbalance and then restoration. That method develops excellent control, and it's safe, but it takes months if not years."

"So what are you going to do?" I asked. I didn't have that kind of time. If Zakiyya was alive, if I was going to stop Shahid, and the Servants—

"The other way to develop some control of the humors is to experience extreme imbalance in every way possible, and come back from it. This process instills a natural feel for the humors within you. If you survive it, it allows for modest brute force control," she said.

"And that's the price of speed or strength? A risk of death and less control?" I asked. Nothing more than I'd already faced.

"Say any final words now," Sajda said, as she grabbed my arm.

I opened my mouth but before I could ask if she was serious, her fingernails dug into my flesh.

"Oww—ahhh . . ." My pain was cut off by a sensation of buoyancy. I felt like everything would be okay for the first time since I entered the bag. I felt connected to Sajda, Zawar, to Saim, to everything around me. The way I was feeling, even the monsters could be my friends. I was raw energy, wrapped in warmth. I snuggled in the blanket of the pleasant sensation, so smothered by it I couldn't even form a thought to ask what was happening.

And just when I surrendered everything to the warmth, a chill crept up my bones. It felt like they might crack from the abrupt temperature change. I was thinking quickly, hyper-aware of the fact that my mind was working. *What's happening to me?* I asked, but my thoughts were too fast to translate to my tongue. My mouth went dry, my limbs shook from feebleness. The bag's fabric was oppressive, shadows consumed Sajda's face. *Is she going to kill me? Why am I still alive in the first place?*

My fear and trembling turned to rage. I saw red and burned like dry tinder. I struggled to break Sajda's grasp, and it took all her strength to hold me firm. My teeth gnashed, my eyebrows knitted together, my blood boiled—there was steam in my veins.

My cracked lips became moist once more. I couldn't remember what I was so angry about, I could barely even remember that I'd felt angry. All words died, and I settled into a reserved silence, barely registering the pain from Sajda's grip, barely registering anything at all.

Sajda let go, and every emotion I'd ever felt, and so many I could never name, flooded over me. She caught me before I collapsed and laid me gently on the ground.

***

I woke up a full day later to the sound of Shaykh Nariman's whistling snores. He'd been waiting by my sickbed the whole while. My head pounded, my stomach growled, and I couldn't move without Sajda's help, but I was alive.

"I surprised you so your body couldn't prepare defenses," she said. "I'm glad you're alive. Saim is happy too, but it will probably be a few hours before he speaks to me or you." I noticed tiny tooth marks on her finger—Shaykh Nariman's angry work.

She launched into a complex explanation that I had her repeat three times. "Yellow bile gives power, but as it increases, its opposite, phlegm decreases. Blood gives energy and speed, but at the cost of black bile—its opposite. Black bile gives intellect, at the cost of blood. And phlegm provides defense, at the expense of yellow bile. That's power at the cost of defense, defense at the cost of power, energy at the cost of intellect, and intellect at the cost of energy. Increase yellow bile and blood, and you can raise your temperature—at a high level of control you can manipulate it within your own body. Increase black bile and phlegm, and you can control cold . . . " I had a headache by the time I understood it all.

She explained the consequences of imbalance. "Too much black bile leads to extreme anxiety, fear, and depression; the body desiccates and freezes. Too much yellow bile ends in anger—and burning. Too much blood results in joy but is coupled with the loss of thought and self. Too much phlegm brings tranquility, quiet, and then a total lack of feeling.

"Generally speaking, even after attaining the ability to control the humors, one predominates," she said. "Shahid leaned toward phlegm, though he liked manipulating heat with blood and yellow bile. Sadeeqa had a strong propensity toward black bile. Zawar has an affinity for blood, and Saim for yellow bile."

Was Saim passionate because he used yellow bile more or was he able to use yellow bile more because of his passion? Did phlegm explain Shahid's quiet tone or did his quiet tone explain his skill with phlegm? "And you?"

Sajda smiled. "I have total mastery." She wasn't bragging.

I propped myself up against a clump of black fabric.. The majority of the bag's surface was smooth, but fuzzy disturbances dotted the landscape, like knots on a wool thobe.

"You know the concepts," Sajda said, "but the best way to learn is experience. You need to *feel* the different humors. Take a moment to relax your body."

My body took that as permission to let go. There couldn't be nightmares worse than—

"No—don't nod off again," Sajda scolded. "Let your limbs go loose, un-tense all your muscles . . . feel them go slack, one by one. Imagine a warm summer breeze or the undulating flow of a pure stream."

I closed my eyes and tried; I couldn't manage the images or sensations but my breathing softened. Yet I wasn't at peace; there was a knot inside my chest that I couldn't unwind. A twisted, sour knot.

"Feel the warmth beneath your skin," she said. "The airy liquid trickling between your limbs, circulating in minuscule tombs around and around your body. Ibn al-Nafis mapped the flow of blood , but you don't need an accurate picture. Imagine a small splash of the liquid swirling around like the wind and trace its movement . . ."

I looked within myself. I could hear my own heart beat, felt the pumping of liquid, but I couldn't follow it. My heart was locked.

Sajda continued, "Feel the blood breeze by your lungs. Breath in and out, follow the wind as it fills you, and the blood as it brushes by. There's a thick, viscous liquid within your lungs. That's phlegm. Feel it splash every so slightly as your chest moves up and down. Feel it beckon like the ocean."

My lungs inflated and I tried to follow the wind, or the ocean, or whatever simile she was pushing now, but I was lost.

Sajda kept going, "On your left side, below your heart, at the bottom of your ribs. There's a cold, clay sac. Your spleen. It spews a dry, black powder. Scoop it up like soil, examine it in your imagination's fingers—"

"Don't make him do this on an empty stomach!" Zawar interrupted and my eyes fluttered open. He had fresh scratches I hadn't seen before, including a long shallow on his left cheek. While I was knocked out, he'd gone hunting. He held a silver chalice in one hand and clutched something in the other.

My stomach growled; too bad it wasn't the origin of one of the humors, I could it sense easily. "That's okay—" I began.

"No," Sajda said, "Zawar is right. You've been furrowing your brows together—I doubt you've sensed anything. It should be easy after the shock to your system, but maybe it wasn't enough . . ."

I flinched. Sajda gave me a sympathetic smile. "Don't worry. There's no point in doing it twice—it's not as effective the second time. And the survival rate is much lower."

She gestured to Zawar and he unfurled his hand, revealing

a small, deep red fruit shaped like a rounded pyramid. It was coated with countless bumpy seeds.

"What is this?" I asked Zawar as I handed it to me. Its smell was similar to cherry, but softer.

"No idea," he said. "The bag originally belonged to Khidr, you have to remember. It contains things we've never seen before. All sorts of food items were stashed away—and nothing goes bad. The monsters ate most of the goodies but we found this fruit tucked away."

He handed over the chalice. A pure white liquid sloshed within it, dribbling over the silver edge. "You have to try it with milk!"

"You really found milk here?" I asked..

"A whole basin. Don't know how the monsters missed it. It's impressive—ancient milk, yet fresh as the day it was produced," Zawar enthused.

I nibbled and a splash of pink sweetness blossomed against the inky black within me. The nibble turned to a chomp. I washed it down with the cool, creamy milk, and paused, unable to speak. There might have been something in my eye.

"Tastes like life has meaning, doesn't it?" Zawar said.

"Aren't you going to have any?" I asked him.

"No, no, we're good . . ." Zawar said.

"You can be frank and say that was the last of those fruits and you have an allergy to dairy," Sajda said with a sigh. "Zawar is essentially a mother who would starve herself so her children can eat. Even when she doesn't need to."

"Hey!" Zawar said with mock affront. "Is that any way to talk about your mother?"

Sajda turned to me. "This wasn't just a pleasant diversion. Everything can be educational. The red fruit and milk are both cold and wet. So which humor do they help produce?"

"Phlegm?" I said, still basking in the aftertaste.

"Breathe in and out deeply—" Sajda instructed me. "Focus on the breath and your lungs. You should sense the slightest accumulation of phlegm. Push against it, tense your chest ever so much—"

I filled my lungs with air and exhaled. I sensed nothing. I set down the chalice and tried again. And again. And again. Failure was turning the sweet taste bitter.

"Let's try a more direct route," Sajda said after I did nothing but pant for half an hour. "Zawar—" she called out, but he was already gone.

He sprinted back with a woven reed basket. I sniffed and was greeted with an explosion of flavor which ripped through my moodiness. The hot tang of pepper, the sly sweetness of cinnamon, the earthy simplicity of coriander, and the powerful push of cardamom all swarmed me, along with a dozen other spices. It was a treasure trove.

"Monsters don't have good taste," Zawar chuckled. "That's why they eat people but ignore this."

"Coriander first," Sajda said. Zawar pinched some with three fingers.

"Open wide," he said.

Before I could articulate anything more than, "Uhh," he sprinkled the coriander into my mouth. It leapt out of his fingers in an artful arc.

The dried spice melted on my tongue. I coughed as I swallowed.

"Dry—and cold," Sajda said. "Do you feel that lump of cold clay within you? Your spleen? Reach for it like you're groping in the dark."

At this point she had to be making descriptions up. But there it was—an icy, dark powder below my chest, billowing like sand in the desert at night.

"Feel it, will it to flow, to increase." She pumped a fist in the first.

My eyes had widened—that's why she was celebrating, she knew the dilation meant I had a breakthrough. It all began to make sense: my eyes widening, her happiness—my whole body was aware, not instinctively, but through a rapid, conscious process of intuition and hyper-focus. I willed the black bile to surge, and I saw how Sajda's smiles contained a hint of mourning, how Zawar's friendliness masked the fear of further loss, and how Saim's heat and hunting were his way of avoiding what had happened to them.

Of course we were all suffering. We were trapped in a twisted dimension, cut off from the world, with only monsters and each other for company. My mouth went dry. My skin prickled with goosebumps.

"Stop," Sajda said.

Is she really worried about me? Or about how she would feel if something happened to me?

"KHURAFA, STOP!" she yelled, grasping my shoulder with a warm hand.

The powder's flow dimmed. The world became less focused. Like it usually was.

It took a couple minutes for the clamminess to dissipate. Zawar went off to fetch a cup of water.

After I drank, Sajda's smile returned. "Now do it without the coriander as a catalyst to locate the black bile," she said. "Will it to happen, but slowly. And pull yourself back—sense the warmth around you, taste the moisture in the air."

***

My dreams were consistent. The cloth closed in, a dark shroud smothering me. I could feel a serpentine creature on the other side, pressing down. It had grown into a thick, constricting snake. It wrapped its body around the cloth, around me, and squeezed. My bones creaked, my blood vessels tightened, my heart pounded as if beating a door, pleading for a means of escape.

The nightmare motivated me, but in three days I still only barely managed to manipulate black bile.

At least I was back on my feet.

"I think it's time for a practical exercise," Sajda said when she saw me stretching my legs.

"There are things hidden in the pockets where the fabric bunches together." She walked briskly. "Undisturbed items . . . and creatures in the folds. We have a pretty good idea of what's behind this one." She put her hand on the woolen black surface and pushed. The crease opened up to a rattling sound, a clanking of hard surfaces as something came awake.

"What is . . ." My voice trailed away as Sajda took a defensive position behind me. Something rushed toward me. I swerved before a long, outstretched hand could scrap my skin. The hand was devoid of flesh. The whole body of the creature was bare, even the ligaments connecting bones were worn away. The skeletal monster was an upright, clattering collection of bones held together by invisible string.

The skeleton swung its hand down toward my head—if it wasn't for the speed, it would've looked like a starving man reaching out for help. I dodged.

I charged the skeleton—it had no weapon, and based on its slapping motions, it couldn't close a fist. But at the instant before impact, I saw the spindly edges on its brittle bones. Ready to impale me.

My hands flailed, shielding me from the impact. My body remembered its training. The flow of black bile increased.

The creature was a dead thing. Fleshless bones. The barren, dry remnants of a body. If it dried out further, if the last echoes of life were sucked out of it, it would be dust.

I drew the life and moisture away from my hands upon contact. The skeleton's ribcage shattered into infinitesimal shards when I touched it. The skeleton jerked back in an attempt to save itself, but I had a savage handle on dryness now. Everywhere I touched the skeleton, it faded. I turned its spine into bone meal with barely a squeeze.

The bits of bone quaked after collapsing, floating as they failed to jump back together. They went still.

I let the life back into my hands, let the moisture collect once more. I toppled to the ground, crunching the fractured femur before me. My head pounded, my blood rushed. The words *Die die die!* thundered in my mind. It was all I could do to not vomit. This was not how Amir Hamza or Rustam would have felt.

"What," I panted, my mouth dry. "What was that?

"A ghoul," she said, "a spirit creature possessing the remains of men and animals."

"It's a jinn?" I asked. Shaykh Nariman answered with a tinge of squeaky affront. "A ghoul is to a jinn as a monkey is to a human. It's not unintelligent and there is a relation yes, but its levels of thought and self-awareness are different. It's an animal, a hungry creature."

"How was it supposed to eat me?" I asked; it was just bones.

"The . . . non-material components can dissolve flesh,"

Shaykh Nariman explained, shifting around ivory shards.

My head throbbed. "A little warning might have been nice," I grumbled.

"You need to react without thought, but instead you thought very fast," Sajda said. "Still, you moved even when surprised—you didn't freeze up. That's good. And you made the right choice—dryness." She handed me a waterskin and despite the thirst I drank slowly, the trauma of near-drowning from a waterskin still written into my flesh.

"You know why I am giving you water?" she asked. "And how it was easy for you, when thinking fast, to enact dryness?"

I hesitated. "Black bile . . . is dry, and it's associated with intellect. I was probably imbalanced toward it to begin with, so that made dryness easy to manipulate."

"Precisely." Smiled approval. "Now you have three more humors to work on, not to mention heat and wetness to master. And black bile still needs more work. Luckily there are many practical exercises available in these parts." Many ways to kill me, she meant.

Chapter 22

I took a walk while toying with black bile a few days later. My mind ran laps as my lips went dry.

She's dead, you know. She's dead. Did Shahid's baraka disappear the moment he touched that old man, or was it after he stabbed her? Why didn't you pay attention?

Why are you the one who's alive?

"We should move away from here," Shaykh Nariman interrupted the dark mass infecting my mind. I needed to fight, to learn, to lose myself in training. Those were the only times the mass subsided.

I don't think Sajda knew the real reason I took to black bile easily.

My walk ended near the opening. It was an area cleared of monsters, but the pillars felt it wasn't safe. They couldn't always watch me though, and didn't try to. Sajda believed in trials by fire. Her warnings about dangerous folds in the bag were undermined by her excitement.

My foot struck giant bones, the remnants of the filshad which killed Sadeeqa.

They kept her body in a fold because there was no soil in which to bury her. The pillars made daily trips to offer prayers. It was the only time everyone was quiet. I went on my own once, following the dimmed spicy scent of stack. She was wrapped up in a series of sheets like all Muslim corpses.

I pulled the white shroud from over her face. It was still intact. Nothing decayed in the bag. Her skull was crushed, like the rest of her body. Her knobby nose, kind round cheeks, her soft jaw. They were all indented like a pothole on the road.

I ran. It took time to slow my breathing and realize I forgot to fix the shroud. When I reentered the fold, her face was already covered.

Unlike Sadeeqa, the filshad lost all its flesh. I couldn't lift a femur, so I selected a chunk of the spine. I slashed the air, uneven bones burrowing into my palms.

Incoming footsteps crunched ceramics. "We ate it," Zawar said. "We ate the very monster that killed one of our own." He smiled. "It didn't taste great. But it lasted over a month. The flesh never rotted."

"That explains it," I said, swinging the spine again.

"You usually use the staff?" Zawar asked. "Is this how you do it?"

I nodded.

"You hold it by the top when you swing?" he asked.

"If I strike with the bottom tip, it splits things," I said, relaxing black bile. The bag brightened.

"When you fight living things, it has no effect. So why not hold it from the small end, the tip, and use it like a proper club, batting things with the heavier top?"

"Huh," I held the bones from the other end. The spine was uniform unlike that staff so it made no difference.

"A staff is not a sword," he said, "you shouldn't think of it like one. Use it as a club, or try holding it from the middle."

I adjusted my grip on the spine as he suggested, imagining

the staff. "Now you can use the tip if you need to split things or the top if you need to give a strong blow. There's not as much leverage for your swings, but it has its advantages—"

He swung a femur toward my shoulder and I reflexively blocked it with one end of the spine.

"This hold facilitates defense," Zawar said. "Your staff is well-suited for defense. Not sure if you noticed, but it's indestructible." I wondered what that was like.

He swung again and I parried. We practiced over and over until the spine fell apart and my palms started to bleed.

***

"We need you for this one," Sajda said as she wrapped salve on my hands. The prickling cuts were met with soothing cold.

I flexed my finger and balled my fists. "Can you first tell me what it is this time?" I asked. I seemed to vaguely remember an idea called 'caution.'

"You won't be fighting it alone. That's too risky this time," she frowned. *She* was calling it risky?

"It's called an Umm Sibyan," Saim said. "Another distant relation of the jinn. It only preys on children. It avoids adults, so it would be hard for us to corner without you."

"You're still young enough." Sajda's frown curled into a smile. "Just barely," she added to pacify me.

"You're using me as a lure again?" I asked. I was more excited than incredulous. It didn't matter what she said, I felt older, stronger.

This time I could do something.

"Saim forgot a detail," Zawar interrupted amiably. "It preys only on *sleeping* children. This won't be pleasant."

"Forgive us in advance," Sajda said. Forgive them for what? My usual drowsiness would finally come in handy.

They set me up on a pallet in the middle of an empty, cavernous section of the bag and left to hide in a fold. Even Shaykh Nariman skittered away from me.

My eyes fluttered as I looked toward the fabric sky. Fuzz particles drifted in the air. I tried to count them until I slept, but I had too much adrenaline this time.

I stretched. There was no Kedi to lull me to sleep with warmth and purrs.

It must have been two hours before I dozed. Maybe aging isn't all its cracked up to be. Everything was dark and quiet. Then a streak of light entered my vision. I tensed within my dream. Sleep hadn't made me forget that the Umm Sibyan sought me. The serpentine forms of the Servants had tormented me for months. This was nothing in comparison.

I was ready for a monster.

Instead, I saw my mom. Safety, love incarnate. Her curls danced as she threw back her head and laughed. "Why do you look so scared?" she asked. Her eyes crinkled.

I stood and approached her, a slow steps at first, and then a run. "What's gotten into you?" she asked.

"You've been gone," I cried. I'd waited to dream of her for so long.

"You've been gone. You've been gone." I locked her in a tight embrace.

"What is it that Mawlana Rumi said?" She asked, stroking my hair. 'She will walk three hundred miles to find her kids/crying and moaning all the way. Smoke and fire fly from her trunk/don't touch those kids of her!'"

"You're not an elephant," I chuckled as the tears streamed down.

"But I'm a mom. Not even death can keep me away," she

smiled, a wide, open smile. A smile which could consume all my worries and pain.

Her teeth were too sharp.

"No," I said. "No, no, no." She bit down on my shoulder and I couldn't resist. My limbs were like water.

Her head jerked back. The smile became a scream. The curly black hair turned white, her light brown skin paled, her laugh lines were ravaged wrinkles.

I held the Umm Sibyan as it fell to the ground, two arrows burrowed into its back.

I looked down at the corpse. It sizzled and started to evaporate. Sweat dripped down my limbs. Sajda and the other pillars ran toward me.

"What—what happened?" I asked. I tried taking a step, but my foot missed the ground. Zawar caught me.

"You were sleeping. All of a sudden you stood and sleep-walked. You stopped moving, but there was nothing in front of you," Zawar said.

"The Umm Sibyan wasn't visible to us," Sajda explained, "but we knew it was there—immaterial. Otherwise why would you have stopped—"

"And if it hadn't been there?" Saim growled at her. "Your arrows would have pierced him. They would have—"

"I know what it looks like when a child thinks they're with their mother," Sajda said softly.

"You could have told me that," I said, too drained to muster anger. "Could have told me it takes the form of the prey's mom . . ."

"If you knew, it wouldn't have come. It can tell when a child doesn't believe the illusion," she said, steadying me as I staggered, "and I know it hurts. But seeing her again is worth that, isn't it?"

I didn't answer. She was right. I'd wanted to continue that false embrace to the very end.

"How did it know what my mom was like? How did it—" I sank to the ground.

"It didn't know. It's not something it does intellectually. It makes your memory and imagination fill in the gaps." Sajda sat down on her knees and let me lay down. She rested my head on her lap, brushing away my tears. It was the second time she'd comforted me.

Zakiyya wasn't around, so there was no reason to feel embarrassed.

No one would make fun of me.

Chapter 23

I joined in a hunt for another ghoul, helped take down a particularly stunted, scaly ejderha, and slew a bayi raksasa all by myself. It looked like a baby crawling and crying for help, but the moment I got close it turned into a pink mass of muscle with teeth.

Things need to stop trying to eat me.

After weeks of training, I had a good grasp of black bile and dryness. Everything else was touch and go.

Zawar, Sajda, and Saim worked their way through a full bestiary including flesh eating worms, a chimera, and a demonic tortoise we made into soup. It was not the most pleasant meal.

My clothes were torn and worn by the end of the first month, and Zawar replaced them with an old regal outfit found in a fold, red and gold clothes with elaborate embroidery. It was a sassanid lord's getup deposited by some mythic user of the bag. I had to tear some of the seams so I could move in it.

Sajda entrusted me with a steel dirk. I shined it a little too regularly.

When the three pillars hadn't found anything to fight for three days, Sajda announced that we were nearly ready to open the bag. At long last.

Zawar and I shared a centuries-old watermelon that had been preserved in a pocket. Watery red juice leaked down my chin and stained my hands for the first time since the caravanserai. Shaykh Nariman nibbled on a fleshy piece and laid down with a sigh.

Saim's padded footsteps broke the reprieve.

"Everyone to the opening. You've got to hear this," he said.

I wiped the watermelon juice on my fine laces. We followed him to the thin rift in the impenetrable fabric, where a sliver of light entered. The crevice was too small to hear anything through for everyone but Saim.

He narrated what he could make out. *"An unfamiliar voice is speaking—It's cold, threatening. Like falling into a frozen lake. It's saying, 'Months, Bayan. Why did it take you months?'"*

Shaykh Nariman crawled closer, his every hair raised.

Saim continued, *"Now Shahid is talking—there's smoldering venom in his voice. He says, 'I wanted to eliminate some threats; I possessed the wrong man in the right place. He had enough baraka to suppress me without even realizing I was present.'*

The other voice says, 'Then how am I talking to you now?' It's chuckle sounds like ice cracking.

Shahid responds, 'Despair. Despair dimmed the baraka just enough. Faith is built on hope, is it not? News of Mongols removed it for a moment—long enough for me to rid us of a few potential enemies. But the control waned. I waited months until he felt despair again, strongly enough for me to take charge. I learned much in the background.'

'Learned what?' the chilly voice asks.

'There are those living today that know about us. The ones I encountered were children—and a certain jinn . . .' and that's it, they're too far from the bag now for me to hear."

"One of The Servants," Shaykh Nariman said, breathless, his little pink paws clutched together in angst. "One of The Servants—Bayan—possessed Shahid . . . He was with us all that time, in Shahid's subconscious. And Bayan was speaking to . . ." His snout quivered. "He was speaking to Mughirah, their leader. I've heard him before. Ice is right. The bag is in their lair."

"Then we come out now, ready to strike," Sajda said, as she restrung her bow and counted her arrows.

"We don't know what we'll be facing," Zawar countered, a contemplative look on his face. "And we don't know what the enemy's capabilities are. We need to gather more information."

"Shahid is possessed. He's a prisoner in his own body," Saim said. "Can you imagine . . . I actually doubted him. Thought he was a traitor."

"The sooner we can do something for him, the better. They said despair allowed for possession. If he sees us again—if he gets back hope, he can take back control. We'd have another ally," Sajda said.

"We do have information," Shaykh Nariman added, looking stricken as he did so. "Mughirah is there. His plan is to resurrect the people of Ad—it's what he planned centuries ago. I don't think God would allow a true resurrection by Mughirah's hand, so we can assume he has magic that allows him to puppeteer the dead."

He turned to me, "'Bayan' is what he called Shahid . . .If Shahid doesn't recover, we will contend with any enemy of immense power. Bayan was Mughirah's second-in-command." His voice turned into a stern whisper. "We also know another member of The Servants we've been pursuing: the poisoner.

He can cause people to go on a rampage and corrupt their minds."

"What about the rest of the servants? Where are we even?" Zawar asked.

"I haven't heard anything distinct before this," Saim said. "Maybe people hawking goods. In Persian and Arabic. A decent amount of hustle and bustle. I'd say we were traveling intermittently at a lower elevation for the past couple weeks. Might have heard a seagull or two. My guess is we're near Basra or elsewhere on the sea coast."

Shaykh Nariman ruffled his snout in thought. "The bodies of Ad are in Iram, somewhere in the empty quarter of the Arabian peninsula. Traveling by ship across the gulf to the Peninsula makes sense."

"Should we wait 'til we're at sea?" Sajda asked, slinging her readied bow behind her back.

"Then we'd have the greatest number of them, contained in one confined space . . . with no escape," Zawar said, coming around to the plan, at last.

"And if they leave the bag behind . . ." Sajda wondered.

"We break out and find time to gather allies," Zawar finished for her. "Even if we are left behind, we know their destination is the empty quarter in the peninsula. They'll be searching for the legendary city of the people of Ad in Iram."

"Does anyone know where it is?" I asked. I'd heard the story before, of the giants with the elegant city carved into stone, who defied God and deified themselves, and were felled by a cold, violent wind.

"Our teacher . . ." Zawar began, "visited once. He wandered the desert in his youth. It left a mark on his soul. The places of punishment—something lingers there."

"We can worry about where it is *if* we are left behind," Sajda said, drawing Zawar back to the present. "We're all agreed—you use the staff to split the bag when we are on the boat. Saim will give the signal."

Saim nodded his agreement and the rest of us murmured assent.

Shaykh Nariman, whispered to himself, "So we will meet again at last."

I went to sort through our supplies while Zawar sharpened everyone's weapons. Sajda drew invisible marks in the ground with a stick, experimenting with battle plans.

"We won't have to wait long!" Saim called out. "I heard a sailor curse about the wind. And I can hear waves! We've boarded. Another hour and we'll be out to sea. They might toss us into storage so it will be hard to know for sure."

"An hour works," Sajda said. "It's in God's hands. Now, here's the way I see this going. When you split the bag, it's not certain exactly how much of the contents will get out, whether it will all come out in one spot or be flung apart. If everything in the bag pours into the boat . . . It will sink."

I gulped.

"That's not a bad outcome," Sajda continued. "If the boat sinks out in the waters, we've stopped them. But if the boat doesn't sink . . . that's the situation we have to worry about. We know Mughirah is there, the chief. Whether we are in the storage or on deck, we'll have the element of surprise on hand. I'll go for him."

"If you can figure out who he is," I pointed out the flaw in her plan. "If he's in any random person's body you won't be able to tell."

"That's not a problem," she said. "My firsat is that I can

always tell someone's identity. Not a name if it's not integral to who they are, but impressions of character, a sense of self. It will be enough to find him. Someone who wants to resurrect Ad will be brimming with ambition and madness."

How did she fail with Shahid?

"I'll go for a killing blow. No time to interrogate, especially if he might leap bodies." She gave Shaykh Nariman a look.

"Zawar, you take care of Shahid. Bring him back to us—the shock of seeing us should do it. If there are members of The Servants we don't know, you tank them until the rest of us are free. Saim, you take the disease guy. He'll use others to do his bidding from what we've heard, so you have to outmaneuver him."

"These are simple assignments," Zawar chuckled. His eyes were afire despite his jovial tone.

"I'm not finished," she said. "Everything needs to be done within a few minutes. If not, then boy . . ." she leaned in and whispered her instructions into my ear. My grip on the staff tightened.

"Gather round," Zawar said. He raised his hands and all of us followed suit. "O Lord, guide our steps, guide our hands, make us instruments of your justice and embodiments of your mercy . . ." He went on for a few minutes, all of us chiming *amen* in unison . . . He set a clay stone before him, and led us in one final prayer, holding us in the prostration for several dozen heartbeats. I never figured out how they determined the prayer direction within the bag.

Saim skipped off toward the opening. I patted the dirk at my waste, adjusted the satchel over my shoulder, and readied the staff. Zawar twirled his blessed blade with a flourish while Sajda tested the weight of the arrows she carved out of monster bone and other ancient ones made of extinct wood that she uncovered.

Saim returned with a report. "Shahid . . . er, *Bayan* set the bag down. It's on the ship deck." He was carrying a person-sized burden wrapped in three white sheets of cloth—he'd made a detour to the one fold they visited daily. We weren't leaving anyone behind.

"Bismillah," *in the name of God*, we all said at once.

I poked the staff into the fabric and it tore—revealing more fabric beneath it.

I jabbed again at another location, and a full chasm opened up, a mini-canyon, composed top to bottom of fabric.

"Now we know for certain this is another realm," Saim said, the load he was carrying muffling his satisfaction. "When you split the fabric, you're splitting ground in the realm, not barriers between the realms."

"So what did we defeat those monsters for?" I said dumb-founded. "In the end we're stuck here . . ."

"What did I tell you about losing hope?" Sajda said, stalking off toward the opening. We all followed.

"Slam it here," she said. "This is the entrance. If we split this, we're splitting the barrier between the realms.".

"Bismillah," I murmured again, ramming the tip of the staff just below the opening.

Chapter 24

A tiny tear appeared in the fabric. It grew, and grew, until the whole space burst at its seams. The explosion forced the staff out of my hand, flinging me and the three pillars back. We landed hard. On solid wooden planks, smelling of brine and fish.

Ancient Persian clothes, broken axes, monster corpses, a cacophony of vegetables—the whole millenia of minutiae that occupied the bag was hurled up into the bright blue sky. Most plopped into the water but enough landed on deck to rock the boat violently. My staff got caught in the railing.

Threads of black fabric littered the deck, more cloth than the external bag contained but less than the pocket reality. I didn't have time to ponder the discrepancy. The corpse of the borz fell right on top of me. I struggled beneath its weight.

Sajda got to her feet first, too far away to help me. She tore through the debris toward the cabin where a pale boy stood, dressed in black. His skin was a fiery red from sunburn, but his voice was impeccably cold, and decades older than his body.

"Is that you Nariman?" he asked. The Shaykh stiffened.

Sajda loosed an arrow as she ran. The boy—Mughirah, leader of The Servants—caught it by the shaft without looking. He twirled it around playfully, using it to kick aside Sajda's second bolt.

Shahid, who was closest to the bag when it burst, stood shakily. Zawar rushed toward his former comrade.

"Za-zawar?" Shahid's voice boomed. Tears welled up in his sallow, sleepless eyes. "You're alive! God, what have I done? What came over me . . . But you're all here. Thank God."

"It's not your fault," Zawar declared. He embraced his friend. "You were possessed in your despair. But we're alive—hope never disappears brother, never—"

"He's not asking about Sadeeqa!" Sajda shouted at the same time that I yelled, "There's no scent of daisies! No baraka!"

We were too late. Shahid/Bayan stabbed Zawar in the gut. The crystalline dagger was coated in scarlet. Zawar never had the chance to pull Zuhrmehr out of its scabbard.

I screamed and flailed, only managing to free one arm from beneath the borz.

Saim set down his burden, and moved to help up a fallen sailor with big ears and a large nose. Baraka visibly oozed from Saim's hand as he reached out. He had no idea whether the sailor was under compulsion, but it couldn't hurt to be safe.

Except, actually, it could.

A needle held in the palm of the sailor pricked his helping hand.

Monsters are predictable. Humans however, are devious, and those that choose to become monsters even more so.

Saim's hand went limp. His whole body shuddered. "Poison . . ." he gasped. "Normal poison . . ." He crumpled to the ground.

The sailor grinned "I imagine you've seen my previous work? Can't have you washing away *sihr*. It's always good to mix things up. An artist must stay fresh."

I strained against the borz, slipping my other arm free. I closed my eyes, pushing all my focus toward drying the corpse, willing it to crumble.

Its flesh was too well-preserved.

Zawar was bleeding out. Shahid/Bayan chuckled as he removed his dagger, stabbing a second and third time. "Your friend didn't just recede into the background when I took control this last time," he said. "I spent time smothering him. It was hard, let me tell you. I can't believe I forgot about the staff . . . keeping the thought from me might have been his last act. How noble." He removed the dagger again and aimed for the throat.

Zawar vanished—he disappeared right before the blade cleft his throat apart.

"Well, I'll be," Shahid/Bayan grinned. "Looks like that innate *tayy al-ard* defense is real! Warping away before dying must be lonely."

Saim, who'd sunk to the deck, green in the face, also evaporated. The sailor frowned. "Someone with that much baraka would have made a fine test subject."

Mughirah walked slowly to Sajda, catching arrow after arrow and flicking them away. "Nariman," he said, ignoring her desperation. "Why the cold greeting after so long? I must say this rodent form suits you."

Shaykh Nariman quaked in my satchel. "What really happened to Haziq?" he asked.

Mughirah walked up to Sajda, arms outstretched, like a little kid reaching out for a hug. She plucked her shortsword from her belt and slashed at the demonic boy faster than sound. He dove for her leg.

It burst into flames.

She tried hacking at him again, stifling her screams, attempting to counter the blaze with humoral cold and moisture. The flames spread, and before her blow could land or Mughirah could dodge—she flickered out of existence. Warped away, to safety or agony, leaving only bits of ashen flesh behind.

"These saints don't amount to much these days, do they?" Mughirah said. He turned toward Shaykh Nariman and I. "Haziq was a phenomenal vessel. Housing nine souls! I really didn't think it was possible. We drowned him out long before the body gave way. Too much crowding. Yes he suffered, but he was honored to serve."

I felt the violent tremors rippling through Shaykh Nariman as I managed to push the borz off me at last. I scrambled to my feet, rushing for the staff, dodging debris with nimbleness I'd never had.

A tall, familiar lady, blocked my way. Aunty Naama, the matronly disciplinarian from the Khaniqah held a rusty scimitar. I edged closer. Her scimitar wasn't rusted; the orange-and-red coating was old blood.

"Not surprised to see you again. You did quite the damage to my little cult. I'd picked out Saf so carefully too," she sighed. "I wouldn't have expected 'heroes' to kill so many innocents."

"What are you talking about?" I asked, summoning black-bile intellect, using it to scan for an opening and stifle my panic.

"When you kids caused the structure to topple. How many people died? Ten? Twenty? It ruined that experiment completely," she said.

"Zakiyya said no one was hurt," I said. *Why would she lie to me about that? To protect me? But why couldn't she trust me?*

What else could she have lied about? Was anything real—

I let my black bile falter.

Aunty Naama rushed toward me with the scimitar and I brought up my dirk to parry. The force of her blow carried the blade out of my hands. It clattered far behind me.

"That Banu Sassan tramp lied," Aunty Naama said with a wicked smile. She raised her scimitar for the killing blow. I picked a monster thigh from the ground, flung it at her, and skirted to the right, closer to the railing . . .

And slipped. Not on a monstrous corpse or ancient minutiae but plain old sea water. My satchel was thrown off and the *Stories of the Prophets* book Zakiyya and I had received ages ago tumbled out, page-first onto the wet deck.

Aunty Naama approached and stopped before the book. She edged back, discomfort on her wrinkled face.

The smell of tulips emanated from the text. I'd forgotten about its baraka. But now its blessings flared up all at once, as if it knew it was needed.

I snatched it up, holding it open and shoving it toward Aunty Namaa. She took another step back.

"Will this one teleport too if I strike him?" the old lady asked.

"No," Shahid/Bayan said. Bones crunched beneath his heavy steps, and with a small smile, he kicked the white-clothed lump Saim had carried. "Cut the boy up all you want and he'll stay right here. He's a clumsy little rat, so he'll likely fall and defeat himself, but why not make sure the job gets done?"

She hesitated in front of the book.

"Oh, for the love of . . ." Shahid/Bayan scoffed. "You can't face the text, so attack *behind* it. Watch."

He launched himself toward me and I flailed the book his way—away from Aunty Naama.

The opening lasted a split second, and she made one swift sweep of her scimitar.

My hands still held the book tightly. But they were no longer attached to me.

I stared in utter disbelief at my bloody, leaking stumps. My hands were gone. My hands. That meant no more gardening. No more carrying the staff. No more fighting.

Shahid/Bayan laughed, clutching his belly. Aunty Naama smiled, sweeping in for another slash. I stood paralyzed, shock disassociating me from the searing pain. My humoral knowledge was pointless. I couldn't staunch the blood, couldn't dry the wound, couldn't do anything. I was useless.

Aunty Naama's blade drew closer and there was no chance of me warping away. The blade drew closer and I was too insensate to notice whether my life was flashing before my eyes.

The blade drew closer, and a ball of white and gray fur jumped in the way.

Shaykh Nariman was cut nearly in two, his spine hanging together by a thread. No blood issued forth; he was a jinn. But smoke wafted from his wound.

What does it mean for smoke to pour out of a being made from smokeless fire?

Shaykh Nariman sailed back against me. He was so light, but the tiny thud brought me to my knees.

"Mughirah will be mad at you," Shahid/Bayan scolded Aunty Naama. "He wanted to talk to Nariman, for old time's sake."

Blood leaked from my stumps, life ebbing away. "I'm sorry boy," Shaykh Nariman wheezed.

"Ah well," Aunty Naama shrugged, angling the scimitar for a clean sweep of my head.

A wave struck the ship. The world lurched, but Aunty Namaa's feet were firm. She cackled as I staggered.

But I wasn't the only one unbalanced. The shaking dislodged the staff from the rail.

I launched my body against it, falling on purpose for once in my life. I smashed the staff into the deck as Sajda had planned.

"Maybe I stumble because I'm meant to be walking in paradise," I said as the wooden planks below me were rent apart. "Or maybe I'm a clumsy rodent. But either way, I'll fall and get back up as many times as it takes to make this world better."

Shahid/Bayan's riposte was drowned out by the boat creaking and splitting in two.

I splashed into the chilly depths, praying that everyone else sunk. The staff floated away, but Shaykh Nariman's two halves clung to me. Another wave bobbed my head back above water.

The sharp pain of the sea salt entering my stumps kept me awake. But it wouldn't be for long.

Shaykh Nariman climbed on to my head, both his halves moving in delicate coordination. My ears were clogged with the tide, yet I still heard his squeaky words.

"I'm sorry my boy. Please don't die. I'm sorry," he said. "You weren't supposed to be here. The truth is . . . you weren't chosen for this. The dream you and Zakiyya had . . . that wasn't your dream. It was my dream and my burden. I projected it onto the two of you because I wanted help. The sleeping minds of children are easy to implant things into. I didn't have the skill to influence an adult. The jinn corpse in the river was a vision I gave you too—based on what I thought had happened. The Servants were executed off the coast of the Euphrates, not the Tigris as you saw. And the garden, that was me. I used the last of my strength to burn it so that you would join me on this quest. I'm sorry my boy. I'm sorry. I'm so sorry."

Even at the very end, he couldn't help but lecture and overexplain.

I coughed up water and phlegm. I'd lost my hands, I was about to drown at sea, and my only companion was telling me with his dying breaths that everything was a lie, that all the things which had nudged me along this journey were manufactured.

Maybe it would have been better if he'd been a hallucination all along.

But endings matter, and I wouldn't let mine be tarnished by hate or despair. I sputtered 'til I could voice my last words. "Having a dream doesn't make you chosen to do something. Having the will to do it does."

"But we failed," Shaykh Nariman said, his voice fading, "this won't kill them. My selfishness led to this."

How long would it take to meet my parents in the hereafter's garden? Maybe my flowers would all be there. And Zakiyya . . .

"We don't do things because we'll succeed," I said, as the world went black, "and we don't do things just because of duty. We do them because they are right and we want to do what is right, regardless of what happens next . . ." water poured into my open mouth and I could say no more.

All was washed away.

Epilogue

"Zakiyya would have roasted me—my final thought was that my last words were pretty epic." Khurafa yawned.

"After that I woke up here, with you birds pecking at me. Last time I was paralyzed, back in the Khaniqah, Shaykh Nariman helped me get up. But I knew this time, he wouldn't be coming," Khurafa said. "Honestly, that's the whole story and I'm all out of words. If you're gonna peck me to death, might as well get started. Oh wait, I can just count out numbers to keep you off! One, two, three, four . . ."

"Humans really love to talk," the larger vulture sighed.

The smaller one responded, "haywan al-natiq—the rational animal . . . the speaking animal . . . the blabbering animal?"

"Twelve, thirteen, fourteen—I'm hallucinating you speaking now, wow. Fifteen—" Khurafa rasped.

"This place is called a tower of silence, though I think of it as a home," the first vulture explained. "You mistakenly call them fire-worshippers, but humans are most ignorant of each other. The followers of Zoroaster leave the bodies of their dead here to be consumed by scavengers and the elements. They place them on indentations in the ground, and after the corpses are picked clean they slide into the pit. Water and lime wash the rest away. They are so careful about purity. They would be horrified to see the effects of the horsemen's arrival. This place was abandoned. Neighbors who didn't know the customs, placed bodies from the

aftermath everywhere, without any plan. What's left is gruesome, but there is a beauty to it . . ."

"Yes," the second vulture leered, "beautiful in that it reveals the true decay inherent in humankind. Clay rots."

"Thirty, thirty-one, thirty-two—" Khurafa continued.

"That's enough," the first vulture said. The second vulture pecked the boy's nose, drawing blood and growling, "Shut up."

"Why can't I hallucinate something more pleasant." Khurafa failed to raise his stub and nurse his nose. "Oh well."

"Thirty-three," he began again.

"We are jinn," the second vulture spat. "Nariman the traitor called for us."

"Thirty-four—wait what . . ." Khurafa said.

"From your story we see you don't know the truth, though he told you the start of it at the end,"the first vulture said slowly. "500 years ago, Nariman was one of us."

"One of the best of us." The second vulture leered. "Until he started dabbling with your kind!"

The first vulture gave his companion a beady-eyed glare. "Nariman fell in with Mughirah and The Servants. They were enchanting and he was enchanted, they were charming and he was charmed. Nariman brought many other jinn into fellowship with them, working toward their dream of a world without rules or strictures, where the wisdom of man and strength of jinn is in natural, perfect accord with the will of the divine. Or at least that's what he thought they wanted."

"Lies like most of what mud-kind says," the second vulture scowled.

"Nariman was tricked. Mughirah, Bayan, the Servants—they didn't want to work with the jinn, they only wanted our power. They found ways to suck us dry, to imbue themselves with our skills *while retaining their wits. Our elders did not find out until the deed was already done and the imam and the saints had dealt away with the Servants." He paused, his glowering eyes misting. "Most of the youth who joined Nariman were recovered as barren shells. Nariman's younger brother Haziq was never found. Nariman was left alive, reduced but alive, swearing he knew nothing, promising us he had been deceived."*

"He was exiled, on pain of death," the second vulture sneered. "Even to contact another jinn would be to forfeit his life. He avoided all graves where we might reside except one he claimed when Baghdad formed, and stayed clear of most ruins. He did not enter or approach the places we make our homes . . . So when we heard him calling, I was surprised it was to help one of the mud-kind— one he manipulated and betrayed."

"He—he contacted you," Khurafa stammered. "You killed him? That's why I haven't seen his body?".

"He was already dead when we arrived. You should have drowned in the sea. Your medicine is not evolved enough to understand, but the lack of air should have killed the components that make up your brain. He converted himself into air and brain matter for your consumption and repair. He stemmed the bleeding of your wrists with his own being. He gave the little that was left of himself to preserve you. When you washed up on the shore, the merging was still under way. Those that found you thought you dead. Your clothing, that of the dhiqans of old, suggested you were one of Zoroaster's follower, so they left your body here. And when you woke, we came."

"But—but why come as vultures and strike me? Why explain this now?" Khurafa asked.

"Tormenting mud-kind is a favorite past-time of mine," the second vulture laughed.

"No more," the first vulture scolded him. "He's an idiot human, but he's suffered enough. Nariman gave his life for him and for us to hear this story."

"You'll help? The jinn will fight The Servants?" Khurafa asked, his lips quivering.

"The jinn will do nothing. Engagement with humans is risky and our kind is fewer than we once were," the first vulture said solemnly. "I, however, will do what I can. Nariman was dear to me before his fall, and his brother Haziq grew up at my knee. The Servants used him as a vessel for their souls to survive the destruction of their body—they violated him and consumed his power. I will see they are held to account, in this life and the next."

The larger vulture roosted on Khurafa's gangrenous right stump. Khurafa winced but couldn't move his body. The vulture's form melted away, and the gangrene receded. A molten hand took form and solidified.

"This is temporary," a disembodied voice uttered, "but for now, rely on my strength. I am called Zal."

"You literally lent me a hand . . ." Khurafa said in wonder. "You're a part of me now—does this technically count as possession?"

His hand involuntarily curled up into a fist in response.

Khurafa's body creaked as he finally managed to sit up. He looked expectantly from his remaining stump to the other vulture.

"One hand is enough," the smaller vulture spat and flapped its wings. "I will tell the others what has happened. But expect nothing, mud-kind. Zal is sentimental. But we are fire, and I am still wroth at your kind." He flapped his wings to leave.

"He says that," the disembodied voice of Zal said, "and it is true. But he came because of his love for Nariman. His death-call reached us all, but only the two of us chose to respond."

"What now?" Khurafa asked, closing his eyes to the sunset.

"I inform you of a few more things that Nariman neglected to say; then, we leave and let the tower of silence be silent once more," Zal said. "It is important you know—the enemy lives, though this was a setback for them. At least some must have lost their bodies—perhaps one is gone for good. I cannot say how much time it buys you. Once they reach the graves of Ad and Thamud, all may be over."

Khurafa inhaled deeply and his face broke out into a bright smile, unbecoming of the chamber of gloom. A faint fragrance of honeysuckles and catnip had wafted through the decay from far away. And from farther off still, a trio of familiar scents left a tenuous trail.

"They are called The Servants," Zal said, oblivious to Khurafa's change in mood. "Have you not wondered about whom they are the servants of?"

Glossary

Ad and Thamud- ancient tribes of Arabia destroyed for their wickedness. Often believed to have been giants.

Amir Hamza- fictional, romanticized version of the Prophet's uncle Hamza, who engages in numerous adventures in the medieval and early modern epic Dastan-e Amir Hamza/ the Hamzanameh.

Baraka- 'blessing,' a mystical force given by the Divine to whom he wills. Similar to the english 'grace' or 'charisma.'

Banu Sasan- the tribal-style appellation for collections of tricksters across the middle east known in poetry and plays for theft, cons, and their own argot.

Borz- a 'wolf' in chechen. Name of a fictional werewolf monster in this story.

Firsat- literally 'occasion,' or 'opportunity,' but in the magic system of this book, it refers to a baraka-based perceptual ability, e.g. smelling baraka, reading minds, etc.

The Five Pillars- the five major ritual acts in Islam, but in the context of this story, a group of five holy warriors with baraka, galenic skills, and more, who combat monsters.

Galenic Medicine/Humoural Theory- a medical theory proposed by the greek anatolian Galen, which aims for a balance of the humours (vital substances in the body). A major part of Unani Islamic medicine. Adapated into a magic system in this story.

Gog and Magog/Yajuj Majuj- apocalyptic tribes who will consume much of the world, sealed behind a wall by the enigmatic Dhu'l-Qarnayn, often believed to be Alexander the Great.

Ghoul- a monster from middle eastern lore, often associated with graves.

Imam- a religious leader of prayer or the community more broadly. Refers to great legal scholars as well as the Shi'i Imams, believed to be inheritors of the Prophet's mystical knowledge and worldly authority.

Jinn- supernatural beings in muslim and middle eastern lore, who are made of smokeless fire, have free will like humans, have immense power, and are generally hidden. Often associated with ruins.

Kitab shahadat al-Hazred/ the book of al-Azif- the Necromincon, the evil grimoire penned by H.P. Lovecraft's character Al-Hazred. Altered significantly in this story.

Mawlana Jalal ud-Din Rumi- a 13th century Poet from Afghanistan, who migrated to Anatolia. He lived during the Mongol conquests.

The Mongol Conquest of Baghdad- the Ilkhanids laid siege to Baghdad in early 1258. The conquest of the city saw widespread looting and massacres, as well as the de facto end of the Abbasid caliphate.

Obur- a vampiric monster mentioned by the 17th century traveler Evliya Celebi, its appearance and mechanics are altered somewhat in this story.

The Prophet- The Prophet Muhammad, peace be upon him, the progenitor of Islam, who passed away in the first half of the 7th century.

Rabia al-Adawiyya- an 8th century Muslim saintess known for her wisdom, poetry, and love of God.

Rustam- the greatest hero of Firdowsi's poetic epic of Persian civilization, the Shahnameh.

Saints/Friends of God- great lovers of God/beloved ones of God, known for their spiritual excellence and sometimes miraculous acts.

The Servants- a group of nine sorcerers from the 8th century who attempted some form of rebellion, threatened to resurrect ancient giants, professed controversial beliefs, and were ultimately executed by immolation according to the historical sources.

Shaykh- literally 'old man,' implies a scholar or teacher.

Sidi- literally 'my master,' but colloquially can be the equivalent of sir.

Sohrab- Rustam's son, a tragic hero in Firdowsi's epic.

Tayy al-Ard'- a miracle associated with some saints, where they can warp away/ essentially teleport.

Umm Sibyan- a monster from middle eastern lore; similar to La Llarona, it preys on children.

Zambil- a bag with seemingly limitless capacity gifted by Khidr to Amir Hamza in the Hamzanameh.

Acknowledgments

Thanks first and foremost to Allah, who gave us the pen (and computer) to write, who created us, sustained us, and taught us the best of stories.

To my father who regaled me with tales of clever hares and complicated pasts, and encouraged me to live the morales I listened to.

To my mother who helped me to read and then confiscated books when I binged too late at night.

To my grandfather who introduced me to rumi and wisdom. "There was a lion..."

To my older sister Safia, who read me my first fantasy novels, and kept me up with wild imaginings.

To my younger sister Attiya, who edited my terrible high school novel and somehow still thinks what I have to say is worth listening to.

To my cat Sufi who briefly let me focus on something besides her.

To my beloved wife Sabiya, who believed in me when I didn't believe in myself. She's rolling her eyes at this cliche.

To say this would not be possible without you all is an understatement- I would not be possible without you all.

This book, and the growth of my writing, owes much to my incredible beta readers, writing group colleagues, and friends: Sarah Mokh, Kyle Smith, Safa Kaleem, Javeria Ahmed,

Furkan Senturk, Abby Gancz, Daniel Reiland, Lillian McCabe, Erum Marfani, Jessica Pirilampa Lee, Sarah Decker, Joni Cole, Marjorie Matthews, Casey Dennis, Donald Kollisch, Edward Corley, Micki Colbeck, Betsy Vereckey, Khadija Ali, and Kelsey Graywill

This work was published with the support of my incredible Kickstarter backers:Nesreen Itani Osman,The Creative Fund by BackerKit, Talal, Hasan Siddiqui, Nitasha, Furkan Şentürk, Safa Kaleem, Thomas Gray, Muhammed Catovic, Kelsey Gray-will, Connor Martini, Sabiya Ahamed, Libby Burnette, Ebrahim Varachia, Sana Siddiq, Sandra, Elsherif Mahmoud, Abdullah Siddique, Huda, Thalha, Scott Casey, Omar Sajjad, Omar Elsayed, Arkam Muhammad Javed, Harley Shaff, Faisal, Calvin Lee, Saminah Munshi, Eric de Roulet, Donovan Lawrence, Touhid Jamali, Austin Knode, Niwal, Erum Marfani, Talal Javed Qadri, Maimuna Hossain, Milton Syed, Timothy Smith, Marjorie Nelson Matthews, Yusef, Beate Brückner, Laura, Taylor Lampasona, Khalidah Ali, Adnan Rokadia, J.D.L. Rosell, Duncan Wilcox, Karen Tan, Rebecca Bradeen, Efe Akengin, Leezanne Zeng, Aadil Iqbal, Nish___daa, Luke Shindle, Yovana Cortez, Lori, Amin Gharad, Cailyn, Khan Shairani, Austin Zhu, Charles Dennis, Guy Collins, Tajuddin Ingram, Kyle Smith, Cynthia Zava, Zahra Rasouli, Huma Chaudhry, Julian, Nazia Tabassum, Kelly McMahon, Saffana Humaira, Hamid Ali, Francesco Tehrani, Naseer Ahmed, Brandon, Kaleem Ahmed, Gadisti Aisha, Richard L Ashenoff, Al Webb, Anthony Brende, Jay, Leena Elsadek, Mark R Garcia III, Aiman Mimiko, Catie George, Zach, Kip Corriveau, G, Carissa Brunick, Abubakr Ziaullah, Darla Novotny, Nicole Tirol, Laila, Hameem Rahman, Henry, John Anthony Sullivan, Elise Bader-Saye, Qasim Qureshi, Shabbir, Michele Predmore, Quasistar, Emily

Pearson, Rifat Rahman, Audra Bass, Edward Maher, Anj, Blake B., Christopher Ogden, Clara Mora, Farhad Jaan Dokhani, Clayton Smith, Bilaal Saif, Charles Lucas Tart, Garrison, Khaled Itani, Asiya Ahamed, Shajuti, Tayyab Wasim, Brandy Pastore, Usman Qadri, Aaron Thomas, Mustafa, The Selkie Delegation, Christy Lohr Sapp, Emily Arotin Wagner, Daniel Esparza, Sydney Baker, Ameer A, Khadeeja Majoka, Shireen, Patrick D'Silva, Emma, Hamza AlHasanm Raza Samimy, Daniall Masood, Muttaqee, Daniel Santoro Reiland, Matthew Recker, and Steven Byrd.

As the Prophet, peace be upon him, said, "Whoever does not thank people, has not thanked Allah."